LEGACY OF THORNS

KINGDOMS OF LEGACY WORLD

KINGDOMS OF LEGACY

Legacy of Roses: A Beauty and the Beast Tale (Book One)

Legacy of Glass: A Cinderella Tale (Book Two)

Legacy of Thorns: A Sleeping Beauty Tale (Book Three)

Legacy of Gold: A Rumpelstiltskin Tale (Book Four)

Legacy of Locks: A Rapunzel Tale (Book Five)

Legacy of Ice: A Snow Queen Tale (Book Six)

TETHERED HEARTS

Ties of Legacy: A Companion Novel

LEGACY OF THORNS

A SLEEPING BEAUTY TALE

KINGDOMS OF LEGACY BOOK 3

MELANIE CELLIER

LUMINANT PUBLICATIONS

*For my niece Primrose Eloise Grace,
who will soon grow out of her naps
but not out of the joy she brings us all*

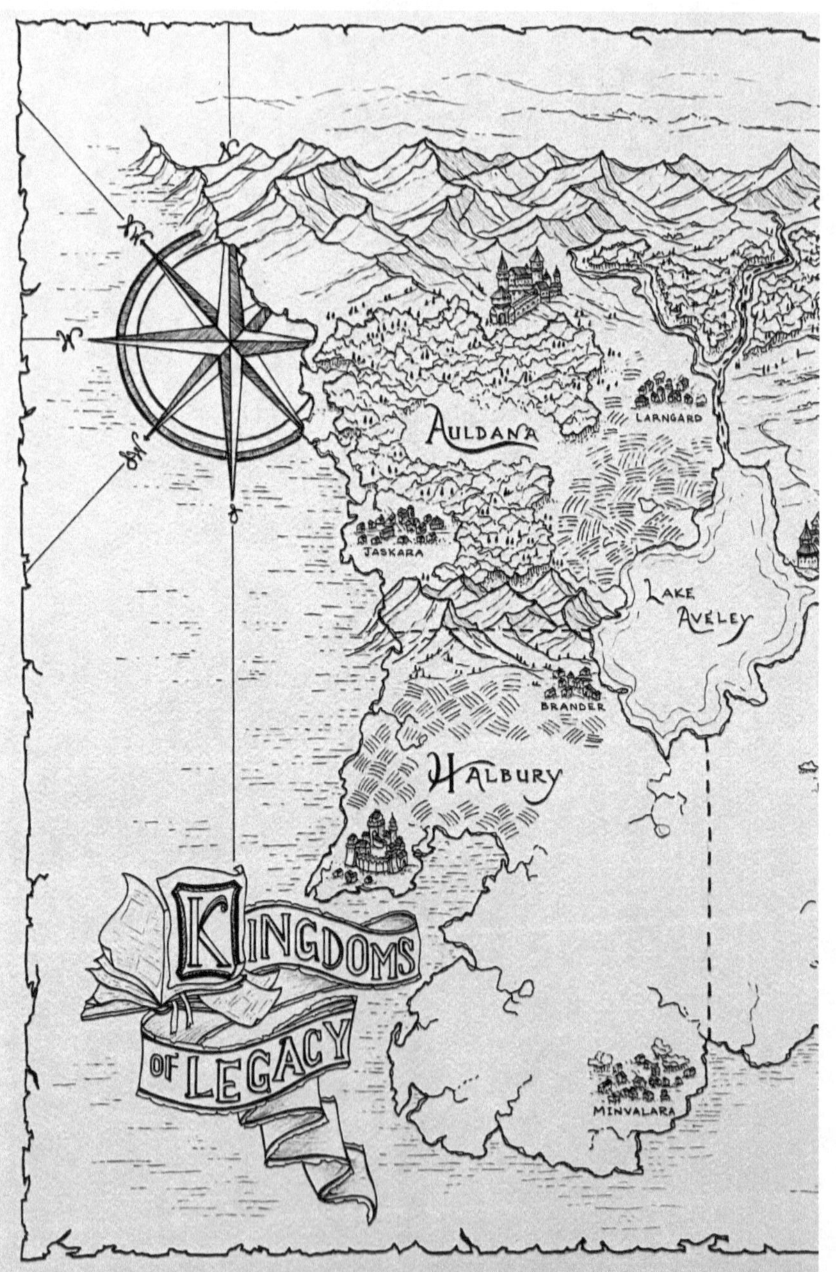

AULDANA
LARNGARD
JASKARA
LAKE AVELEY
BRANDER
HALBURY
MINVALARA
KINGDOMS
OF LEGACY

MOUNTAIN COMMUNITY
GLENALTA
BOLIVERE
THEBARTON
STONYFELL
GLANDORE
KLYMPTON
ETHELSON
MARLESTON
OAKDEN
SOVAR
HENTON
MIRANDAR

PROLOGUE

"It's that one." Nisha pointed at a large house with an attached yard.

The house in question bordered a deserted lane, which increased the possibilities for entry, but Finley still hesitated. When he didn't move, Nisha took the lead, marching down the lane. Finley followed far enough to find a secluded vantage point that still allowed him to watch the main street.

When a middle-aged woman hurried past the entry of the lane, a bag in her hand, Finley drew himself up. He glanced at Nisha.

"Are you sure this is worth it?" he asked. "It won't help Archie if I end up getting caught."

"I'm not at all sure," Nisha said matter-of-factly. "But you asked for the best lead I have, and that's it." She pointed at the house again. "The housekeeper wouldn't say where the old man has gone, but he may have left some record of his destination in the house."

"But you're sure the housekeeper is the only one living there at the moment?"

Nisha shrugged. "That's what I heard. Can't say for certain."

Finley closed his eyes and drew a long breath. He should have known better than to seek empty reassurances from someone as literal as Nisha. He already knew he was clutching at straws, but he couldn't do nothing. Not when his younger brother was counting on him.

"Hold on, Archie," he muttered as he ducked down the lane and swung himself over the fence, "we'll be coming for you just as soon as we can."

Inside the yard, he found no sign of anyone. He chose to take it as a positive sign that the housekeeper had indeed been the only one left in the large house.

Retrieving the lock picks that he kept in the lining of his jacket, he set to work on the back door. It didn't take long for it to click open. He slipped inside, closing it gently behind him without making a sound. As far as he knew, he was alone, but old habits were hard to shake.

He prowled through the house, peering into various rooms until he came to a large study. A cold fireplace occupied a central place along one wall with several comfortable chairs drawn up before it. The rest of the wall space was covered in bookshelves.

The room had the kind of cozy, appealing vibe that was foreign to Finley after the last six years. But it also had a large desk, standing proud in the center of the room, and he went straight for it.

"What do you have hidden away in here, old man?" he murmured as he tried the drawers.

Only two were locked, and he immediately focused on them, making short work of the first lock with his picks. The drawer held bundles of letters, but one glance showed their age. They wouldn't have any bearing on the old man's current location, and as soon as Finley realized they were love letters between the man and his deceased wife, he threw them down as if burned. He was there to invade one portion of the man's private life and one portion only.

He took the time to re-lock the drawer before unpicking the other. At first glance, the second drawer was an even greater disappointment, with not a single paper in sight. But Finley's eyes lingered on the locked drawer's only contents anyway: a miniature dagger in its own scabbard. Why would the old man have bothered to lock up a tiny dagger?

Finley's eyes focused in on the intricately crafted hilt, his eyes narrowing. With a soft indrawn breath, he scooped it up, his expression turning eager.

A closer inspection only increased his certainty. He recognized the work. That particular dagger hadn't come from a weapons master but a herbalist. And that meant it was no ordinary dagger.

His hand closed around the hilt, acting before his mind was fully made up. It wasn't a replacement for his own full-sized dagger—a beautiful weapon whose loss he grieved daily. But it would certainly go some way toward making up the shortfall.

With a slight shake of his head, he stashed the dagger

in his boot. The miniature size made it perfect for such a hiding place, and he suspected it had been made with that in mind.

Now to look through the papers in the unlocked drawers. Hopefully one of them would give some hint of the reasons for the old man's precipitous departure—and more importantly, where he could be found.

A sound in the corridor made Finley freeze. He hadn't heard the front door, but someone was definitely in the house. Before he had time to conceal himself, a hand pushed the study door fully open, and someone stepped inside.

He'd been caught.

CHAPTER I

DAPHNE

Daphne gazed across the river at the far bank. Oakden. The kingdom where she had been born and, therefore, the kingdom whose Legacy had claimed her. She hadn't seen it in twelve years.

Daphne had spent all twelve of those years knowing she would one day return. Given how deeply the claws of Oakden's Legacy were sunk in her, it had never seemed like a choice. And yet she lingered on the Sovaran side of the river. She was traveling alone, and the carriage which had brought her this far had already departed, so there was no one to see her uncharacteristic moment of cowardice.

She yawned, eyeing a nearby patch of soft-looking grass. Her mind was sharp enough, but if she lay down on the grass, she would be asleep instantly. It had been like that for the last twelve years—ever since she had dared to leave Oakden. The Oakden Legacy had punished her for her departure by saddling her with the constant burden of sleepiness. None of the Legacies approved of their citizens leaving the bounds of their birth kingdoms.

Resentment surged up, but Daphne took a deep breath and let it drain back out. She had long ago rejected resentment—if she hadn't, it would have swallowed her whole years ago. What was the point in railing against something she was powerless to change?

She yawned again, her eyes once more drawn to the grass. But she resolutely turned her gaze back to the water. Naps could be excellent tools for avoiding certain situations, but on this occasion, a nap would provide nothing more than a pointless delay.

Twelve years had brought Daphne to this shore, and a few minutes of sleep wouldn't change that. It was time—and past—for her to cross.

As if in tune with her thoughts, a small rowboat pulled up to the riverbank in front of her. The man inside touched his cap in her direction and smiled.

"Are you lost, miss?" he asked. "That's Oakden across there."

Daphne smiled back at him. "I know. I'm headed to the other side."

"To Oakden?" The man's brows rose, and he scratched his head. "What do you want to do that for?"

"I'm Oakdenian," Daphne said simply.

Shouldn't he have been able to tell? Wasn't it blazoned across her face? For most of her life, she had worn that label—always pointed out as a curiosity. A girl who had moved between kingdoms and who dropped asleep in any and all circumstances was unusual enough to be noticed wherever she went.

But all of that would change when she stepped foot on Oakdenian soil again. In Oakden, she would be just like everybody else.

"Ah, that will explain it, then," the man said. "You must be anxious to get back. I'll row you across for a coin, if you like."

Daphne accepted the offer and climbed into the boat, taking a seat across from him with her back to Oakden. She had already gazed at it for long enough.

"There's not many as cross just here," the man said, making cheerful conversation as he pulled on the oars and sent them shooting across the river. "Most cross at the Marleston ferry down south or else they go upriver to the Glandorian capital and take the ferry there."

Daphne shrugged. "I'm heading for Ethelson."

"Even so," the man said. "It isn't as if Ethelson is right on the river, so most traffic heading that way crosses at Marleston and takes the river road north to Ethelson."

He looked at her expectantly, clearly hoping for an explanation, but Daphne remained silent, gazing south down the river. After a long pause, the man huffed and turned his conversation to the weather. Apparently it had been a late spring in Oakden.

Daphne had no intention of telling her life story to a stranger. Traveling between kingdoms already made her remarkable enough—she didn't want to advertise the fact that her cousin had just married the crown prince of Sovar. Daphne's royal connection had given her the use of a carriage for as long as she was on the Sovaran side of the border. So it had made sense to cross the river into Oakden as close to her destination as possible. But that hadn't been her true motivation for crossing so close to Ethelson. Once she stepped foot in Oakden again, she wanted to reach the town as quickly as possible.

Lorne was in Ethelson, and Lorne was much more than just one of her several godparents—more than an offer of accommodation, however welcome. As much as Daphne yearned to set foot in Oakden and be normal again at last, she also feared that nothing would change after all. And no matter which way it went, she would have questions for Lorne. The old man had more experience with travel than any Oakdenian she had met. If anyone could understand her situation, it would be him.

As the boat pushed further into the water, Daphne focused less and less on her companion's monologue and more on her own body. Was she less sleepy?

She eyed the hard wooden bench beneath her. The narrow plank of wood shuddered and pitched with the movements of the boat, but she didn't doubt her ability to lie down on it and go to sleep. At least, she could have done so inside Glandore or Sovar. But what about now?

She had heard that the border rivers carried power from the Legacies of both kingdoms that touched them and could therefore be used by the citizens of either side with comfort. Shouldn't that mean she was already back in Oakden as far as the Legacy was concerned?

But when she concentrated, she could still feel the ever-present pull that lingered at the back of her consciousness, pushing her to lie flat on the seat and close her eyes. Was it just long habit, producing a familiar feeling that wasn't really there?

She shifted, preparing to lie down and test it, when the boat lurched, nearly sliding her off the seat altogether.

"We're here," her personal ferryman said with enthusiasm.

She stood quickly and placed the promised coin in his outstretched hand. He nodded acceptance and farewell, leaving her nothing to do but scramble out of the boat, her pack clutched tightly in her hand.

Dimly she heard the boat depart, but her eyes were on the ground beneath her feet. Oakden. She had finally returned home.

"Home." The word tasted sour in her mouth. Glandore was her true home.

But Glandore was behind her now. She shook her head and focused on the road that ran alongside the river. It was smooth and flat, bordered by the river to the east and a forest to the west. But her eyes traveled north along it only to where another road branched off, heading westward into the trees.

She had thought her memories of her childhood were hazy, but now that she was here, she easily recognized the road and where it led. Ethelson—the town of her birth.

Daphne hoisted her pack and took the branching road, walking toward the town that was tucked away from the river among the trees. No signpost guided her, but she didn't need the reassurance. She could vividly remember traveling the same road in the opposite direction. She had ridden at the front of a cart on that occasion, the tray behind her piled high with all her family's possessions.

Her mother had been crying, and seven-year-old Daphne hadn't asked why. Even then she'd understood it was a perilous topic. Unlike Daphne, her parents had been born in Glandore and had chosen to move to Oakden as adults. But after ten years of living with the Glandore Legacy's burden, her parents were returning in defeat.

In the years since, she had come to understand why they had returned—the aching pain caused by the Glandore Legacy had seemed light at first, but after years it had worn away at their endurance, growing gradually more and more unbearable. Daphne had also come to realize that her mother had been crying for more than one reason. The relief at returning home was mixed with defeat at having failed and, of course, guilt. Her mother was about to be relieved of her burden, but in doing so, she was transferring that same burden to her young daughter.

But the punishment enacted by the Legacy was not only different for each kingdom, but also for each individual, and Daphne's burden had been one of sleep, not pain. Her parents had rejoiced when they found out, and in the face of their relief, Daphne had forced herself to be glad as well. She had smiled and assured them that she didn't mind constantly napping in odd places. Most days it was even true.

Ethelson came into view suddenly among the trees— the bustling town unleashing another wave of memories.

Daphne stood just beyond the outskirts of town and let the memories come. Her lips curved upward.

She had enjoyed her years in Ethelson. Her days had been spent running free through the streets with the other local children, who had accepted her without question. Her parents might have been foreigners, but Daphne had been born in Oakden and that made her one of them. She had been full of energy then.

An uncomfortable feeling grew inside her, an angry rumble she couldn't afford to entertain. She pushed it down. There was no use dwelling on the past. She needed to focus on her new future.

Without even noticing what she was doing, Daphne put her pack down at the base of a tree and sank onto it. As her head tipped sideways against the trunk, dismay filled her. *This wasn't supposed to be happening. This wasn't the future she had come to claim.* And a final thought...*Was she even safe?*

She tried to reach for some of her earlier tumult of feelings, but it was no use. The darkness claimed her, and her thoughts slipped away.

Daphne's eyes slowly opened, and she stretched and yawned. There was still no sign of anyone else on the road with her, and she didn't think much time had passed. She glanced up at the sky above. It was hard to see the position of the sun through the canopy, but her naps often lasted no more than ten minutes.

But even so, for those ten minutes she had been alone and vulnerable in a kingdom that had become strange to her. She didn't usually spend much time alone, and there was a reason for that. When you could fall asleep anytime, anywhere, it wasn't exactly a wise idea.

But she wasn't supposed to have to worry about that particular concern once she crossed into Oakden. And yet, she had just fallen asleep despite her efforts to stay awake. And in doing so, she had lost something far more important than ten minutes of her time—she had lost her hope.

In Oakden, Daphne was supposed to meet her true self —the self she was without the burden of the Legacy. But nothing had changed.

Pressure built up behind her eyes, but Daphne shook it away. Breaking down in the middle of the road outside town wouldn't help her in the least. Sleepy or not, she needed to find her godfather's house. Perhaps he would even have answers for her.

Lorne had experienced what it meant to return to Oakden after many years away. He would be able to explain why the Legacy's burden hadn't lifted.

CHAPTER 2
DAPHNE

Daphne hurried into Ethelson, intending to head straight for Lorne's house. But her memories were years out of date and everything looked smaller than in her mental images. It took her two wrong turns and a great deal of backtracking before she found the street she sought.

Turning onto it, she breathed a sigh of relief to see the familiar building at last. When she had lived in Ethelson as a girl, Lorne's wife had still been alive, and the couple had been two of her parents' closest friends, despite the generation gap between them.

There weren't many people driven to travel despite the Legacies, and they tended to find each other. Lorne—who had long ago given up any significant travel for the sake of his wife and children—always said that surrounding himself with people from other kingdoms was almost as good as traveling to those kingdoms himself.

When Daphne had written to Lorne of her intention to

return to Ethelson, he had immediately invited her to stay. He lived with only his housekeeper now, but his daughter lived nearby and from the sound of it he had a constant stream of grandchildren in and out of his house daily. He insisted that Daphne, as his goddaughter, was just as welcome as any of his grandchildren, although Daphne was sure he had to have many godchildren—given the Oakdenian love of godparents. His warm welcome had touched her, and she had gladly accepted his invitation.

She hadn't known the exact date of her arrival when she last wrote to him, but she had given a general idea of when she expected to be there, and she was confident he would be delighted to see her turn up at his door.

But when she knocked on a door painted an unfamiliar shade of green sometime in the past twelve years, no one initially answered. She put her pack down and knocked again, waiting.

The door finally swung open, and Daphne smiled in relief. But it wasn't Lorne's face gazing back at her. An unfamiliar middle-aged woman started at the sight of Daphne on the doorstep, clutching at her heart. She had a bag of her own looped over one arm, and appeared to be on her way out. Apparently she hadn't heard Daphne's knocks.

"Who are you?" the woman asked, still a little out of breath.

"I'm Daphne." Daphne paused, but there was no sign of recognition on the woman's face, so she continued. "I'm one of Lorne's goddaughters. I wrote to him that I was coming, and he said I was welcome any time."

"How unfortunate." The woman seemed to be paying little attention to her own words as she bustled out of the house and closed the door behind her.

It shut with an ominous note of finality.

"Is Lorne not inside?" Daphne asked, pushing down her dismay.

"Gracious, no, child," the woman—who must have been his housekeeper—said. "He left days ago and in that much of a hurry. Would have dashed off without so much as a hat once he got the message, I've no doubt. But thank goodness I was here to make him see sense. I got him properly packed up and on his way."

"Has something happened to one of his family?" Daphne asked, her mind leaping to the obvious conclusion. The message must have contained something terrible to send Lorne off in such a state.

The woman gave Daphne a closer look. "You've some sense about you, I can see. That's it precisely. His son." She shook her head. "A sad business."

"Not dead?" Daphne asked. Lorne's son lived in Klympton, in western Oakden, so Daphne had never met him, but he was only the age of her own parents.

The woman shook her head. "Lorne feared the worst, but Master Gordon has so far pulled through. So Lorne has sent for me to help with the nursing. And I've a coach to catch, so you'll have to excuse me, miss."

"You're leaving, too." It wasn't really a question. Daphne had suspected it since first seeing the bag on the housekeeper's arm.

"Yes, dearie, and I really must run. But I'll tell Lorne

you stopped by. Daphne, was it?" She didn't wait for Daphne to answer before continuing. "You must visit again sometime when he's back. He's always happy when his godchildren visit."

"Actually, I'm..." Daphne's words faded to a murmur as the housekeeper bustled off down the street. "I'm supposed to be staying with him."

Despite everything, Daphne's mouth twitched into a smile. What ridiculous and terrible timing. The momentary amusement faded, and she considered her situation. She had barely set foot in Oakden, and already nothing was going to plan.

She had some coin with her, so she didn't need to worry about the immediate specter of sleeping on the streets. But her funds wouldn't be enough to secure long-term lodgings. She had always intended to find a job once she arrived, but she had been relying on Lorne to not only house her in the short term but also provide a reference and some direction on securing a decent position. Now she was a stranger, alone in a town that no longer remembered her. Who would want to hire her on the spot without any credentials?

She slowly turned to look back at the house behind her. The large, empty house. What a waste that she needed somewhere to stay and it was just sitting there empty.

One side of her mouth tugged up, and she picked up her pack. She would have to break in, but if someone challenged her, she had a letter in her pack from the owner of the house claiming her as his goddaughter and saying she was welcome anytime and could stay as long as she liked. He hadn't said a word about her only being welcome if he was there himself.

She circled the house, relieved to find the gate to the rear yard had only a simple latch. She closed it carefully behind her, preferring to avoid notice if possible. Hopefully once she was inside, she would be able to find a spare key that would enable her to make further exits and entrances through the front door.

In the meantime, she would likely have to make do with a window. Her eyes narrowed as she examined the windows she passed at the back of the house, distaste filling her at the thought of squeezing through one. Daphne always preferred to avoid excessive effort if possible.

Pausing by the back door, she shrugged and tried the handle. To her astonishment, it turned.

"Well, that was easier than I was expecting," she muttered, wondering why she didn't feel more pleased.

She stepped inside and put her pack down in the back hallway. She would explore the house first, and once she found a guest room, she'd come back for it. With any luck, she'd find a key along the way.

She walked down the hall, examining the rooms that lined it. Guest rooms would be upstairs, but she was on the lookout for anywhere likely to contain a spare key, and her eyes caught on a door standing half ajar, giving a glimpse of bookshelves beyond. The sight brought back the sound of a crackling fire, the smell of books, and the voices of her parents, talking and laughing with Lorne and his wife. Lorne's study.

She quickened her pace, picturing Lorne's large, sturdy desk. He might keep a spare key in one of the drawers.

She thrust the door the rest of the way open and stepped inside. Unlike the front door, nothing in the study had changed in the years of her absence, and a wave of nostalgia washed over her, making her falter.

Then her eyes reached Lorne's desk, and she froze. A man was bent over one of the drawers. He had paused at her entrance, raising his head to look directly at her.

That, Daphne thought to herself, *is what comes of making assumptions.*

Lorne might be gone, but one of his sons remained in his house. But, no. Lorne only had one son, and he was in Mirandar recovering from some unknown illness or injury. Daphne stepped further into the room and got a better look at the man behind the desk. He was too young to be Lorne's son anyway. He had to be a grandson—one of Lorne's daughter's many children. They had probably played together when they were young, although she didn't recognize his adult face.

"My apologies," she said with her friendliest smile. "I hope I didn't startle you."

The young man straightened but said nothing, continuing to stare at her. She really should have tried knocking at the front door again.

"I'm sorry to appear unannounced," she continued with a confidence she didn't entirely feel. "I'm one of Lorne's goddaughters, and he invited me to stay. But it seems I have poor timing. The housekeeper didn't even have time to introduce me before she had to rush off."

The man's eyebrows shot up at her speech, but she kept her face calm and added, "I'm Daphne."

She wracked her brain to remember the names of Lorne's grandchildren, but the only one she could remember was Mary—the girl who had been closest to her in age.

"Your sister Mary might remember playing with me when we were children, though I haven't been in Ethelson since I was seven."

"Ah, Mary." The young man finally spoke, his voice deep and smooth. He was still looking at her with bemusement, but at least he wasn't denouncing her as an intruder.

"I realize it's not the most convenient time for me to stay," Daphne said with her most winning smile, "but I don't have anywhere else in Ethelson to go. Your mother might also remember me," she said with a flash of inspiration. "She knew my parents when we lived here."

A flicker passed through his eyes, but it was gone before she could identify it.

"You've come to stay with...Grandfather?" the man asked slowly, his eyes narrowing slightly.

Daphne nodded. "I was sorry not to find Lorne here. Sorry on your uncle's behalf, of course, but also on my own. I was wishing to consult with Lorne on an urgent matter." At least, it felt urgent to her.

Lorne's grandson continued to stare at her, and a

flicker of doubt whispered across Daphne's mind. Was it possible this wasn't—

"If you've come to stay with Grandfather," the young man said with more urgency, "does that mean you're the goddaughter he's been talking about? Princess Olivia's cousin?"

Daphne breathed a sigh of relief. The man was Lorne's grandson, and Lorne's family was expecting her, even if his housekeeper had forgotten. It would make her stay in the empty house a great deal less awkward.

"Daphne," the man said with the beginnings of a smile. "You're Daphne."

"I'm afraid I've forgotten your name," she said apologetically. "I remember Mary had a collection of brothers, but apparently you didn't leave a strong impression." She gave him a mischievous grin, hoping he would respond in kind and lighten the mood between them.

As she hoped, he smiled back, stepping around the desk and finally approaching her. When he held out his hand, she put hers into it, but he neither shook it nor let it go. Instead, he clasped it warmly, his eyes twinkling down into hers.

"I'll forgive you for forgetting my name, if you'll forgive me for being so startled by your arrival. I'm Finley and apparently we're godsiblings—or cousins, perhaps? It's a bit confusing."

Daphne smiled back. "I think I'm actually your godaunt."

He blinked and laughed, and Daphne almost laughed with him, responding instinctively to the warmth that emanated from him. It reminded her of Lorne, even if his looks did not.

His cropped curls were so dark as to be almost black, but his eyes were light, their color somewhere between blue and gray. Of course, Lorne may once have shared his grandson's coloring—his hair had been white as long as Daphne had known him and she'd never asked its original color. But Lorne had never had the height of Finley, of that she was certain. And neither did he possess the chiseled jaw or the straight, masculine nose.

She guessed his age to be within a couple years of her own, and she could hear her friend Rosalie's voice in her ear as she gazed at him. Her best friend from back home in Glandore would have a lot to say if she knew Daphne was standing with her hand clasped by a man who looked like Finley.

Daphne whisked her hand away. Along with his chiseled jaw, Lorne's grandson sported a black leather coat with a high neck and moved with the sort of quiet grace that Daphne imagined an assassin would possess. And yet, his smile and the slight point to his ears lent him an air closer to that of a charming rogue. All together it spelled one thing—danger.

Daphne considered herself far more sensible than Rosalie, but she wasn't sure even she was proof against Finley. And that made her very wary indeed.

Finley looked down at his empty hand, but his smile only quirked and didn't disappear.

"You mentioned you have an urgent need to consult

my grandfather," he said. "Would you like me to take you to him?"

Daphne's head snapped up, her concerns over Finley momentarily forgotten. "We could go to him? Is that really possible?"

She felt no pull to stay in Ethelson if Lorne wasn't there. She had come to see him more than the town. And she didn't care how dangerous Finley might be to the heart of any girl he came in contact with. Daphne had survived plenty of attractive men—the Sovaran court was full of them—and she could handle one more if it meant getting answers about why her sleepiness hadn't lifted.

CHAPTER 3

FINLEY

"I could certainly take you to him," Finley said, adding silently, *if I had any idea where he is.*

"Is he not in Klympton?" she asked. "Has your uncle moved?"

"From what I've heard, he was traveling when the accident happened." Finley repeated the gossip Nisha had managed to pick up. "He's in a small hamlet near the crash site."

"Oh, how awful." Daphne's hand came to her mouth, her eyes full of sympathy.

They were lovely eyes, too—green with flecks of gold, framed by long dark lashes and distinctive brows. Paired with her button nose and luscious lips, she was undeniably stunning. But Finley couldn't afford to get distracted by a beautiful face. Archie couldn't afford for him to get distracted.

So he maintained his charming smile and tried not to

flinch at the lies. Despite the practice he had accumulated in the last six years, Finley had never liked lying.

"I was actually already on my way to join him this afternoon," he said. "You'd be welcome to accompany me."

Daphne's brows rose slightly, and she regarded him with an assessing gaze.

Finley grinned at her. "Not just with me, of course. We'll be traveling with two of my grandfather's associates, who are hoping to be of assistance to him."

He definitely didn't imagine the look of relief on her face. He must be losing his touch if she felt that unsure about him.

"I was just dropping off some papers." He gestured toward the desk. "And now I'll be on my way to meet them." He stepped toward the door before looking back over his shoulder with a perfectly calculated grin. "Are you coming?"

She looked back at him with a level gaze, her eyes hard to read. "Yes, I think I will."

He faced forward again, hiding his look of triumph. It wouldn't do to get overconfident. For a girl who didn't look much over eighteen, Daphne was astonishingly cool and collected. He was going to have to work hard to keep her on the line.

She collected a pack from the hall near the back door and followed him outside. When he shut the back door behind her and strode toward the yard's front gate, she didn't follow. He paused and glanced back.

She was watching him with a frown. "Shouldn't you

lock the door? The housekeeper might not be back for weeks."

"Oh, yes." He walked back to the door. "Foolish of me. I've been so distracted."

She seemed to accept the excuse, but she kept her eyes on him as he fumbled in his pocket and drew out a key. It wasn't the key to the house, of course, but he angled his body so she couldn't see the keyhole as he pretended to put it in.

When he turned back to her, his smile was perfectly calculated—relaxed but a little sheepish. She smiled back and finally followed him out of the yard.

Nisha stepped out of the lane to join them. "Who is that?" she asked in her usual blunt way.

"This is Daphne. Daphne, this is Nisha. She's one of those associates of my grandfather's that I told you about."

Nisha turned a blank expression on him, and he directed his next words at her, trying to give her a significant look as he did so. "Daphne is Grandfather's goddaughter and has just arrived to stay with him, not realizing he's out of town. We ran into each other in the house. I've offered to be of assistance."

Nisha's brows shot up. "You mean she's—"

"My godsister, of sorts, yes," Finley said quickly. "And she's coming with us to see Grandfather. I hope you don't mind."

Nisha blinked several times and shut her mouth. After a moment, she nodded solemnly, and he breathed a sigh of relief. Dissimulation wasn't Nisha's strong suit. She usually left that to Finley and Archie.

"It's nice to meet you." Daphne smiled at Nisha, seeming calm and confident although he suspected she was relieved at the early proof that his claimed companions did, in fact, exist.

"Are you sure you don't mind me traveling with you?" Daphne asked as they led her through the streets of Ethelson. "I would hate to be an imposition."

"Of course not!" Finley said. "The more, the merrier."

They walked on in silence for another minute before Daphne asked abruptly, "Why is Lorne's housekeeper traveling by coach instead of going with you?"

Finley kept his expression steady as his mind raced. The housekeeper had been on her way to join the old man? Blast! That explained the bag. Daphne had mentioned her leaving in a rush, so the woman must have been hurrying to catch the coach.

He laughed easily. "Perhaps I should have mentioned that we're walking. I hope that won't be a problem?" He phrased it as a question, but he had no doubt she would assure him of her capability.

"Walking?" Unexpected disdain dripped from the word. "How dreadfully fatiguing! Whatever for? Why didn't you take the coach with the housekeeper?"

Nisha gave a snorting laugh. "The coach? That wouldn't work for us. You'll understand when you see Morrow. We'll be meeting up with him in a few minutes."

Daphne's eyebrows rose. "You see me besieged with curiosity." Her tone sounded closer to boredom—with a hint of suspicion—and Finley regarded her from the corner of his eye.

She filled him with curiosity, sparking an interest he couldn't afford to indulge. He'd never met someone quite like her, though, so he couldn't entirely suppress it either.

Despite her claim of being easily fatigued, she kept up with them despite Nisha's determined stride. But her dismay at learning they were to walk had seemed genuine. Should he hire a cart and horse?

He blinked. Where had that thought come from? He wasn't one to use coin so carelessly. It wasn't as if she'd said she wouldn't accompany them on foot.

Of course, if she did refuse to walk, he might be forced into hiring a cart after all. Whatever happened, he couldn't let her slip through his fingers.

"We'll meet Morrow just out of town," he told her, uncomfortable with the silence that had fallen. "He took our packs ahead while I detoured to Grandfather's house."

Daphne nodded and made no demur as he led her through the outskirts of Ethelson and onto the road that led southwest through the forest. They found Morrow just outside the town, sitting on a small mound of packs. He lumbered slowly to his feet at the sight of them, his eyes fastening on Daphne.

"This is Daphne," Finley said quickly. "I met her at my grandfather's house." He gave Morrow a warning look. "She's a friend of his and is eager to see him, so I've offered for her to come with us since we're going to him anyway."

Morrow took the new information in stride more easily than Nisha had. Despite his appearance, he had always been more attuned to emotional nuance than she was.

"It's nice to meet you." Morrow held out his hand to Daphne, and she took it slowly.

"And you." Her eyes traveled up and down his vast bulk, and she gave a sudden laugh.

The musical sound made Finley smile involuntarily.

"I can see why we aren't traveling in the public coach," she said.

"Ha!" Morrow joined in her laughter with an easy smile. "I would have to buy out all the seats, and then where would my friends be?"

"I heard you're an associate of Lorne's," Daphne said. "Are you a traveler like him? My parents were also, which is how I came to know him as a child. But they found it too difficult and returned to Glandore twelve years ago, so I've been living there ever since."

"Glandore?" Nisha shot a look at Finley. "I thought you were from Sovar?"

He glared at her. It was still early days and any questions needed to be handled with finesse. Daphne wasn't easily charmed, and they all needed to tread carefully.

Finley did want to know the answer, though. If he'd brought the wrong girl, they'd have to find a way to shake her off. And then they'd be back where they started— worse than where they'd started, in fact, because at least they'd started with the hope of finding Lorne's houseguest.

"Glandore is my home," Daphne said, "but I've been in Sovar for the last six months. My family has an unusual history of traveling between kingdoms—my grandfather was originally from Sovar before he moved to Glandore and had my mother. Then when she was grown, she decided to move to Oakden." Daphne shrugged. "It didn't stick in her case, but I was born during the ten years they spent here. I always intended to come back after I turned eighteen, but I made an extended detour to Sovar on the way at the request of my cousin, Olivia. She and I have always been close, despite living in different kingdoms."

"Ah, Princess Olivia that would be," Morrow said with enthusiasm.

"Yes." Daphne shook her head. "I'm still getting used to that." She gave Finley a sidelong look. "It seems Lorne made particular mention of that part."

Finley grinned apologetically. "Apologies. I hope you don't mind that I told them about you. Grandfather was very proud to have a royal guest coming to stay."

Daphne snorted. "I'm not royalty."

Nisha and Morrow exchanged worried looks that Finley hoped Daphne didn't see.

"Royalty-adjacent, then?" he suggested with a grin. "Close enough by my book." That's what he was counting on, at any rate.

"If you say so." Daphne sounded like she certainly didn't say so but also couldn't be bothered arguing the point. "Are we starting out immediately?"

"Food first!" Morrow declared authoritatively, and Daphne brightened.

"You're a sensible man with excellent priorities," she

told Morrow gravely and put her pack down next to their pile.

Finley felt a ridiculous pang of jealousy. Why did she seem to approve of Morrow more than she did him? New acquaintances always liked Finley—he'd worked for years to ensure that.

He tried to tamp down the feeling while he listened to Morrow and Daphne discuss the food supplies. Apparently Morrow had already prepared a meal and was refusing all Daphne's efforts to contribute. Finley's spirits lifted somewhat. The portions were always generous when Morrow was on food duty.

As long as Daphne stayed with them, it didn't matter what she thought of Finley. In fact, it might be better if she didn't like him too much. The better she liked him, the greater her sense of betrayal would be when she found out the truth.

He might find her interesting, but there was no point getting attached in any way. She was going to hate the lot of them soon enough. And that wouldn't matter either— as long as she saved Archie.

Morrow soon had them seated in a circle, eating the bowls of stew he handed out.

"So you're Oakdenian, but Glandore is home," he said through a mouthful. "Sounds confusing."

Daphne sighed. "Most people seem to find it so."

"Do you miss Glandore?" Morrow asked. "You've already been away six months."

Daphne's lips tightened slightly. "Sometimes." She sighed. "My best friend, Rosalie, is still there, and it's been strange not to spend every day with her. She's more like a sister than a friend, in truth. But she's married now, so I'm sure she's busy enough without me."

Finley watched her closely, trying to read the air of melancholy that hung around her.

"Do you dislike her new husband?" he asked, taking a guess.

Daphne looked up, clearly surprised. "Oh no, not at all. He's a wonderful man. Dimitri is an excellent match for Rosalie."

Finley's brows had drawn together at her first words, but her final sentence put paid to any notion that she might be pining after her friend's groom for herself.

"Rosalie got her happy ending," Daphne murmured, "and I'm overjoyed for her. I suppose I just want to get mine too."

Morrow chuckled and threw a sly look at Finley. "Looking for romance, are you?"

Finley pointedly ignored his glance, and thankfully Daphne seemed oblivious to it.

"Oh no!" she said. "That wasn't what I meant. I was thinking of the Legacy."

"The Legacy doesn't give people happy endings," Nisha said shortly. "I think it must enjoy pain and suffering."

Finley rolled his eyes at the uncharacteristic flight of fancy from Nisha. Was she upset about Archie?

"The Legacies don't have minds or emotions," he said, not wanting Daphne to get a strange idea of them. "You know that. They may plague us, but that isn't their intention."

The Legacies were nothing more than the remnants of the enchantments that had once plagued the original royal families of each kingdom. They had sunk into the land itself, changing the landscape of each kingdom in strange ways and affecting even the animals. And they had a similar hold on their citizens—not just making it difficult to travel outside the kingdom's borders, but constantly trying to force their lives to follow elements from the original histories.

Although Nisha was right that the Legacy didn't necessarily give the happy ending—just whichever elements of the tale happened to fit the circumstances in question. Which was exactly the reason he was there now, forced into lying to Daphne—who seemed like a perfectly nice girl and not at all deserving of their deception.

"It is possible to get the happy ending," Daphne said quietly. "I've seen it with my own eyes."

Her words sent a shot of hope through Finley. Daphne clearly already had plenty of experience being at the center of the Legacy's power. Surely she could manage it one more time.

"And the Legacy's effects aren't all bad," Finley added, wanting to support her. "All the kingdoms have found ways to turn their particular quirks to advantage. The Sovaran economy makes good use of their ability to blow flexible glass with fantastical properties. And everyone benefits from the sleeping potions that Oakden sells to foreign doctors." The sleeping herbs required for the draft only grew in Oakden and had been put to good use by his kingdom for generations.

"Some of the Legacy's effects are good and some of them are less ideal," Daphne said, caressing a flower that grew next to her. "I'll admit it's nice to see flowers other than roses."

In Glandore, where she had lived most of her life, it didn't matter what seed you planted—the only flower that would grow was a rose.

"Ouch!" Daphne pulled her hand back and frowned at the prick in the tip of her finger. Her voice turned wry. "I could do without the thorns."

Just as Glandore grew only roses, Oakden had more than its fair share of thorns. They grew on flowers that had no business having thorns.

Daphne shook her head, returning to her stew. "Thorns aside, the real problems all come from the hold the Legacy has on the people."

Her three companions all nodded, none of them seeing anything to dispute in her words. They had all seen people suffer from the whims of the Legacy. They were currently some of those people. And Daphne had apparently been one of those people for years—ever since her parents had forced her away from her birth kingdom as a young child.

Something uncomfortable shifted in Finley's gut. He recognized it at once and pushed it away. He couldn't afford the luxury of guilt.

It wasn't as if they intended to harm Daphne. They needed her assistance, but after that, she would be free to go anywhere she wished—they would even deliver her back to Ethelson if that was her preference. Although Finley suspected she would want nothing to do with them at that point.

Nisha began gathering the empty bowls for a quick clean, and Finley turned to take Daphne's. They had been speaking only moments before, but she had since lain down in the grass by the side of the road and was somehow already asleep.

"Is she...sleeping?" Nisha asked. "Right there? Just like that?"

"I..." Finley shrugged, for once having no idea what to say. She certainly appeared to be sleeping.

"Well, that's going to slow down our progress," Nisha said, stacking the last of the bowls.

CHAPTER 4
DAPHNE

Daphne lay on the grass, her eyes closed and her breathing even. She had slept for a few minutes and woken again—but without giving any indication of having done so. It was an art she had mastered years ago. A lot of interesting things could be learned—and tiresome situations avoided—by appearing to be asleep.

And now that she was—for the first time in her life—traveling without someone she knew and trusted, the skill had become vital. She needed to know what these people said and did when they thought her vulnerable and unable to hear them.

Only a second's mental catalog told her that she hadn't been harmed or even moved. She turned her attention outward.

"Everything's clean, and I've repacked," a woman's voice said. Nisha. "Should we wake her?"

"But she looks so peaceful," Morrow protested.

"Isn't that a bit odd, though?" Nisha again. "Is there something wrong with her?"

"She's been out of Oakden for years," Finley said more quietly. "I guess now we know what price she's had to pay for leaving. It must have been hard for her to live like that all this time."

Tears pricked at Daphne's eyes, and she struggled to keep her breathing in the correct cadence. It made sense that Lorne's grandson would understand her struggles—he must have watched his grandfather suffer every time Lorne left the kingdom. But she hadn't expected her own response to such immediate understanding and sympathy.

She stretched and yawned, finally opening her eyes. "Is it time for us to go?" She rose slowly to her feet.

"Yes, the washing up is just finished." Finley grinned. "Very convenient timing."

"I do my best," Daphne said calmly.

She hadn't been able to help falling asleep on that occasion, but there was no use protesting her innocence when she had done exactly what he suspected on more than one occasion. She didn't even feel bad for using her frustrating circumstances to her best advantage where possible.

They all shouldered their packs and took to the road, Morrow in the lead. Finley and Daphne walked side by side behind him, with Nisha behind them.

Daphne glanced back at the other woman, concerned

she might be unhappy with being relegated to the rear. But Nisha walked in a state of alertness, her eyes busy scanning the forest on either side of them. Daphne followed her gaze but noticed nothing out of place.

Most Oakdenians lived life at a slower pace than in other kingdoms—their Legacy had a tendency to slow everything down before you even realized it was happening. But Nisha—who Daphne guessed at about thirty—seemed to have her own supply of coiled energy. She wore her dark hair in a practical bob and the muscles in her arms and legs proclaimed she wasn't used to a life of indolence.

In front of Daphne, Morrow moved comfortably despite his size, his fair hair ruffling in the spring breeze. Daphne had never seen such a mountain of a man. And yet, his good nature seemed equally oversized. She placed him as mid-forties—still with plenty of strength in his frame—and she easily could have felt intimidated by his mere presence. But despite his appearance, she didn't. And Daphne generally had good instincts about people.

She threw a sideways glance at Finley. So why did she feel so wary of Lorne's grandson? He had been nothing but friendly so far—even charming. But her usual assessment was thrown off by how disturbingly attractive he was. She couldn't tell if she felt uneasy because he was hiding something or because she mistrusted her response to her own feelings of attraction.

All together, the three of them were an oddly matched group and equally unexpected as associates of Lorne. But perhaps it wasn't so surprising after all. Daphne had first-hand experience that Lorne welcomed everyone with open arms.

The spring air was pleasant, and she enjoyed looking for the spring blooms that poked through the forest litter on the ground wherever possible. Despite her concern for Lorne's son and her worry over her own continuing sleepiness, Daphne felt light. It was the perfect day for a walk through the forest.

Morrow broke into sudden song, his voice infectious and joyful. Nisha immediately joined him, the rich notes of her low alto merging seamlessly with his unexpectedly smooth tenor.

They sang a traditional Oakdenian song that Daphne remembered from her childhood. As they reached the chorus, she couldn't stop herself from joining in. Her voice merged with the rich melody they were making, soaring over the road as they sang together.

When the song wound to a close, Morrow began another one, and both women joined him immediately. Daphne's heart swelled, her earlier pleasure in the day growing with the simple joy of making music. She'd almost forgotten this part of life in Oakden. So many people had beautiful singing voices, and the people loved to sing. You never knew when someone would break into song, the people around them joining in.

Morrow embarked on a third song, and Daphne regretfully fell silent. It was one she didn't recognize, and she was too out of practice to join a song she didn't know.

She glanced across at Finley, whose lips had remained stubbornly shut throughout the impromptu choir performance.

"How can you not get caught up in the song?" she asked quietly beneath the singing of the others.

"Is it a crime not to enjoy singing?" Finley protested. "You're looking at me as if I just kicked a puppy!"

"A crime?" Daphne's eyebrow rose. "Of course not. But it does make me question your character."

Finley winced, but Morrow broke off his song mid-word to give a low chuckle.

"Don't blame Finley. You should thank him instead. He's refraining for all our sakes."

"People assume every Oakdenian can sing well," Finley said ruefully. "But some of us had godparents who didn't give that particular gift. Of course, some are naturally gifted anyway, but then there are some of us who...aren't." He shook his head. "Living in Oakden, having a poor singing voice is practically a curse. I could demonstrate for you, but—"

"No, don't!" Nisha and Morrow cried, almost in unison.

Daphne rolled her lips together, trying not to laugh.

"I thank you for your sacrifice," she said gravely.

"Clearly you're one of those who were gifted with song, like Morrow and Nisha," Finley said. "How many godparents do you have?"

"Four," Daphne said with a small wince. "And I know that's considered tempting the Legacy by most locals. But my parents were overeager at the prospect of an Oakdenian baby."

Almost all children born in Oakden had godparents chosen by their parents. The main role of these individuals was to speak a blessing over the baby in their first weeks of life—a gift chosen from the list given to Oakden's famous sleeping princess. No one risked having actual christenings, of course, or making any formal occasion out of it. They already had enough trouble with the Legacy when it came to party invitations. No matter how carefully hosts prepared, someone important was always left off every party invitation list made within the kingdom's borders.

But parents were eager to make the most of the Oakden Legacy's history of gifts for newborn babies, so they had developed their own traditions that didn't require a formal event. The chosen godparents would visit individually and speak their gift over the baby's cradle. No one had all six of the gifts given to Oakden's historical princess, as that was considered too great a risk. In most parts of Oakden, two was considered standard, three greedy, and four or more foolhardy.

Of course, the value of the gifts was debatable. Some argued they did little beyond make the parents feel good. But most people agreed they had some effect on the child—the strength of that effect depending on the general power of the Legacy in the area at the time of the blessing.

"Let me guess..." Finley said slowly, a smile in his eyes. "You were given song, grace, beauty...and wit."

"Should I be offended by that hesitation?" Daphne asked, hiding a smile of her own.

Morrow glanced over his shoulder. "Ignore Finley. Clearly the power of the Legacy was strong in Ethelson at the time of your birth."

"Thank you, Morrow," Daphne said gravely. "From the sound of your voice, it must have been overflowing at the time of yours."

Morrow laughed. "That's what my parents claim, anyway. Although my mother always complained that she'd told her sister to give me wit, not song."

"She certainly didn't give you beauty," Finley remarked, earning a narrow-eyed look from Daphne.

But Morrow just laughed again. "You're just jealous your godmother gave you beauty instead of song, my friend. Unlike beauty, the gift of song is a gift to oneself as well as others. That's what my aunt always said."

Daphne gave a snort of laughter. "Finley got beauty?"

Despite her teasing, she wasn't actually surprised. If anyone represented masculine beauty, it was Finley, with his sharp lines and strong brow.

"I didn't only get beauty!" he protested, but the combined volume of three people's chuckles drowned him out.

The moment of friendly teasing filled Daphne with more joy than the variety of flowers beside the road. But the happiness unsettled her even as it brought a smile to her lips. Just as when she had first seen Ethelson, the unexpected moment brought a rush of conflicting emotions. She had resented the Legacy for forcing her to leave her true home in Glandore to return to Oakden—she still did—but it had been years since she had laughed with friends over their respective birth gifts. It was something no Glandorian would understand. Glandore might have become home, but a part of her would always be Oakdenian.

The afternoon's walking passed with stretches of silence, stretches of song, and stretches of light conversation. Twice they stopped to rest, and both times Daphne napped—although she no longer felt the need to pretend extended sleep in order to test her companions.

"How much longer until we reach Lorne?" she asked as dusk began to fall.

"We won't reach him tonight," Finley said. "Possibly not even tomorrow. His new nurse will arrive faster in the coach, but I'm afraid we're stuck at the slow pace."

Daphne considered the information, comparing it to a map of Oakden in her mind. Their destination must be inside the forest, which meant Lorne and his son must be in one of the forest hamlets that nestled among the trees. Had Gordon been traveling between the capital and Ethelson when the accident occurred?

As they all worked to set up a camp for the night in a small clearing near the road, she asked Finley about her assumption.

"Does your uncle live in the capital now?"

Finley paused in unrolling his bedroll and frowned at her, his eyes confused.

Daphne's brows drew together. "Your Uncle Gordon? Given our direction, it seems like he must have been traveling through the forest from the direction of the capital, not Klympton."

"Oh, right." Finley resumed arranging his bedroll, hiding his face from her. "Yes, he was coming from the capital."

Daphne finished laying out her own bedroll—putting it with Nisha's on the opposite side of the fire to Finley and Morrow. As she worked, she threw covert glances at Finley. He hadn't actually answered her question. And he'd seemed confused by it as well.

Despite the dedication he was showing in traveling to his uncle's sick bed, Finley didn't seem very concerned about the man. Was Gordon unlikable in some way? Was it only Lorne Finley cared about?

As they worked together to build a campfire and prepare an evening meal, Daphne continued to watch Finley from the corner of her eye. As far as she could see, he behaved normally, but she couldn't shake the certainty that something was off. What was he hiding from her?

Or was her certainty that he was hiding something merely an excuse—a reason to watch him constantly? It was certainly no hardship to look at him. He moved with a lithe grace that was mesmerizing, and she didn't doubt he was a skilled fighter. One of his birth gifts had clearly been grace.

She tore her eyes away from him when she realized the direction of her thoughts. She was alone in a kingdom that was no longer familiar—alone if she didn't count her new friends, and she wasn't completely sure she should count them yet—and she couldn't afford to be distracted by an attractive face.

But what if it wasn't a distraction but a genuine instinct for trouble? The question kept her awake for some time after they had said goodnight and climbed into their bedrolls. And she noticed that while Nisha and Morrow were both snoring quickly, there were no sounds of sleep from Finley either.

CHAPTER 5
FINLEY

Daphne had been watching him all evening. Surreptitiously, but she was watching. Why? Did she suspect something?

Finley turned in his bedroll, frustrated that he couldn't get comfortable. They were so close. It would only take one more day to reach Archie, and he was sure Daphne would help them when they did. Mostly sure.

If she didn't...His eyes drifted to the boots beside his makeshift bed. They still concealed the tiny dagger he had taken from the old man's desk.

He would do his absolute best to persuade Daphne to help willingly, but if she wouldn't...Well, there was another use for the famous Oakden sleeping herb beyond the sleeping potions made and sold to doctors. When it was infused into the blades of weapons, those weapons could send someone to sleep with the smallest prick.

Not permanently, of course. Finley had no desire to

harm Daphne. He wouldn't even have lied to her if it wasn't for his brother.

If the herbalist who used to live south of Ethelson—the one who had sold Finley his old dagger—had still been in his old workshop, Finley wouldn't have had to take a dagger at all. But the herbalist was gone. From the look of his house, he had been driven away by a fire, so it wasn't likely he was coming back. And Finley needed the advantage an Oakdenian blade could provide.

As always, he had done what he had to do to keep his brother safe. And yet, it was a long time before he managed to drop to sleep.

The next morning, he woke abruptly with the dawn as he always did. He was used to waking up first among their group, but this time one bedroll was already empty. Daphne's.

Finley sat up, immediately alert. Had she waited for the rest of them to fall asleep so she could run from them in the night? What had tipped her off?

But a moment's reflection calmed his anxiety. If she had fled, she would have taken her bedroll and pack.

So where was she? He pulled on his boots, considering the possibilities. Despite the presence of her possessions, he wouldn't rest easy until he had seen the girl herself.

He prowled through the trees, moving noiselessly as he listened for any sign of another person. He could hear none. That didn't mean she wasn't there, though. Like Finley, Daphne had received the birth gift of grace, and if her beauty was any indication, the Legacy's power had been strong at the time of her birth.

The slightest rustle of leaves met his ears, and he tensed. The rustle sounded again, and he turned in its direction, catching sight of movement through the trees. As he crept closer, Daphne came into view.

She stood in a small clearing set back from the road and didn't appear to notice his approach. Her focus was turned inward as she glided through a practiced series of long, flowing movements.

Finley's brows rose as he watched her. He knew those movements. He had done them himself, morning after morning, holding each one until his muscles quivered with the strain. They were more difficult than they appeared, although Daphne made them look easy and smooth. She was completing the solitary practice dance of a fighter who had no companion to spar with.

For a girl so prone to naps, she was a master at the training dance, and apparently an early riser as well. Finley guessed she must start every day the same way. At every turn, she grew more fascinating.

And more appealing. He was honest enough to admit that, even if he knew his acquaintance with the girl from Glandore was about to come to an abrupt end.

But it hadn't ended yet.

Before he had consciously decided to do so, his body moved forward. Emerging from the trees, he slid into the space beside her, mirroring her current movement.

She nodded slightly to acknowledge his presence but didn't pause. He had expected her to be startled, but she responded as if she'd known he was there the whole time. Perhaps she had.

He joined her pattern, moving through the oft-practiced poses with ease. He was taller than Daphne, so at first he had to work to stay aligned with her pace, but he soon fell into the rhythm of it.

As the minutes ticked by, Finley's muscles began to ache, twitching as he tried to hold himself steady. Daphne, however, neither faltered nor slowed. Finley hadn't been practicing enough lately.

He pushed on anyway, realizing how much he had missed it. The stillness of the morning seeped into him, relaxing his worries of the night before. The repetitive movements and even the strain of his muscles had a meditative effect. Or maybe it was the girl at his side who made the experience so peaceful. Enclosed by the trees, at the cusp of the day, they felt alone in the kingdoms, and he felt each one of her deep, even breaths as if it was his own.

Did she feel his? Did she feel the unexpected communion of the shared moment? Would she still feel it when it came time for him to ask for forgiveness?

He straightened abruptly, breaking the flow of the movements only beats before the training dance ended. Daphne glided to a more gentle close, gazing at him quizzically.

"We need to get moving," he said roughly, striding off toward their campsite and leaving her to trail behind.

He couldn't afford to lose focus or to waste time on a fool's hope. Protecting Archie was what mattered—not the forgiveness of a bright-eyed girl with honey-brown hair and hidden depths.

He strode out of the trees to find Morrow awake and

preparing a hot breakfast. Finley would have preferred to get moving immediately—the turmoil inside him demanded forward progress. But he pushed the feeling down, well practiced from years at concealing his true emotions.

He half expected Daphne to quiz him on his unexpected appearance in the forest, but she ate breakfast and helped pack up camp as if nothing had happened. She wasn't entirely unaffected by her morning's exertions, however. After rolling up her bedroll, she sank onto the ground, placed her head on it, and fell instantly asleep.

"Is she napping already?" Nisha paused halfway through putting the cooking dishes in her pack to stare at Daphne. "She just woke up."

Finley shrugged. Daphne had expended enough energy in the forest to earn a nap, but he found himself loath to speak about their shared morning training.

His own muscles already ached, although they hadn't even started walking for the day. He couldn't have settled to sleep, though. Restless energy buzzed through every line of his body.

He gazed at Daphne. She looked utterly peaceful. Apparently the training dance hadn't affected her the way it had affected him.

She woke with a stretch and beamed beatifically around, apparently pleased to find their camp fully packed and the packs ready to go.

"Are we ready to start?" she asked as if she hadn't just slept through the last of the morning's work.

Finley smiled reluctantly. He should have felt irritated

with her, but somehow it was impossible. And from the smiles Nisha and Morrow were hiding, he wasn't the only one who felt that way.

On the road, they fell into the same walking rhythm as the day before with one notable difference. Finley still walked in the middle, but Daphne positioned herself at the front, beside Morrow, leaving Finley to walk alone. He tried not to let that sting. As long as Daphne remained with them, nothing else mattered.

At the midday meal, Daphne produced a cheese from her pack to share. It was greeted with enthusiasm by Morrow and Nisha, and even Finley couldn't help smiling as he ate it. Judging from its quality, she must have brought it with her from the Sovaran palace.

With lifted spirits, they made good time after the meal, and it was only mid-afternoon when Finley spotted a small road branching off from the main one and disappearing into the trees.

"That's our road," he called to Morrow, and his companion nodded, turning toward it.

It was smaller than the main road south through the forest, but it led to a small town and was well maintained. At sight of it, Daphne perked up, clearly eager to arrive at their destination. Her enthusiasm sent another stab of guilt through Finley which he had to work to suppress. At least his deception was nearly at an end.

Morrow led them down the smaller road, and Daphne dropped back to walk beside Finley again. The new path wasn't wide enough for anyone to walk comfortably beside Morrow's broad frame.

Finley smiled warmly at her, but her initial enthusiasm had dimmed, and she barely seemed to notice. Each step made her more quiet and thoughtful—even tense. Did she suspect something? Had the time come to tell her the truth?

But before he could make up his mind to speak, the road bent to the right and the village appeared before them, nestled among the trees. Daphne brightened at its appearance, but her mouth soon turned down as Morrow led them off the main road to circle around the town. She cast glances between the three of them but remained silent, waiting to see where Morrow was leading.

When a large manor house appeared before them, her brow cleared. "Are they accommodating Gordon at the manor? That's kind. I'm sure Lorne will be much more comfortable there than at the village inn."

Finley said nothing, not willing to lie yet again when he was so close to confessing the truth. Nisha and Morrow both remained silent as well, and a small line appeared between Daphne's brows.

Finley tensed, but she didn't push him for answers. Neither did her steps slow, although he caught a bright, alert glint in her eyes that was at odds with the already familiar languor of her manner.

When they skirted the house to weave through the trees, however, she stopped. The rest of them stopped as well, Morrow several beats behind the others.

"This doesn't look like the path to the front door," she said, an amused lilt in her words despite the wariness in her eyes.

"He's not in the main house," Finley said. "He's in an outbuilding to the rear." The words weren't technically a lie, given he didn't clarify who *he* was.

Daphne sighed. "Not as generous as I thought, then," she muttered to herself, moving forward again.

Finley let out the breath he was holding. He didn't know what he'd been thinking earlier. It was much better to wait and tell her the truth when they were actually at the barn.

When they made it to the back of the sprawling manor, Daphne turned toward the structure that housed the manor's outdoor servants. But the others held their course, heading for a large, wooden barn.

Daphne hesitated for a moment before trailing silently behind them. The old barn was set back from the main building and hadn't been used for horses in generations. Trees had grown up between the two structures in subsequent years, and no one was likely to notice or disturb them out there.

When they stopped in front of the worn double doors, Daphne shook her head and spoke flatly. "Lorne is not out here."

Finley wasn't sure if she was speaking from actual disbelief or if she intended the words as an indictment of the local lord. Such a lack of hospitality would certainly have reflected poorly on him if he had actually been guilty of it. But as far as Finley knew, the manor's owner wasn't even aware of the occupant currently slumbering inside the wooden walls of his storage barn. Finley didn't think he'd even noticed the theft of the items within.

Morrow and Nisha both looked from Daphne to Finley, and he sighed. He couldn't put it off any longer.

"No, Lorne isn't here," he said. "My brother is. And we need you to save him."

Daphne tensed, her eyes jumping from Finley to Morrow and then Nisha. They all looked back at her gravely.

Her eyebrows rose. "Why is one of Lorne's grandsons in there?"

Finley grimaced, and Daphne's eyes hardened, although her voice remained level and light.

"I should perhaps mention that I'm not a doctor," she added, "and I don't think I'd make a good nurse, either. I fall asleep a little too easily to keep a bedside vigil."

"Archie doesn't need that kind of help." Finley hesitated. "And he's not Lorne's grandson."

Daphne took a step back, understanding igniting in her eyes. Finley's story had been one big lie, and now she knew it. She didn't look outwardly angry, but there was a whisper of hurt on her face that hit him harder than anger would have.

It's for Archie, he repeated silently to himself. *You had to do it for Archie.*

"So you brought me here for this," Daphne said slowly. "Perhaps you'd care to explain why." She looked between them. "Unless you want someone who's very good at napping, there's nothing special about me."

Finley was increasingly convinced that wasn't true in the least. But he hadn't lured Daphne to his brother's side because of her personal qualities. She was there because of her royal connection, and it should have been a simple matter to say so. But somehow his voice wouldn't speak the words.

"You're the cousin of a princess," Nisha said when the silence drew out. "We're hoping that will be sufficient for the Legacy."

"I'm here because of Olivia?" Daphne frowned. "You know she wasn't born a royal, right? I have no royal blood."

"Unfortunately there weren't any actual princesses lying around," Morrow said with a cajoling smile. "We won't blame you if it doesn't work. We just thought it was worth a try."

He gazed at her hopefully, but she didn't smile back. Instead, her eyes cut to the closed stable door.

"We're in Oakden right now, so if your brother has fallen afoul of the Legacy and you're looking for a royal to rescue him, I can only assume he's asleep in there." She gave a snorting laugh of disbelief. "Did he seriously prick his finger on a spindle? Don't they teach you anything in school? Isn't that like a Glandorian child being foolish enough to pick someone else's rose?"

Finley ignored the deliberate provocation of her barb —he had been entertaining similar frustrated thoughts about his brother for weeks. But the truth was that he didn't know how it had happened. Archie had been alone at the time.

"It shouldn't have happened," he said grimly. "Even if he encountered a spindle..." He trailed off and shook his head. "He's just an ordinary boy, so I don't know why the Legacy responded so strongly."

One of Daphne's brows lifted. "If the Legacy's power has latched onto your brother so strongly, won't you need actual royalty to free him?"

"Do you happen to have a royal to hand?" Some of Finley's frustration leaked into his tone. "We've been looking for weeks now, and you're the best we've found."

His eyes held hers steadily. He refused to weaken. He was too close to rescuing Archie.

Daphne gazed back at him, and he had the sensation of being weighed and measured, although her expression was hard to read.

"You can't move people after they fall into a Legacy sleep," she said after a moment. "So your brother must have been pricked inside that barn. What was he doing there?"

The challenge in her eyes told him she already suspected the answer, so he remained silent.

"He was stealing from the local lord, wasn't he?" she asked at last.

Morrow winced visibly, and she seemed to take that—along with the continued silence—as confirmation.

"What about Lorne?" she asked. "Where is he?"

"I have no idea." Finley forced himself to hold her gaze. "All I know is the gossip we heard in Ethelson. His son was traveling when he had the accident, I know that much, but I don't know where. Lorne could be anywhere in Oakden."

The disappointment that filled her eyes made his chest squeeze painfully.

"In that case," she said, her voice somehow still steady, "I have no reason to be here." She turned and began to walk away.

Finley lunged after her, grabbing her arm and swinging her back around to face him.

"Please, Daphne," he pleaded in a low voice. "I freely admit to everything—I'm a liar and sometimes a thief, and I brought you here under false pretenses. If you never want to speak to me again, I won't blame you. But my brother is different. He's barely more than a child. And despite everything he's been through in his short life, he has the purest heart of anyone I know. If I could wake him up myself, I would—even if I had to bleed out to do it. But I can't. So when I heard Lorne had a houseguest—one who was the cousin of a princess—I had to take the chance."

Daphne looked down at his hand on her arm, her voice turning icy. "Let go of me now before I'm forced to expend a lot of unnecessary effort to make you let go."

Finley dropped her arm and put both his hands up, taking a step back. But he caught her gaze and held it, putting every bit of his desperation into his voice.

"Please, Daphne. Save Archie. You might be his only chance. Don't punish him for my wrongdoings."

Daphne hesitated, and Finley leaped into the opening.

"Just come into the barn and see him for yourself. Please."

Daphne glanced at Nisha and Morrow. Nisha's face

was stiff, her worry for Archie hidden behind a mask, but Morrow's heart was in his eyes.

"He's right about Archer," Morrow said. "Heart of gold, that boy. I should have stopped him going in, but you could never stop Archer when he had it in his head to help someone."

Daphne hesitated and glanced at the barn. "He was helping someone?"

"Just look at him," Finley pleaded again, and Daphne sighed.

"Why do I feel like I'm going to regret this?" she muttered as she stalked toward the barn doors.

Finley breathed a sigh of relief and followed her. He had to pick the locks, fighting to keep his hands steady beneath the judgment in her gaze. But the lock finally clicked open, allowing them inside.

"I guess I know how you got inside Lorne's house." Daphne swept past him, entering first.

She stopped a few steps in, waiting for her eyes to adjust to the dim light. The cavernous space was littered with pieces of old equipment, most of it in various stages of degradation, and in one corner, an entire outdated carriage had been abandoned. But Finley ignored the depths of the aging structure, focusing on the double-sized stalls just inside the doors, one on either side of the large central aisle. The stalls had been fitted with rough shelving and were used for storing items that had no business being there.

Right now they were almost empty, thanks to Archie's

efforts. And he was currently paying the price for his altruism.

Finley unlatched the stall on the left and stood back, gesturing for Daphne to step inside. She paused in the open door, gazing down at the boy stretched out in front of her.

Her face softened at sight of him, just as Finley had expected, and hope filled him. No one could ever resist Archie.

CHAPTER 6
DAPHNE

The boy slumbering peacefully inside the stall looked young, just as Finley had claimed. Perhaps it was the softening of sleep, but Daphne guessed him to be fourteen at most.

The anger and frustration coursing through her lightened the longer she gazed at him, overtaken by her desire to help. But the feelings—directed at herself—didn't entirely disappear. She had known better, she really had. She had sensed from the beginning that Finley was hiding something, and in the past she had always trusted her intuition. But being back in Oakden was interfering with her clear thinking. She had lived so much of her life as if watching from the outside—as an outsider, it was easier to remain detached. But now she had stepped foot into her own life...only to immediately trip up.

Not that she blamed herself entirely. Finley's blasted good looks deserved a significant portion of the blame. She wouldn't have ignored her intuition if she hadn't been confused at the way he made her heart flutter. She would have walked away from him back in Ethelson.

But she hadn't walked away, and now she was staring down at a boy who shared a youthful version of those good looks. But there was something softer about Archer's face—something both boyish and peaceful. He looked like the sort of person who found something positive and hopeful in every situation he encountered.

He certainly didn't look like a hardened criminal. And Morrow had claimed he was trying to help someone.

Daphne glanced around the old barn. It was an unlikely place for the lord to store valuables. What had Archer been stealing?

"Lord Castlerey is a genial person for the most part," Finley said softly from behind her. "But unfortunately he has a large number of grandchildren and is particularly susceptible to the Legacy's influence. Whenever one of his family approaches sixteen, he becomes convinced he needs to act to protect them by confiscating some new household item from all the locals. From what I've heard, he fastens on a different household item each time, and he always comes to his senses eventually and returns the items. But then another grandchild approaches sixteen..." He sighed. "Archie can't abide injustice or the strong preying on the weak. He may have been technically stealing, but he was only returning the items to their original owners."

Daphne looked at the sleeping boy again. "I take it this isn't the first time he's gotten involved in others' troubles —whether legally or not."

Finley winced. "Ever since he heard stories about Lathlain across the northern mountains, he's been convinced he should have been born there instead of Oakden."

Daphne raised an eyebrow. "Stealing from the rich to give to the poor, is it?"

Little was known about the kingdoms that lay beyond the almost impassable northern mountains, but everyone had heard the tale of the thief from Lathlain with a heart of gold. If Archer had been trying to emulate him, it was no wonder he'd gotten himself into trouble.

Now that she had seen him and heard his story, Daphne had lost the desire to walk away or to refuse to help him out of petty revenge on Finley. But Archer was also basically a child. She couldn't possibly kiss him. They needed to find a young girl his own age for that.

"I can't do it," she said, her words short and clipped. "You'll have to find someone else."

But when she turned to go, Finley blocked her path out of the stall.

"I can't let you leave." He sounded haunted but also firm.

"Do you really think you can force me to kiss him?" Daphne asked, her voice tinged with frost.

Something flashed in Finley's hand, but the tiny dagger was too small to incite fear. Her determination hardened.

"Stand aside."

Finley didn't move. "This is an Oakdenian blade, not an ordinary dagger. One prick, and you'll be sleeping alongside Archie." He shrugged. "I don't know for sure if it will work while you're asleep, but I'm hoping one brush of your lips is all he needs."

Daphne stiffened. Why hadn't she seen this coming as well? Finley had already shown himself willing to lie and manipulate to get her there.

Finley sighed. "I don't want to use this against you, Daphne. I swear I don't. But I can't let you walk away from my brother. How can you look at him and just leave?"

"People usually underestimate what I can do."

"It isn't like you have to kiss him on the lips!" Finley cried. "Is it really too much to ask you to brush your lips across his hand?"

Daphne's brows rose, her eyes moving from the dagger in his hand back to the sleeping boy.

"Will that work? Really?"

"I've heard stories of at least two instances where it did," Finley said. "I'm not asking you to do something unsavory. I'm just asking you to save a young boy."

Daphne ground her teeth together. It went against the grain to reward Finley for all his lies, but when he put it like that, she didn't really have a choice. Dagger or not, she had to live with herself, and she wasn't sure if she could if she just walked away without even trying to help. Whatever her feelings toward Archer's older brother, Archer had done nothing to earn her ire.

"Fine." She spun. "One quick kiss, and if it doesn't work, you let me go without another word."

"Of course." Finley's eyes glowed as his gaze fixed on his brother's prone body. "One kiss is all I ask."

Daphne sighed and knelt beside Archer. His hands had been neatly folded on his stomach, but she didn't like the idea of kissing one of them—as if she were a courtier flirting with a princess.

Her eyes drifted to his boyish face. The forehead would be better—as if she was kissing a child awake. It wasn't hard to muster maternal feelings at the sight of the innocently sleeping boy.

Leaning jerkily forward, she pressed her lips against Archer's forehead. She didn't linger, pulling back quickly and looking for signs of life. Behind her, there was no whisper of sound from Finley. Apparently he was holding his breath.

As they both waited, disappointment seeped through Daphne. She had been tricked off course for nothing.

The boy opened his eyes. In wakefulness, he looked even more like his brother than he had while asleep, although his blue eyes lacked the greenish tinge that made Finley's stand out. He also looked older.

Daphne, still crouched beside him, rolled back on her heels. His eyes latched onto hers, growing slowly wider and wider.

When he pushed himself into a sitting position, he seized her hand, moving too quickly for her to whisk hers out of the way.

"My lady!" he breathed.

Daphne tugged her hand free and scrambled to her feet. "I'm no lady."

Archer followed her up, his eyes still fixed reverently on her face. "Yes, you are. You're the lady of my heart."

Daphne snorted as inelegantly as possible. "Aren't you fourteen?"

Awake, she was doubting that estimate, though. Archer puffed out his chest and rejected the suggestion with force.

"I'm sixteen and more than old enough to court a beautiful lady."

Daphne's eyes widened, and she let out a crack of disbelieving laughter. Court?

She looked desperately back at Finley, but he wouldn't meet her eyes. Earlier, she had been too frustrated with herself to have much anger left for him, but this time a wave of outrage swept through her.

Clearly Finley, unlike Daphne, hadn't forgotten his old school lessons. Those unfortunates who fell prey to the Oaken Legacy's enchanted sleep fancied themselves in love with the person who woke them—a fancy that was strengthened by the Legacy. And while the Legacy couldn't actually control someone's actions—or even thoughts—those who were susceptible could fall prey to its influence. And apparently Finley's sixteen-year-old brother was extremely susceptible to falling in love.

She glared at Finley, but he brushed past her, seizing his brother in a choking embrace. "Archie! Do you have to play the fool every time I leave? What were you thinking?"

Archer grinned and clapped Finley on the back, but when he pulled away, his eyes flashed to Daphne.

"I'm sixteen now, brother," he said. "I'm too old to be called Archie."

"Oho," Finley said. "I'll believe that when you stop

getting yourself into scrapes and needing your big brother to come to the rescue."

"Actually," Archer said, "it was an angel who rescued me this time, not you, Fin."

"And who do you think brought the angel to you?" Finley asked dryly.

"Don't call me an angel," Daphne said firmly, "unless you want me to start calling you Archie as well."

Archer straightened. "Of course not, my—"

"Don't call me a lady either," Daphne said promptly.

"Then what should I call you?" The twinkle in his eyes reminded her too much of Finley.

"Nothing," she said. "You're awake now, which means I'm leaving. And with any luck, I'll never see either of you again."

"No!" Archer seized her hand and gazed soulfully at her from eyes that resembled a puppy's. "You can't mean that. Unnamed Lady, you wouldn't leave me when I've just found you!"

"Her name is Daphne," Finley said from behind Archer.

The suppressed laugh in his voice made Daphne glare daggers at him. It would serve him right if she dumped him on his rear for getting her into such a ridiculous situation. Except she'd seen his experience with the training dance, and she was afraid it might take more effort than she was willing to expend.

"Is he awake?" Morrow called hopefully through the barn door, and Archer finally let go of her hand.

"Morrow!" He bounded out of the stall and toward the bear of a man.

Morrow pulled him into a rough hug, pounding him on the back with such force that Daphne winced involuntarily.

"The lad's awake, Nisha!" Morrow called through the open barn door, and Nisha appeared in the gap.

She held out a hand to Archer, who had managed to disentangle himself from Morrow. Archer seized Nisha's forearm with a grin, and she grasped his back, their grips firm as they nodded at each other.

"Nisha isn't really a hugger," Finley murmured beside Daphne.

She wheeled around to glare at him, her eyes narrowed almost to slits. "You knew this was going to happen."

Finley ran a hand down the back of his head. "I knew it was a possibility. Archer is a romantic at heart, and you are very beautiful." His words sounded too apologetic to be a compliment.

"I'm also nineteen!" she hissed. "I don't want a sixteen-year-old boy following me around and confessing his enchanted love. Rejecting him is like kicking a puppy!"

"I see you understand how he manages to make my life so difficult," Finley murmured. "And how he has Morrow, and even Nisha, twisted around his little finger."

Daphne groaned. "I'm leaving. Immediately. Maybe I can slip away without him noticing."

From his expression, Finley wanted to protest. But she held his gaze, her own full of accusation, and he looked away.

"I can distract him while you sneak past, if you like," he offered.

Daphne rolled her eyes but didn't reject the offer outright. It would be easier for everyone if she succeeded in getting away unnoticed.

But she'd hesitated too long. Archer turned back to her, his eyes shining.

"Have you already met Morrow and Nisha, Daphne? Did you travel here with them? Thank you for coming to rescue me. Not that I'm surprised," he hastened to add. "I can already see that you're full of compassion and goodness."

Daphne managed a weak smile. "I'm glad you're awake, but I really do have to be going. Right now."

"But how will you get back to Ethelson, Daphne?" Morrow asked, his brow creased with concern. "Surely you won't walk back on your own? Do you have enough coin to book a seat on the coach?"

"Did you come from Ethelson?" Archer asked. "Of course you can't go back all that way on your own! Anything might happen to you!"

"Anything already did," Daphne said caustically, throwing a sidelong glance at Finley. "But it's still a good point." She turned to face Finley fully. "I think you at least owe me coach fare back to Ethelson. Don't you?"

He had the grace to look shamefaced before her single raised eyebrow.

"I'm sure I owe you far more than that," he said softly. "Won't you allow me to escort you back? I'd feel better if I knew you made it back to Lorne's house safely."

"Unfortunately for you, I'm not in the least interested in making you feel better," Daphne said coolly. "I'll take the coach fare and be on my way."

"I'm not sure that's a good idea." Archer's voice caught her attention, his words sounding more like a reluctant confession than a lovesick plea.

"What do you mean?" she asked.

"Did you all walk here together from Ethelson?" Archer asked, looking from Daphne to the others. "You brought her from there to rescue me?"

Morrow nodded. "Her cousin is a princess."

Archer's eyes lit up at the supposed confirmation of Daphne's high status. She sighed, but she also didn't turn and leave. Something in Archer's manner had her on edge, and after ignoring her instincts before, she wasn't going to do so again in a fit of pique.

"If you came together, people must have seen you." Archer met Finley's eyes. "They'll think she's one of us."

Finley's brows snapped together. "Do you mean they're here? In this area? I think you'd better tell us how you came to prick your finger, Archie. Right now."

Archer bit his lip. "Maybe Nisha should come inside first. And lock the door behind her."

Finley's face hardened even further, but he didn't protest. Daphne watched nervously as Nisha promptly obeyed, removing the lock from the outside of the stable door and using it to secure them inside instead.

"Why is that necessary?" Daphne asked.

Archer hurried over and took one of her hands in both

of his. "I'm so sorry we've dragged you into our troubles, Daphne. But I won't let anyone harm you. I swear it."

Daphne pulled her hand free and stepped back, looking from him to Finley. "Why don't you start by telling me who would want to harm me?"

"Are they really here, Archie?" Finley asked sharply.

Archer nodded. "I didn't notice them at first, unfortunately. I was too busy ferrying all the looms out to Morrow and Nisha to pay full attention to my surroundings." He looked at Daphne. "I always insist they stay outside in case I get caught. I'm much better at charming my way out of trouble than either of them."

The charming grin he flashed at her was an exact match for Finley's, except his jaw hadn't quite reached the full definition of his older brother's. The effect was still devastating in an entirely different way, however—making her heart melt rather than flutter. She could well imagine an adult letting the charming lad go with a stern warning.

"So I was taking the looms out to them," he resumed, but Finley cut him off.

"Did you really have to get involved, Archie? You know what Lord Castlerey is like. He would have returned the looms eventually—once the latest grandchild turns sixteen without incident."

"But I met the sweetest grandmother, Fin," Archer said. "Did you know they took the knitting needles as well as the looms this time? Think of all the grandmothers left with idle hands! And some of the villagers relied on those tools for their income, too. I couldn't just abandon them to wait for months!"

Finley sighed and rubbed his eyes. "Of course you couldn't."

Daphne was starting to understand why Finley had said his brother was simultaneously a thief and a pure-hearted child. She could only imagine how devastating the local girls must find such a lovable rogue. Which only made it all the more farcical that the Legacy was encouraging him to think himself in love with her.

"None of that explains why I'm in danger," she said, eager to get to the main point.

"Right." Archer turned sorrowful eyes on her. "I got all the looms out safely—" he paused to look at Morrow and Nisha. "You distributed them?"

"Aye, lad," Morrow said. "We knew you'd want us to. They got back to their homes safe enough."

"Good." Archer smiled before resuming his tale. "I came back in for the last of the needles, and that's when they came in the other end of the barn." He threw a look toward the darkness in the depths of the barn, beyond the abandoned carriage.

"What?" cried Finley. "They were here? They got that close?" He looked furious and dangerous, and Daphne's heart skipped a beat.

Just how bad were these unknown villains?

Archer nodded. "I wasn't sure if they'd seen me, so I snuck into the back of the stall and tried to hide. But it turned out there were a few odd spindles still back there from a previous confiscation." His expression turned rueful. "It shouldn't have mattered except I'd completely forgotten what day it was."

"What day?" Finley stared at him for a second before he groaned. "Don't tell me this all happened on your birthday? You really are a fool! What did you expect to happen when it was your sixteenth birthday? I'm surprised the spindle didn't fly out and prick you itself! No wonder the Legacy responded with so much power."

Archer winced. "It was a little forgetful of me, yes." He shrugged and brightened. "But it worked in my favor in the end. Once I'd fallen asleep, I was safe from them. The Legacy doesn't allow those in an enchanted sleep to be moved far."

"That's true enough," Nisha said. "Otherwise we never would have left you behind when we went in search of Fin. Morrow could have slung you over his shoulder easily enough."

Daphne had no trouble believing that, but Archer looked a little abashed at Nisha's assessment.

"My sleep brought Daphne to me, as well," Archer added, looking at her with an expression of adoration that made her cringe.

"As lovely as it was to meet you," she said, "it's time for me to go. Whoever the people are who came after you, they're not here now, so I'm sure I'll be fine." She turned to Finley. "Open that lock, if you please."

"No." He crossed his arms over his chest, his face implacable.

Daphne's scalp prickled. "No?" she asked, her voice

deceptively light. "I believe we had a deal. Your brother is now awake, and you need to let me leave."

It wasn't too late to dump him on his rear if he kept refusing.

His face softened. "I'm sorry, Daphne, but I can't let you go. For your own safety."

Her brows rose. "Oh, is that the new excuse? And what will the next one be?"

"Daphne." His voice dropped lower, more intimate, pleading. "It isn't an excuse. I swear. If I could give you the coach fare and let you walk away, I would. But I can't let you walk straight into danger. Not when I'm the one who put you at risk."

"It's true, Daphne," Nisha said, her matter-of-fact manner more convincing than Finley's pleas. "Now that they've seen you with Finley, you'll be a target. They'll think if they get their hands on you, he'll fall in line."

"And they'd be right," Finley muttered, the words barely reaching her ears. But they did nothing to soften her anger.

"And you knew that?" She turned from Nisha to Morrow and finally to Finley himself. "You lied to me and dragged me here under false pretenses, knowing the whole time that it would make me a target?"

"What?" Archer glared at his brother. "You lied to her? Finley, how could you?"

"No, I didn't know," Finley said quickly, his eyes on Daphne. "I had no idea they were even in the area."

"We didn't know either," Morrow said regretfully. "Nisha and I came in looking for Archer eventually, but they'd gone by then. We had no idea how he'd come to prick himself." He gave Archer a chiding look. "We didn't even realize it was his birthday."

Archer grinned. "I'd lost track of the days myself, so I'm not going to blame you for that." His expression turned more serious. "I also had no idea they were in the area until they appeared, or I would have been more careful." He looked at Daphne. "We don't know who they are, but they've been coming after Finley and me for years. It's a miracle we haven't been captured."

"Actually, you have been," Morrow pointed out. "Twice."

"Yes, but we escaped." Archer grinned. "So those don't count. And they tried to take Nisha once, but—"

"I don't like strange men who try to abduct me," Nisha said calmly, one hand straying to the hilt of the sword at her waist and the other to one of the daggers she kept thrust into the right side of her sword belt.

"She wasn't the soft target they thought she was," Archer chuckled.

"They'll find I'm no soft target either." Daphne tried to sound braver than she felt.

"Even with all her expertise," Finley said, "Nisha might have been taken if Morrow hadn't showed up to help. It's not safe to be alone if you're on their list, Daphne. And it's not safe for any of us to be here right now."

"Are you sure it isn't the law chasing you?" Daphne asked tartly. "Since you seem to make a habit of stealing."

"I wish it was." Finley's voice was too serious. His gaze

turned to Archer. "How long did it take them to show up last time? How long did you have from when you first arrived to when they appeared?"

Archer responded with certainty. "It was twenty-two minutes." He glanced at Daphne. "I always keep count from the moment I break in anywhere. Just like Finley taught me."

Why was Daphne not surprised to hear that Archer learned thievery from Finley?

"It's not like that," Finley murmured to her, but she turned her back to him. He sighed and spoke in a louder voice.

"We've already been here too long in that case," he said. "We need to leave quickly." His voice lowered again. "Please, Daphne. You have to come with us."

"Come on, lass," Morrow said more gently. "We can sort it all out when we're somewhere safe."

Someone rattled the door, cursing when they found it locked from the inside. Daphne's heart jumped, speeding fast enough to make her decision for her. Whether or not she trusted Finley and his crew, she wasn't staying behind to face whoever was on the other side of those doors alone.

CHAPTER 7
FINLEY

"The other door," Morrow said urgently, turning toward the depths of the barn.

But Nisha shook her head. "If they're trying this door so openly, they'll already have the back covered."

"Then we go out the side." Finley pointed at a ladder that led up to a hayloft above.

Archie grinned and immediately began climbing. "Don't worry, Daphne," he called quietly over his shoulder. "I'll test that it's safe for you."

"I'd better go last." Morrow eyed the simple wooden ladder with misgiving.

But Finley was only half aware of his familiar companions and their expected reactions. His main focus was on Daphne. If she insisted she wasn't coming with them, he would use the dagger. He wasn't going to leave her behind to be captured because of him—even if that meant carrying her out over his shoulder.

But Daphne's expression was serious, even grim, and she put her hands on the ladder to steady it as Archie scrambled over the top. As soon as he had disappeared into the loft, she wrapped her skirts firmly around herself and began climbing after him. She didn't once look at Finley, and he had the impression that wasn't by chance. But she was escaping with them, and that was all that mattered.

Nisha stepped up to the base of the ladder in Daphne's place, holding it steady for her as Daphne had done for Archie. When Finley took his place at her side, she threw him a single look.

"Now that," she said, "is a lady worth admiring."

Finley's neck went red, but Nisha didn't wait for an answer, ascending upward so quickly that he barely had time to steady it before she disappeared over the top. He climbed after her, emerging into a dusty old hayloft that looked less sturdy than he would have liked. He peered back down at Morrow.

"Careful, friend. There's no one to steady the ladder for you."

"That's for the best," Morrow huffed, already several steps up. "If it can't hold my weight, I'd squash them like a pancake."

Finley grinned reluctantly, his concerns alleviated by the sight of the ladder holding firm, despite Morrow's sturdy bulk and dire predictions.

On the far side of the hayloft, a dirty window let in streaks of light. As Finley glanced at it, Archie punched out the glass, his fist wrapped in an old piece of leather.

Finley rushed to his side. "That isn't the best way to do that."

"I know." Archie grinned at him affectionately. "But it was the only thing I could find up here. I didn't think moldy hay would do the job."

"It did the job well enough," Daphne said evenly. "But I hope you have a better plan for what comes next. I have a strong aversion to leaping blindly out of windows."

"Don't worry," Archie said. "Finley always has a plan. And they're usually brilliant."

Finley's jaw tightened. It was hardly the moment for Archie to boast about him to Daphne—Finley had done nothing to impress himself to her so far.

The wooden floor of the hayloft creaked as Morrow clambered onto it, giving Finley fresh nightmare fuel. They needed to move quickly.

"Pull up the ladder," he instructed Morrow, stepping forward to receive the end from him.

Daphne took his place at the window, leaning out to peer downward. "That ladder won't reach all the way to the ground if that's your plan," she said over her shoulder.

Archie pushed up beside her to peer out as well, although Finley suspected him of doing it just to be near her. His hands tightened on the ladder.

"See that rock?" Archie murmured to Daphne as Finley gruffly instructed them both to move out of his way.

They did so, Daphne's expression one of almost reluctant admiration. But it was much too early for Finley to feel any pleasure at the sight. He hadn't gotten them safely out yet.

He maneuvered the ladder through the window, lowering it carefully until it was fully extended through the window, the base only just reaching the stone positioned carefully below. He dragged the two points of the ladder's base until they settled into the grooves he had carved out earlier, after Morrow helped him roll the stone into position. It was fortunate that the rock was large enough to have remained in place since their last visit when Finley had undertaken proper preparation. Usually he never went into an uncertain situation without first preparing an escape route.

"You go first again, Archie," he murmured. "And then you can hold the ladder steady for Daphne."

Archie's half-formed protest died at the mention of Daphne, and he clambered out the window in due haste.

"Don't worry, Daphne," he whispered, before his head disappeared out of sight. "I'll make sure you get safely down."

Finley shook his head. If Archie hadn't yet recognized Daphne's competence, his younger brother must be more Legacy-addled than Finley had realized. Daphne might wear an air of sleepy detachment, but she didn't need help climbing down a ladder.

This time she didn't follow straight in Archie's wake, however, instead stepping back and gesturing for Nisha to descend ahead of her. From the pained look on Daphne's face, she didn't want to climb straight into Archie's arms. Nisha seemed to understand since she bumped Archie out of the way and braced the ladder for Daphne herself, an unusual grin lingering around her lips.

Finley was glad someone was finding Archie's enchanted puppy love amusing because he certainly wasn't.

It didn't take long for all five of them to reach the ground, Morrow coming last and sliding most of the way down in his rush. Nisha led the way into the trees, the first three already disappearing between the trunks before Morrow was off the ladder.

But even with their haste, they hadn't moved fast enough. Finley had only just stepped between the first of the trees when a yell sounded from inside the barn. A flurry of shouted words followed, and a man appeared around the end of the barn. He caught sight of them and gave a louder shout.

"Blast!" Finley took off running, Morrow behind him. "Run!" he called ahead to the others, and both women did so without a backward glance. Even Archie instinctively picked up his pace, although he did take the time to look worriedly over his shoulder toward Finley.

With his longer legs, Finley could have outrun them all, except perhaps Nisha. But he moderated his pace, maintaining his position at the rear of the group. If their pursuers caught up, they would have to go through him before they could touch the others.

Thankfully it was taking the men time to close the gap, although he could still hear the sounds of pursuit. Most of them must have still been inside the barn when Finley was spotted, slowing them down. It was just unfortunate that a full speed flight through the forest made enough noise to be easily tracked. On the other hand, if they slowed enough to reduce the noise, they would be overtaken before they had a chance to lose their pursuers.

Ahead of him, Daphne caught the arms of Nisha and Archie, pulling them both to an abrupt stop. Finley nearly ran into the back of them, only just sliding to a halt in time.

"What are you doing?" he gasped out between sharp breaths. "We have to stay ahead of them!"

"And where exactly are we going?" Daphne was breathing heavier than Finley, but she didn't look too exhausted to continue. So what did she hope to gain?

If she thought the men behind them could be reasoned with, she was wrong. Finley had already tried. Twice. And Finley was good at talking people around.

"We need a better plan than run until we all keel over," Daphne said when no one responded to her question.

"Do you have one?" Archie's voice was filled with excited anticipation, his faith in her complete.

To Finley's surprise, Daphne nodded. "Of course. I don't like running."

She turned to a solid patch of brambles with wickedly long thorns. The type that littered the forests of Oakden. "This should work well."

Archie let out a soft, wordless cry of caution, but she had already reached her hand toward the greenery. The leaves and branches stirred, pulling back from her touch. As they moved, they picked up speed until a path had formed leading into the middle of the bramble patch.

Daphne turned a satisfied expression on the rest of

them. "Well, come on! We don't have long!" She stepped between the brambles.

Morrow and Nisha exchanged a look before both shrugging and following her. As she led the way, the brambles continued to move until they revealed a central hollow in the middle of the patch.

Archie gave a silent whistle and followed, his adoring eyes fixed on Daphne as he slipped between the brambles. When he reached her, he sat on the ground, alongside Morrow and Nisha, ensuring their heads stayed low and out of sight.

Daphne remained standing, however, her gaze turned back toward Finley, a challenge in their depths. Shaking his head, he followed his brother.

As soon as he reached the hollow, she touched the brambles again and they closed behind him, leaving only the central space that sheltered them. It was large enough for all five of them to sit, but only just.

He and Daphne had only just settled on the ground when footsteps raced past, voices calling to each other. The five inside the brambles kept quiet, and Finley held his breath, straining his ears as he listened to their pursuers stream by. There seemed to be more of them than he had seen before.

He turned his gaze to Daphne, hoping she couldn't read his feelings on his face. Once again she had surprised and impressed him. Without her assistance, they would have been in serious trouble.

When the forest settled back into silence, he ventured

a whisper. "How did you do that? Do brambles usually part at your touch?"

"I don't know." She shrugged. "I've never tried it before."

"You've...never....tried it before?" he repeated slowly, his admiration turning to indignation.

"I don't like running," she repeated. "This seemed much more efficient."

"We could all have been caught if it didn't work," he growled.

"We would have been caught eventually anyway," she said, apparently unconcerned. "You might be able to run forever, but the rest of us can't. Only think of your brother. What state must his muscles be in after sleeping for weeks?"

Finley glanced at Archie and was dismayed to see him massaging his calves. Usually Archie could run longer than Finley.

"Don't worry about me," his brother said with his usual cheer. "The cramps will die down soon."

Finley looked slowly back at Daphne, abashed. She was yawning.

"The Legacy power must have been building in this area ever since Archer was put to sleep," she said. "Probably even before that since it prompted the local lord to confiscate all those looms. So it seemed logical that if I just woke an enchanted sleeper, I should be able to part brambles as well. At least until the Legacy power in the region dies down or decides I'm no longer a focus of its attention."

"That's brilliant," Archie murmured, smiling admiringly at her. "You're as intelligent as you are beautiful."

"You do know it's only the Legacy making you think that, right?" She gave him a stern look. "You should be busy admiring girls your own age."

Archie puffed up his chest. "There's barely an age difference between us! And there's no way the Legacy is the only reason I think you're beautiful. I have eyes in my head." He turned to look at Finley. "Back me up, Fin. Tell Daphne how stunningly beautiful she is."

Caught off guard, Finley coughed.

"Tell her, Fin!" Archie demanded.

Finley's eyes jumped everywhere but Daphne as he managed to croak out, "I'm sure anyone would agree that Daphne has a beautiful face."

His swiftly moving gaze finally fell on her, and his embarrassment immediately melted away. At some point during Archie's speech, she had lain her head on her raised knees and fallen asleep.

"Is it the Legacy?" Archie cried, his voice rising in his panic. "Is she in an enchanted sleep?"

"Hush!" Nisha said sharply.

"That's just Daphne," Morrow reassured him. "She sleeps a lot."

"What? Why?" Archie still watched her with concern. "Are you sure it's not my fault? Because of the Legacy?"

"It is the Legacy, but it's not your fault," Finley said softly. "She's lived most of her life in Glandore, and the effect seems to have lingered."

"But why?" Archie asked, obviously still worried, even if it wasn't his fault.

Finley shrugged. "Maybe because she was so young when she left, or because she was away so long."

"She's only been back a couple of days," Morrow added.

"A couple of days?" Archie's face turned horrified. "How close we came to never meeting her at all! To think I might have gone my whole life without knowing her. What good fortune that she decided to return and that you encountered her immediately when she did."

Finley pressed his lips together, barely refraining from rolling his eyes at the overwrought speech. But he couldn't dispute their good fortune in finding Daphne. He didn't know anyone else with a royal cousin.

Daphne had given him his brother back, and he had repaid her by bringing her into their troubles. And the worst of it was that he had no idea how to get her back out of trouble again. The best he could do was keep her with them and protect her himself.

It was a solution he found all too appealing—a point that would likely count against him with Daphne. She was going to be even more suspicious of him than she currently was. He sighed and ran a hand through his already messy hair.

Everything was his fault. He shouldn't have gone off alone in the first place. He should have known Morrow and Nisha wouldn't be able to stop Archie dragging them into some foolish scheme or other. The boy was too soft-hearted for his own good.

Finley had left, and their enemies had found Archie. If Archie hadn't happened to prick himself on that spindle... Finley tried to shake away the thought. It was too terrible to bear thinking of. The last two times they'd been captured, Finley had been there, at least, and he'd been able to help Archie escape. If Archie had been captured without him...

He had failed his brother, and now he had failed Daphne. He ground his teeth together. He needed to find out who was pursuing them and why so he could end the matter for good. But attempting to discover that information was what had led him away in the first place, and look where that had gotten them.

His eyes traced Daphne's face where it rested on her arms. He couldn't deny Archie's claims. She was achingly beautiful. But she also thought Finley was a villain—and she was justified in thinking so.

He shifted, turning slightly away from her and forcing himself to look at a solid wall of brambles instead of her face. There was little he could do for her, but at least he could refrain from watching her sleep.

He didn't know if she was truly asleep or faking it, but he was grateful either way. The moment was already awkward enough, and they would have to wait hours more before it was safe to leave the tight confines of the brambles.

CHAPTER 8
DAPHNE

Daphne had thrown her head on her knees and forced her eyes shut as soon as she heard Archie's demand of his brother, but the sleepiness wasn't entirely faked. She had barely been holding off sleep since the moment she stopped running. It had been a while since she felt the pull so strongly.

She slept longer than usual as well, if the crick in her neck when she woke was anything to go by. How much time had passed? It was hard to tell beneath the forest's canopy, but she suspected it had been hours.

She stretched, startling more than one of her companions.

"You're awake!" Archer sounded joyous, and he spoke at normal volume, confirming her suspicion that plenty of time had passed.

"What about our pursuers?" she asked the group in general. "Have you heard anything more from them?"

"They've passed us three times," Nisha answered. "But they've been further away each time, and we haven't heard anything for over an hour. We've just been discussing if it's safe to leave the brambles."

Despite herself, Daphne smiled. She always woke up at the right moment. In this case she'd escaped several hours of simultaneous tension and boredom.

"Excellent." She stood. "In that case, why don't we get out of here?"

"Assuming we can," Finley muttered.

Daphne felt a twinge of unease. Was it possible the strength of the Legacy had faded so significantly in only a few hours? If the brambles no longer responded to her touch, they'd have a long, unpleasant job trying to cut their way out.

She reached out her hand without speaking, brushing it against the closest leaf. A strange awareness blossomed inside her mind, a connection to the greenery that allowed her to send it a silent command to part. For a moment nothing happened, and then the branches in front of her quivered and moved. Their progress was slower than it had been the previous time, and she watched the tangled mass in front of her intently.

Finally the branches and thorns had pulled back far enough to allow a narrow passage to freedom. She gestured for the others to pass through it, keeping her fingers on a nearby thin branch.

"Hurry," she said quietly, and they moved faster in response.

Even so, she could feel her connection to the greenery fraying, and she gripped the branch harder, pushing out her silent command more fiercely. When Finley stepped free of the bramble patch, she finally let go and ran after him. She leaped past the last of the brambles just as they closed behind her with a snap. She really had woken up just in time.

"Apparently that strategy won't work again," Finley murmured.

"But it worked when we needed it." Archer's perpetual cheerfulness was unabated by the near miss.

For a moment they all stood in silence, exchanging uneasy looks as they considered what had just happened.

"Now what?" Morrow looked to Finley.

Nisha watched him too. Apparently he was the leader of this strange gang, despite being years younger than the other two. What had brought them together? Daphne didn't want to feel any curiosity about Finley after what he'd done, but it bubbled up just the same.

He gazed up at the sky. "I'd rather not be out in the open tonight."

The days were lengthening again now that winter was past, but it was still close to twilight after all the time they'd spent in the brambles.

"I once found an abandoned woodcutter's cabin in this area," Nisha offered. "If I remember rightly, it wasn't too far from here, and our pursuers have no reason to connect it with you. I doubt they even know it exists."

Finley nodded decisively. "That sounds perfect. We

can at least spend the night there and reassess in the morning."

Nisha took the lead, Morrow assuming her old position in the rear, his body tense and alert in a way Daphne hadn't yet seen. After the unexpected terror of being chased, she was glad to have his bulk between her back and the descending night.

They moved quickly, but it was still almost full dark by the time a building loomed out of the forest ahead of them. It was neater than Daphne had expected, with wooden slats and a wraparound porch. Was it really abandoned?

But when Finley tried the door, it swung open easily beneath his hand. And the inside showed clearly that no one had been there for some time. The windows were all still intact, so none of the forest had blown inside, but everything was so dusty that Daphne sneezed three times before she'd made it all the way in.

"How tiresome," she said to no one in particular.

It didn't take much rummaging to discover a broom that had been abandoned along with the cottage, and she began to sweep with long, flagging strokes. Despite her long nap, she was already exhausted again. Was it the excitement and emotion of the day sapping her energy? Or was something else going on? The uneasy thoughts slowed her sweeping even further.

Archer intercepted her, wrestling away the broom. "Let me do that!" He plied the tool with far more enthusiasm than she had.

She let him take over, turning her attention to the furniture and shelves instead. Thankfully Nisha unearthed a couple of cleaning cloths from her pack and dipped them both into a bucket of water Finley had managed to produce by working a small, manual pump in the wall.

Nisha nodded toward the water pouring from the spigot. "The well beneath the house is the reason I remembered this place. Very convenient."

"As the one who usually carts most of the water, I appreciate that," Morrow said with a rumbling chuckle.

He had finished clearing the fireplace and was lighting a fire, coaxing it into a small, cheery blaze that gave light to the room. Finley finished with the pump and stepped to Daphne's side, gazing into the fledgling flames alongside her.

"Don't worry," he said, although she hadn't spoken. "The smoke from the chimney won't be visible at night, and we'll put it out well before dawn."

Daphne hadn't been worried. The comfort, light, and warmth of a fire outweighed any small risk—at least in the darkness.

"Enough talking." Nisha thrust one of the wet cloths at Finley and the other at Daphne. "The sooner we get rid of this dust, the better."

Daphne took the cleaning implement without complaint, in complete agreement with Nisha. She was willing to sleep in the dirt when camping outside, but she had no desire to do the same inside the cabin.

While Daphne and Finley dusted, Morrow took over

the pump, rinsing the cloths as needed and periodically dumping the dirty water outside. Nisha, meanwhile, went on a search for anything that could be used as a chair or stool, managing to find several old crates and even two abandoned stools that needed only a small bit of repair.

The larger items of furniture, such as the table and beds, had been left when the house was abandoned—most likely because they were too large to fit through the doorways and too heavy to be easily transported. But all the smaller items, like chairs, had been taken.

Daphne cared more about beds than chairs, however. While she wouldn't admit it, she missed her bed back in her cousin's palace, and was already thinking of the large bed in the room she and Nisha had claimed. The other room had only two narrow beds, but there was room enough on the floor for a bedroll, so the men would fit, even if one of them was relegated to the floor.

By the time the cabin was at an acceptable level of cleanliness, Nisha had found five makeshift seats to place around the table, and the last hints of daylight had disappeared, deep dark falling. Between the forest canopy and what had to be cloud cover above, there was no hint of either stars or moonlight.

Daphne shook out her cleaning cloth for the final time and closed the door firmly behind her. The fire inside burned warm and inviting.

An empty spot in the main room had likely once held a stove, but that had been taken by the departing occupants. The open fireplace stood as a substitute, however, and Morrow had already started preparing the evening meal.

"Why was a neat place like this abandoned?" Daphne asked, as they finally took their places at the table.

"There are dwellings like this scattered throughout the forest," Finley said, "and a reasonable number are abandoned. It isn't easy living such an isolated life, and many people eventually decide to move back to more populated areas."

"I heard Lord Castlerey outlawed woodcutting in this part of the forest years ago," Nisha said around a mouthful. "The inhabitants were cutting from a valuable grove to the west, and he wanted time for it to regrow, so he ordered all the residents to relocate east of the town."

"In that case, there should be little to no traffic around this area," Daphne said hopefully. "It sounds like a perfect place to stay."

Finley frowned. "You want to stay here?"

Daphne took a spoonful of stew. "It sounds more appealing than endless walking." She gave a shudder. "Or worse—running."

"And the people without compunction or morals who are dedicated to hunting us down?" Finley asked.

Daphne swallowed her mouthful, unconcerned. "From what I can gather, they've been chasing you across the kingdom for years. Running around doesn't seem to have done you any good so far. Maybe you should try staying in one place." She took a mouthful.

Archer chuckled. "When you put it like that..." His amusement died away. "It's true that we haven't been able to shake them, no matter what we've tried. Every time we think we've succeeded, they reappear. We once lost them for six whole months, but then…" He shook his head.

"Given your past behavior, they won't expect you to stay in this area." Daphne reached for a slice of bread. Staying would mean fresh bread to replace the single, stale loaf remaining from Ethelson.

Archer looked at Finley, his expression eager. "Given they couldn't find us this afternoon, they must think we've already fled the area. I agree with Daphne—why should we hurry away?"

"Of course you agree with Daphne," Finley muttered.

His scorn didn't hurt because Daphne agreed with it. She would prefer any other champion than Archer. But aloud, she said calmly, "Let them search the rest of the kingdom while we sit here and come up with a better plan than running away from them for another three years."

Finley looked at her, his face hard to read.

"Unless you like running and close escapes?" She twisted off a corner of bread and chewed it. "Personally, I'm not at all fond of either of those things."

"It makes sense," Nisha said after the silence had stretched out for nearly a minute. "And I wouldn't mind a few nights in a proper bed."

Daphne smiled, but her eyes lingered on Finley. His was the vote that counted most. Would he disagree just for the sake of it? He seemed like the kind of man who was used to coming up with the ideas, not meekly following the ideas of others.

But he gave a decisive nod, no sign of disagreement on

his face. "We stay here for now, then." He looked across the table at Morrow. "Unless you have any objection?"

Morrow shrugged. "Our coin won't last forever." He clapped his hands together. "But I've had an idea about that." He turned to Archer. "How are you feeling about our new companion over there?" He gestured toward Daphne. "Still aglow with her magnificence?"

Daphne choked on her sip of water, but Morrow kept his gaze on Archer.

Archer grinned. "I'm aware of her perfection, yes."

"Good!" Morrow clapped his hands together a second time and looked at Nisha. "In that case, we have an opportunity. The Legacy hasn't fully released him from its grip yet. Daphne might not be able to manipulate thorns anymore, but we still have a Sleeping Beauty in our midst."

"I am quite beautiful, it's true," Archer said with a grin.

Nisha's eyes narrowed, her speculative gaze lingering on him. "He was never much good at whittling, though." She tipped her head slightly to one side. "He might cut off one of his fingers by accident."

"I'm not that bad!" Archer protested with a laugh. "I made a very creditable horse for Fin's birthday once."

"That was a horse?" Fin looked genuinely surprised. "I always thought it was a dog."

"A dog?!" Archer stared at him in offended horror. "Of course it wasn't a dog. We've never had a dog. Why would I carve you a dog?"

Finley shrugged. "You'd obviously put in a lot of effort. I didn't want to ask any questions."

"Thankfully, spindles are easier than horses or dogs," Morrow said, not distracted from his original purpose.

Archer turned back to him. "You want me to carve you a spindle, Morrow? Are you in need of some yarn? I'm happy to do it, of course, but you might have better luck whittling one yourself." He threw Finley another wounded look, and Daphne hid a smile.

She would have laughed at the idea of Morrow needing yarn if she hadn't spotted him packing away knitting needles on their first morning. Apparently his vast bulk didn't inhibit the deftness of his fingers.

"It's not for me, it's to sell," Morrow said. "We could always do with supplementing our coin supply."

Finley's eyebrows shot up. "You want to sell something Archer carved? We won't make much that way."

"It doesn't matter how good it is," Nisha interjected, "since it won't be used to make yarn."

"The only other use for a spindle is bringing on unwanted naps," Daphne said. "Or worse than naps for unfortunates like Archer. No one in Oakden has any need for more naps. Life is slow-paced enough here already, thanks to the Legacy."

"Ah, but that's just it." Nisha leaned forward slightly. "We heard a rumor a couple of seasons back. We all know that here in Oakden if we prick our finger on anything weaving or needlework related, we'd better get comfortable for the coming nap—but outside Oakden, pricking your finger has no effect. But Morrow and I heard that a spindle carved by a recent Sleeping Beauty—made while the Legacy still lingers around them—still works outside

Oakden. It's a powerful sleep aid, so it's prized by those who have trouble sleeping. And they'll pay a high price to acquire one since they're so rare."

Morrow nodded. "Issue dropping to sleep at night? One prick on your finger, and you'll be sleeping like a baby."

"Do babies sleep so well?" Archer muttered. "They seem to cry a lot from what I've seen."

Daphne smothered another laugh, but Finley only frowned.

"I've never heard that before."

Nisha shrugged. "Has it ever been relevant before? This is the first time I've known a full Sleeping Beauty myself."

Finley continued to frown, but Archer clearly didn't share his mistrust of the story.

"Why not, I say," he exclaimed. "If the quality of the carving doesn't matter, I could make a dozen. Two dozen! I'll start right now."

"And do what with them?" Finley asked. "We live in Oakden, remember?"

"Ah, see that's where the situation is working in our favor," Morrow said. "We not only have a Sleeping Beauty in our midst but a foreigner as well." He paused and glanced at Daphne. "Or, well...sort of. Close enough anyway."

Daphne's expression didn't change. She was far too used to the label to react to it.

"If we sent them to your parents, would they sell them

in Glandore for us?" Nisha asked. "They would keep a cut of the profit, of course."

"That's your plan?" Finley asked. "And what if the rumor is false? What if they don't work? It's not like we can test them ourselves before we send them."

"My parents could test them when they arrive," Daphne offered, but Finley was already shaking his head.

"Fin!" Archer cried. "Think of all the coin we could make!"

"Think of all the coin we would have to invest to ship them safely to Glandore." Finley gave him a stern look. "All with the chance they won't actually work when they get there. And then how long before we get any coin back, even if they do work? No." Finley shook his head again. "We don't have enough coin to waste on wild, speculative endeavors."

Archer looked like he wanted to protest, but he slumped in his seat instead and said nothing, apparently unable to think of a good counter-argument.

Finley stood. "It's been a long day, so we'll come up with a *proper* strategy in the morning. For now, everyone needs sleep. I'll keep watch for the night."

Morrow stood also, his voice soft. "For five hours, lad. Then I'll take over."

"Make that three each." Nisha rose and began collecting bowls. "That should cover the hours of dark."

"I can take a watch as well," Daphne offered.

"Of course you can," Archer agreed. "And I can join you. Together we won't miss anything." He fixed a pleading look on Finley.

"No—" she started to protest, but Finley's "No" sounded even more loudly over her own.

The look he gave his brother allowed for no argument. "Daphne falls asleep just from blinking, so there's no way we're trusting her to take a night watch. And you were only just woken from an enchanted sleep this afternoon."

Daphne's protest caught in her throat and died. She couldn't deny that she wasn't likely to be a reliable night time sentry. Her eyes were already drooping, requiring more and more effort to open each time. If she didn't go to bed, she was going to end up napping any minute.

She shot to her feet. The sensation of sleepiness was familiar, but it was stronger than she remembered in a long time. She needed to get to bed.

But she couldn't help lingering alongside Finley when she passed him.

"Would it really be so bad to give their idea a try?" she murmured to Finley, Archer's dejected face in her mind.

Finley gave a rough laugh. "You say that because you don't know what Morrow's like when it comes to these schemes. He always has some new, brilliant idea for making money, and Archer is always equally convinced it's a good idea. And while you wouldn't think it to look at her, Nisha is almost as easily persuaded. Why do you think they gave control of the purse strings to me? After the first brilliant idea failed, they decided I should have the deciding vote." His voice lowered even further, the lines on his face deepening. "None of them want to become my Father."

A spurt of interest briefly drove back the sleepiness,

but one look at Finley's expression dissuaded her from further questions. He would tell her more when he was ready.

And when she passed Archer on her way to the bedroom, the boy already seemed to have recovered from his momentary low spirits. He was standing with Morrow, whispering excitedly.

"I could at least carve them. Just in case. As long as I make them right away, they'll be Legacy infused and should store well enough."

She didn't catch Morrow's rumbled reply as she slipped through the door, but the tenor of his voice sounded positive. A smile lingered on her face as she prepared for bed, and within minutes, she was stretched out in bed. Despite her late afternoon nap, Daphne fell asleep immediately—as she could do anywhere, anytime.

~

Daphne didn't stir when Nisha left their shared room for the final watch of the night, but she woke before any of the men. She joined Nisha in the main room, relieved to see the fire was already out and the fireplace cold.

"No disturbances in the night?" she asked.

"All quiet." Nisha was preparing breakfast, her moves practiced and confident.

Daphne joined her, working silently for several minutes before speaking. "How did you end up traveling with Finley and Archer? Are they family?"

"*My* family?" Nisha's hands paused, and she looked up at Daphne in surprise. "No." She resumed her work.

But after another moment of silence, she continued. "I've been traveling on my own since I was twenty. Never had much of a hankering for settling down, but didn't much fancy tangling with the Legacy either, so I've stayed within Oakden's borders. Reckon I've seen most of the kingdom by now."

"Did you find it lonely?" Daphne asked.

She had traveled further than Nisha, but she had never been alone.

Nisha pondered the question, although her hands didn't still. "At times. At other times I enjoyed the solitude. Then three years back, I encountered several men trying to cart off a couple of lads. Couldn't let that stand."

She retrieved plates from one of the packs and used them to set the table.

"Two lads?" Daphne asked.

Nisha chuckled. "Finley was just a lad back then himself, though he doesn't like me to say so. He still is sometimes, though he's past twenty now."

"Oh, of course." Daphne hid a smile, imagining Finley's reaction if he was present. "So you rescued them. But why did you stay with them after that? It's been so long."

Nisha shrugged. "Seemed clear they'd get themselves straight back into trouble if I left, so I said I'd stay until they shook off those men. And here I still am." She smiled slightly. "I guess I must like having company after all."

"They've been chased for so long..." Daphne

murmured as she carried food to the table. "They really don't know why?"

"Not a clue." Morrow joined them, his hair spiking in all directions. "Though Finley's been trying to find out. I joined them six months after Nisha. I was on my own before that as well, but for my part, I never enjoyed it." He scratched his head. "You could say I have a bit of a tendency for getting into trouble when I'm on my own. That's what had happened back then. They found me in a spot of bother, and Finley talked my accusers down, pretty as you please."

Morrow shook his head. "No doubt he was gifted at birth, that one. Never encountered such a tongue in my life. He always gets us out of scrapes, no matter how tight they appear." He shrugged. "So I figured if I was going to get into scrapes one way or another, better to do it in the company of someone who can get me back out again."

"It's the smile as well," Nisha said reflectively as she served the food. "It could charm the most cold-hearted curmudgeon. And frequently does."

"Of course, Archer bids fair to do even better," Morrow added with his rumbling laugh. "He can even charm us."

"More's the pity," Nisha grumbled. "Or he would never have gone into that barn in the first place. Went against my judgment to agree."

"That assumes you could have stopped me," Archer said cheerfully from the doorway of the left bedroom, unabashed to find them discussing him. "And you only agreed in the first place because you knew that if you didn't, I would have snuck off and done it on my own." He swept Daphne a flourishing bow. "Good morning, fairest Daphne."

Daphne sighed. Apparently the Legacy's effect hadn't worn off overnight. Her eyes slipped past him, looking for someone else despite herself.

She stood abruptly. What was she doing? She needed to get outside and clear her head.

"I'm going for a walk," she announced. "And no, Archer, you're not welcome," she added before he could declare his intention to accompany her. "I'll keep an eye out and let you know if I hear or see any sign of anyone."

She slipped out, closing the door on their protests. Breathing deeply, she moved away from the cabin. She wouldn't go far, but she needed a few minutes of space.

Once she was out of sight among the trees, she stopped. She had no intention of risking her safety by going further. Drawing a deep breath, she settled into the starting pose for her training dance. She craved the stability of her habitual morning activity.

As adventurous travelers, her parents had long ago learned how to protect themselves, and they had first taught her the training dance while they still lived in Oakden. Once they returned to Glandore, and Daphne exhibited a propensity to fall asleep at odd moments, they had put even more emphasis on keeping her in peak form.

The familiar movements calmed her, providing an anchor to the life she had left behind. Some things had changed, but not everything.

Footsteps disturbed the peaceful solitude, but they were approaching from the direction of the cabin, so she didn't break from the proper form to look behind her. "I told you not to follow me, Archie."

But the voice that answered was deeper than Archie's. "I thought I might find you doing this."

She almost faltered, catching herself just in time to finish her lunge. Finley.

A half-dozen responses flashed through her head before she settled on silence. The prospect of an argument was too exhausting to contemplate, especially when she'd finally found a moment of peace. She would just ignore him.

Unfortunately, he proved frustratingly difficult to ignore. He didn't speak again, but he positioned himself beside her as he'd done the morning before, timing his movements perfectly with the rhythm she had set for the traditional dance.

It was the place her parents used to occupy, and his presence at her side unleashed a flood of unwelcome emotions. Why did a stranger stand in their place? She should be with her own people, in her own home, not caught up in the troubles of strangers in a distant kingdom.

And yet it had been her own family who had ensured that she could never truly belong at their side. If her parents had only confined their travels to their own kingdom as Nisha had done—

Daphne forced the thoughts down, ruthlessly squashing them. There was no use dwelling on the past or the decisions of others. She was seeking calm, not further turmoil.

She forced her mind to focus only on the trembling of her muscles and the soft sounds of the forest, reaching for her earlier feeling of peace. Her breathing slowed again. As she breathed in and out, her breaths aligned with those of the man beside her, just as their movements aligned. It brought a familiar sense of communion. Together they breathed in the quiet beauty of the morning—a peace that was stronger for being shared.

But it was one thing to feel such companionship with her parents. Sharing it with the man beside her was utterly wrong. Finley was a liar, a thief, and a charming flirt. He had tricked her into a situation of untold danger.

Daphne knew Finley couldn't be trusted. And yet the moment of connection reached deep inside her anyway, as if she was only now seeing his true self. As if it was the lying that was a mask and a facade.

Daphne stopped abruptly, cutting off the dance mid-movement, as Finley had done the morning before. Finley stopped as well, turning to face her, a question in his eyes.

Daphne held his gaze, emotions roiling within her. The earlier anger and resentment burst free, roaring into new life. Finley was a safer and more comfortable target than her parents. He had earned every bit of her ire.

He looked back at her, silent and clear-eyed. She had the sensation that he was waiting for her accusations—that he was braced for the wave of her fury and had no intention of defending himself. He already knew what he had done to her.

The words of righteous fury died on her tongue unspoken. Daphne could no longer tell the true cause or target of her anger, and its mere existence drained her of energy. She let it wash away in a receding wave that left her more exhausted than the training dance. She turned on her heel, still not having spoken a word, and returned to the cabin.

Two minutes later, the cabin door opened, and Finley slipped quietly in after her. If he thought her behavior strange, he gave no indication of it. He gave no indication that they had met in the forest at all.

CHAPTER 9
FINLEY

Inside the cabin, Nisha had laid out their remaining supplies, and Archer was regarding the meager spread gloomily.

"The bread last night was bad enough," he grumbled as Finley stepped through the door behind Daphne.

He instantly brightened at sight of Daphne, though, smiling in a boyish way. Daphne didn't smile back, looking at the supplies instead, although Finley caught the sides of her mouth twitching. It was hard not to respond to Archer's open face.

"Looks like we need to restock sooner rather than later," she said, and Finley couldn't dispute the words.

Morrow offered to go hunting, but that alone wouldn't be enough. Someone would need to visit the local village.

"I should leave now," Daphne said. "It's a long walk."

Finley's eyes snapped to her. "You don't have to be the one to go."

She gave him a look that spoke volumes. He might not

like it, but it was obvious that she was the best one to show her face in town. One or more of their pursuers might still be lingering around, and her face had to be the least familiar to them.

"You're not going alone, at least," he said implacably. He wouldn't budge on that point. "None of us should be alone out there—it's too dangerous. I'll go with you."

"If you like," Daphne said with only the briefest hesitation. Her tone said she didn't care what he did, but her eyes said otherwise.

He wished she had unburdened herself and yelled at him out in the forest as he had thought for a moment she would. Maybe if she let out her resentment, she might move past it and learn to trust him.

"I'll go hunting with Morrow." Nisha stood, taking inventory of her weapons.

"That just leaves me." Archie grinned at Finley. "I'll come with you, since none of us should be alone."

"Archie," Finley said warningly. He knew exactly why Archie wanted to come to the market, and it had nothing to do with shopping.

"He has to go with you," Nisha said firmly. "He's not coming with us."

Finley glanced at Morrow, who was grinning. "You do want us to have some game to eat, don't you?"

Finley ran a hand down his face. "Fine. Archie comes with us." He gave his brother a stern look. "But don't forget we're trying to be discreet!"

"I'm good at lots of things," Archie told Daphne, ignoring Fin. "But not hunting. Morrow says it's because you need to be both silent and patient for hunting." He grinned. "Apparently I'm neither."

Daphne tried to look serious and unresponsive, but the sides of her lips twitched again. Finley tore his eyes away from their curve with considerable effort. If they were going to go, better to do it quickly. With any luck, any of their pursuers remaining in the area had spent most of the night searching and were still asleep.

They weren't the only sleepy ones, though. When he looked back at Daphne, she had put her head down on the table and fallen asleep. Finley exchanged a dismayed look with Archie, but by the time he had gathered together a few items to take with them, she was stirring again.

"Ready to go?" she asked coolly, standing as if nothing had happened. But he thought he caught a note of worry in her eyes, and the feeling reverberated back into him. They couldn't afford any napping incidents in the village given they needed to avoid notice.

The three of them followed the faintest signs of an old path that wound through the trees in the direction of the village. Finley threw subtle glances at Daphne as they walked. What was lurking inside those tightly controlled emotions?

He wanted to ask, but Archie kept up a constant stream of chatter. When he wasn't talking about his and Finley's childhood in coastal Mirandar, he asked Daphne about hers in Ethelson. And when that topic faltered, he flowed smoothly into questions about how Glandore and Sovar differed from Oakden.

"I've seen the giant pumpkins that the children hollow

out and use as boats on the river," he said, "but surely not every pumpkin in Sovar is that size? It is? And the mice? Are they really the size of cats? A horse! Your cousin has a mouse the size of a horse! Does she ride it?"

The flow of words didn't stop. Forty-eight hours ago, all Finley had wanted from life was for his brother to wake up. Now he would have happily put him back to sleep—for five or six hours, at least.

But, loath as he was to admit it, Daphne didn't clam up for Archie as she had done with Finley. Few were immune to his unaffected friendliness, and the further they walked, the lighter her face became. Eventually she was laughing along with Archie as she told him about Glandore and the allure of picking an enchanted rose, assuring him that she had really, truly seen a man turn into a Beast.

Jealousy stirred inside Finley. Not toward his brother, exactly—he knew Daphne saw Archie as barely more than a child. But he wished he possessed his younger brother's easy charm. He had never felt that way before—Finley had taught Archie his charm, for goodness' sake! But Archie's charm was working on Daphne, while she remained immune to Finley's supposed appeal.

Was it the openness and goodness she could see in Archie—that part of him that was all his own? Or was it Finley's lies that had turned her against him? She had been suspicious of him from the start.

What would have happened if he'd told her the truth in that old man's study? Would she have come with him voluntarily to save his brother?

Finley shook away the impossible thought. He couldn't change the past. And even if she'd come willingly, she still would have been justifiably angry to find herself thrust into their endless troubles as reward.

Such circular thoughts would get him nowhere.

At the fringe of the village, he spotted a line of cloaks drying on a row of bushes behind one of the houses.

"Perfect," he muttered. "Wait here."

Checking for watchers, he had the cloaks in hand and was back at their side within seconds. But when he tried to hand the smallest cloak to Daphne, she refused to take it.

"I'm no thief," she said coldly.

"We're not stealing them." Archie gave her a coaxing smile. "We'll return them on the way out of the village. No harm done."

Daphne crossed her arms over her chest. "If we need cloaks, we should have brought our own."

"We need to be inconspicuous," Finley said in a level voice. "Archie and I have cloaks in the southern style and yours is obviously from Sovar. These cloaks, on the other hand, are in the local style and will blend in."

Daphne's lips tightened, but after a reluctant moment, she took the cloak and pulled it on.

"The least we can do is take care not to get them dirty." She gave them both a warning look.

"Yes, my lady." Archie gave her a cheeky grin, managing to wrest a laugh out of her.

"Don't start that again," she said, but she was smiling as she said it.

Finley smiled as well, but his heart wasn't in it. Now that they had reached the village, responsibility for Daphne and Archer's safety had settled on his shoulders much more heavily than the cloak.

"Hoods up," he said gruffly, and they both complied, although Archie did it with a teasing look that made Finley groan internally. He would need to keep a close eye on his brother.

But he needn't have worried. Once they stepped into the village streets, Archie's manner changed. He lingered protectively by Daphne, keeping his head down even as his eyes darted in all directions. Perhaps it was typical for his brother's age, but Finley was always taken by surprise when Archie switched so easily between boy and man.

They followed the trickle of people moving toward the single village square.

"We're lucky it's market day," Daphne murmured. "Stallholders will assume we've come in from one of the outlying areas. Just make sure you both hang back. You insisted on accompanying me, so don't cause trouble!"

"Yes, my lady," Archie said with a wicked twinkle that turned his face boyish again for a moment.

Daphne gave him an exasperated look, but Finley handed her a leather purse before she could retort. Her fingers closed over it instinctively, but her expression turned dubious.

"For the purchases," he explained. Her brows didn't soften, so he added, "It's not stolen."

She raised an eyebrow, but Archie backed him up.

"We earned it honestly, I swear. We do get honest

work from time to time." He grinned again, and Daphne narrowed her eyes.

"I find it hard to believe you've ever done an honest day's work in your life," she said sternly, but her face and posture gave her away. Her shoulders had relaxed, and her hands were slipping the purse out of sight in one of her pockets.

"It's a surprise, isn't it?" Archie's good humor was unabated. "But plenty of people have jobs that need Morrow's strength, and the rest of us tag along. Most recently we spent three whole months hired as guards for a merchant caravan that made the trip back and forth between the capital and the Marleston crossing. They even hired me when they saw I could use a sword." Archie's tone was proud, and Daphne turned her head away to hide a smile.

"Very well, then." She led the way toward the baker's stall. "Just remember—no causing trouble!"

Finley obediently stepped back, he and Archie forming a guard behind her as she greeted the baker's assistant. The lad busied himself collecting her order, giving no indication of surprise at encountering an unfamiliar face. The same thing happened at the next stall and the next. Daphne did all the talking, while the two men hung back and kept their faces shadowed by their hoods.

Finley barely registered Daphne's bargaining, his focus devoted to the market crowd. He caught no sign of anyone he recognized, and no one was paying undue attention to the small group of three, two of whom were growing more and more laden down with packages.

But when Daphne stopped at a final stall near the edge of the market, the stallholder caught his attention. The woman smiled readily enough at Daphne and gathered the requested items without issue, but her eyes kept jumping to Finley and Archie. When she lowered her voice and leaned toward Daphne, Finley came to full alert, his attention focused on the woman.

"Awfully self-conscious for such strapping fellows, aren't they?" she murmured, her voice tinged with excited curiosity.

"Sadly, yes," Daphne replied in a serious tone, not missing a beat. She mirrored the woman's movements, leaning across the stall to close the distance between them and dropping her voice. "It's the hair, you know. A family affliction among the males. I've tried to tell them there's no shame in going bald, no matter your age, but…" She sighed and shook her head.

The woman smiled triumphantly. "I guessed as much! Their egos are fragile when they're young, my dear, so there's no point telling them not to mind it. I know just the type, and I have the very thing for you."

Daphne clasped her hands together, her expression hopeful.

The woman pulled out a tiny bottle with a flourish. "We had roving merchants through town recently, and I managed to acquire a hair tonic from Stonyfell."

Daphne gasped dramatically and clasped her hands to her mouth in apparent astonished delight. Finley growled too quietly for the woman to hear, and Daphne's smile grew. She was clearly enjoying herself.

But she let her face fall, biting her lip and twisting her hands together as she glanced back at the two robed figures. "It would be just the thing, but an item from Stonyfell must be expensive. How much are you asking for it?"

The woman named a price, and Daphne's face fell. She glanced into her purse and then gazed wistfully at the miniature bottle.

"So much..." she sighed.

The woman broke into voluble praise of the tonic and assurances of its rarity, and Daphne sighed again.

"Undoubtedly it's worth it," she assured the woman. "But I'll have to save my coin and come back another day." She leaned forward, talking more quietly. "I'm sure they'll both work extra hard with such an incentive, so hopefully we'll have the coin saved in no time."

The woman nodded, clearly disappointed. "I can't promise it will still be here," she warned. "I was able to spread it across several bottles since you need such a small amount to be effective, but if other customers take them..."

"Of course!" Daphne assured her quickly. "I wouldn't expect you to hold it for us."

She paid for her other purchases and thanked the woman, leading the way quickly out of the market. As soon as they were safely within the trees, Finley pulled back his hood.

"Daphne, you wretch!" he growled. "What were you thinking?"

She turned to him with a look of satisfaction. "It was

rather brilliant, wasn't it? But I didn't expect her to pull out a hair tonic." She pressed her lips together, clearly trying not to laugh.

"You were brilliant," Archie assured her, taking off his cloak and helping Daphne out of hers. "I didn't know you were such a good actress."

"It was my debut performance. Perhaps I have a future on the stage."

"We were supposed to go unnoticed!" Finley cried, his frustration growing in the face of his companions' frivolity. "That woman is definitely going to remember us now."

"Ah, but she'll remember you as the two balding young men." Daphne eyed both of their generous heads of hair with significance. "There's no danger in that. And if there does end up being any talk about the two men in cloaks, she'll spread the rumor that it's because you're self-conscious. It's perfect."

"Maybe we should do it for real," Archie said, entering into the spirit of the moment. "We could shave some of our—"

"No," Finley said firmly. "Absolutely not."

Archie sighed and shook his head at Daphne. "Their egos are fragile when they're young, my dear." He gave such a credible impression of the stallholder that Daphne laughed.

"You're the one who should become an actor," she said. "I bow to the master."

Finley seized the two cloaks from Archie's hands. "I'll

return these," he growled. "You two try not to get into any trouble in the three minutes I'm gone."

He stalked off back toward the village, aiming for the house on the edge where they had found the cloaks. But as he carefully arranged the garments just as they had found them, he had to admit Daphne's reasoning was sound. Their behavior had been just odd enough that an explanation wouldn't do any harm.

He sighed and ran a hand through his curly hair, a wry smile stealing onto his face. Given his reaction to Archie's suggestion, there might be some truth in the mention of fragile egos...Although Finley hadn't thought half so much about his supposed good looks until he had started to wonder what Daphne thought of them.

When he rejoined the other two, Archie was back to his usual chatter, and the three of them turned toward the path home. But Daphne kept glancing his way as they walked, and after a few minutes, she broke into Archie's flow of talk.

"Is that how you always do it?" she asked. "Returning the things you take?"

"As often as we can." Archie threw an expression of affectionate exasperation at Finley. "Fin will only take things in the first place when my safety is in question. But I follow the Lathlain principle." He sounded inordinately proud of himself. "That's why I stole those looms."

"Except we don't live in Lathlain." Finley repeated the familiar refrain in weary tones. "So the Oakden Legacy isn't going to help you with that goal. As you've now experienced firsthand."

Archie grinned at him. "That's why I have you to get me out of scrapes." He looked at Daphne. "Finley taught me everything I know—how to pick locks, how to evade capture, how to blend in, how to make people want to help me."

"Why am I not surprised?" Daphne muttered, but she looked more thoughtful than disgusted.

Finley watched her surreptitiously. He needed to explain the full truth of their history to her—as he had once related it to Nisha and then Morrow. But it wasn't the moment for that sort of conversation.

Or maybe he was just reluctant for Daphne to discover the full truth of who Finley really was.

CHAPTER 10
FINLEY

inley, Archie, and Daphne reached the cabin without incident, and Finley and Archie began putting their purchases away. But though Daphne took a sack of potatoes, she only made it a few steps toward the kitchen before she placed it on the ground and promptly sat on it, resting her head against a wall and going to sleep.

Archie laughed, but Finley eyed her with concern. She stayed upright, however, showing no tendency to topple, so he returned to his task. Daphne woke just as they were storing the last of the packages, hefting her sack and carrying it to them as if nothing had happened.

She poured a stream of potatoes into an empty bucket, declaring her intention to prepare them for the evening meal. Archie stepped in to help her balance the sack, so when a voice hailed them from outside, Finley stepped onto the porch alone.

"Success!" Morrow grinned from the forest floor, raising his voice to add, "Come on, Archie!"

Archie appeared in the doorway behind Finley, moving with uncharacteristic reluctance. Usually he was more than willing to help with the unpleasant task of cleaning and preparing the meat, given he was no use in catching it. But that was before he had someone anchoring him to the cabin.

"I was about to help Daphne peel potatoes," Archie said slowly. "I can't abandon her to do that alo—"

"I'll help Daphne," Finley said, recognizing his opportunity. "Go, Sprout."

Archie shuddered. "That's worse than Archie! I'm not a child anymore!"

"I know," Finley said implacably. "That's why you have to do your fair share—in this case helping clean the carcasses."

Morrow grinned. "We can't have Daphne thinking you're the sort to shirk unpleasant tasks."

Archie's eyes widened, and he leaped off the porch. "You'll have to tell her the truth, Morrow." He gave the man a pleading look. "You know I'm the helpful sort!"

Morrow chuckled. "That you are, lad, that you are. I'll see if I can work it into conversation. Natural like, of course." He winked at Finley and led Archie off.

Finley watched them go with a strange mix of excitement and reluctance. He hadn't expected his opportunity to talk to Daphne to come so quickly.

She appeared in the doorway with a bucket of potatoes on her hip, her lips twitching as she watched Archie's retreating figure. But when she transferred her gaze to Fin, her expression turned more serious. "You don't actually have to help with the peeling. I can easily do it on my own."

"Of course I'll help." Finley took the bucket from her, and she turned back to fetch an empty one for the peeled potatoes. "Shall we peel out here on the porch? It's a beautiful day."

Daphne agreed, and they were soon settled on the porch, their hands falling into a natural rhythm. Fin tried to think of a smooth opening and failed. With a sigh, he gave himself a mental shake and plunged straight in.

"I hope you believe that I didn't mean to involve you in our mess. I thought you would be free to walk away after waking Archie."

Daphne's hands stilled for a moment before she resumed her even movements. "I accept that." She didn't look at him.

He took a breath, grateful she was willing to concede that much. "The current situation isn't what any of us wanted, but there's no denying that you're involved now. So I think I should explain the background more fully."

She looked up quickly, her brows lifting. "I thought you don't know why you're being pursued."

"We don't know the specific offense." He sighed. The words were hard to say. Harder than it had been with Nisha or Morrow. "But we know where it started."

His hand bore down on his potato, accidentally taking off a chunk of the vegetable along with the peel. Grimacing, he forced his hands back under control.

"To explain it properly," he said, "I have to go back to our childhood."

Daphne's brows rose again, but he kept going.

"Archie already told you we grew up in the southern city of Mirandar. What he didn't say is that our mother was both beautiful and kind—the epitome of goodness and love. But our father was not. He never deserved her."

The words came a little more easily now he had begun, but he didn't look toward Daphne. He didn't want to see her reaction. "Father was often absent, off on some scheme or other that always came to nought. And when I was ten and Archie was five, he didn't come back at all. For five years, Mother raised us entirely on her own. I helped where I could, of course, but it was difficult for her. Although she tried her best to shield us from that truth."

He laughed roughly. "She was always telling me to stop worrying and be a child while I still could. But I had to help—of course I did. I couldn't watch her struggling and do nothing."

He risked a glance at Daphne. She had stopped peeling and was watching him instead. He couldn't read her expression, so he grabbed blindly for another potato and kept talking.

"When Archie was ten, our mother got sick and died. The sickness came on quickly, and the local doctors could do nothing to save her. If Father had been there, perhaps he could have gotten her to the capital in time. But even at fifteen, I couldn't manage it on my own. Not when we always had so little coin."

"I'm sorry," Daphne said softly. "If you don't want to talk about this, you don't have to."

He frowned as a droplet balanced on his chin before dropping free. When had he started crying?

He brushed the moisture away angrily. They were tears of anger more than sorrow, but he needed to get himself under control.

"You need to know this." His voice sounded hard even to his own ear. Did she realize his anger and resentment weren't directed at her? "It's the beginning of how we ended up in this predicament. An interfering neighbor managed to contact our father, although I have no idea how. He told him of Mother's death, and Father actually showed up."

He dropped his potato into the bucket of peeled ones and snatched up another, wielding his knife savagely. "We didn't need Father. I could have looked after Archie on my own. But when Father came, Archie was so excited. He barely remembered him from before, and he was desperate to know his father. He'd just lost his mother, so how could I say no?"

"You couldn't," Daphne said softly. "Of course you couldn't."

"The first thing he did was take us away from Mirandar. I could have refused to go, of course. I was old enough for that. But I couldn't send Archie off with him alone." There had been no way he was going to trust Archie to their unreliable father. "So all three of us became homeless drifters. Our father was extravagant, wasteful, and a spendthrift—a man without a practical bone in his body.

But he was also charming and had an unshakable faith that good fortune was just around the corner, so he was always finding people to loan him money." Finley's expression hardened even further. "Of course those relationships always eventually soured. And then we would move on to the next place."

Daphne shifted in her seat as if uncomfortable with his words. But when she spoke, her voice was soft. "That must have been difficult."

Finley couldn't look at her or reply. He needed to get through the story, and her sympathy unraveled him. Nisha and Morrow had both listened in silence.

He cleared his throat. "I got jobs wherever I could, and worked to pay off his debts. But I could never earn enough. Mostly, I did what I could to shield Archie from the truth."

"How sad that your father's optimistic outlook was so misdirected. He sounds like Archie in that regard, except Archie uses his positivity to cheer and help others."

Finley jerked, nearly cutting his finger with his peeling knife. Words of defiance leaped to his tongue. Archie was nothing like their father.

But he swallowed the words down, bitter though they were in his throat. Was she really wrong? Finley might hate to admit it, but her words rang true. If he forced himself to see past the bitterness and anger that clouded his view of his father, Archie was very like the man. But Archie was their father without his fatal weaknesses.

He forced himself to speak, though the words sounded wooden. "Archie has the best parts of both our parents.

The charm and positivity of Father, and the goodness and compassion of Mother."

Daphne tipped her head to the side. "And what of you?"

He frowned at her, but she didn't seem to notice, continuing to muse aloud. "Archie grew to be like your parents, but he took the best of them and filtered out the worst. You, I think, are the opposite."

Finley stiffened. Was she saying that he was the worst of both parents?

But again she continued without waiting for him to speak. "You rejected your father and shaped yourself to be his opposite. You saw his irresponsibility and became far more responsible than any youth should have to be."

Her words resonated somewhere deep inside Finley, brushing against something too painful to be touched. Was that what he'd done? Had he formed himself in reaction against his father?

He shied away from the question. There was no part of his father in him—even in opposition.

"Most people find me just as charming as Archie, you know," he said with a smile that was a ghost of his usual, easy one.

"I know." Daphne continued to gaze at him. "But I think with you the charming rogue role is a mask. Archie might truly be one at heart, but not you."

Finley stared at her, robbed of speech.

Daphne's brow crinkled, and her eyes seemed to turn inward. "You talk as if you hate your father, but surely..." She looked up and met his gaze, her own confused. "He's your father! And he can't be all bad if he managed to raise you and Archer."

"Our mother raised me." His breath sawed through his throat. "And after she left us, I finished raising Archer. We owe our father nothing."

"Nothing?" Daphne sounded genuinely shocked, her emotions rubbing against his newly re-opened wounds.

"You may choose to close your eyes on the truth of your parents," he snapped, "but I choose to see my father clearly, as he actually was."

Daphne frowned at him. "What's that supposed to mean?"

"My father ruined my life, and I won't pretend otherwise. But what of you? Your parents' selfishness ruined your life, too, and yet you pretend it was an unavoidable occurrence. They're the ones who chose to move kingdoms and then to have a child in Oakden. Having done that, they should have endured, no matter what it cost—not run away and forced their child to take the burden in their place."

Daphne pulled back as if struck, and Finley's eyes widened. He had lashed out without thinking. He was no better than a wounded animal, acting as if he had been backed into a corner.

"I'm sorry," he said quickly. "Forget I said that. Your parents and your life—it's none of my business." He hesitated before adding in a much softer voice. "I do think your parents wronged you. But you're the injured party, and the emotions are yours to feel—however you feel them, without any reference to me."

Daphne opened her mouth only to close it again. She didn't unleash the tirade on him that he deserved, but her face still contained the glassy, shocked look. Finley's stomach clenched.

"My life hasn't been ruined," she said with dignity, but there was a catch in her voice as if she wasn't entirely sure she believed her own words.

Fin's stomach twisted tighter. Maybe there was something of his father in him after all, to behave with such unconcern for Daphne's feelings after everything she had already undergone for his sake.

She sighed. "It's true that I could have nursed resentment all these years, as you have done." Her quiet words didn't hold any note of judgment, but they plunged deep into his middle regardless. "But what would it have achieved? My resentment would have served no purpose except to make me miserable. My parents love me and have provided well for me. I'm grateful to them." Her final words were said in a stubborn tone that would brook no argument.

Finley knew he should let the topic go. He never should have brought it up in the first place. But he couldn't stop himself from making a final comment.

"As I already said, your feelings are yours without reference to me," he murmured, "but I just hope you let yourself feel them without reference to your parents either. They were the adults and you the child. It was never your responsibility to make them feel better about their mistakes."

Daphne sucked in a breath. Finley waited, but she didn't speak, so he went on.

"At least in your case, your parents have redeeming virtues for you to cling to. My father had none, even if I wished it."

Daphne's stricken expression softened into something weary and sad. "I wonder if that's really true. You say I don't see my parents clearly, but do any of us? We're all shaped by the decisions of our parents, whether we want it or not."

Finley frowned, his voice unintentionally harsh. "Well, it's my father's fault that I have no chance to discover hidden virtues in him—given that three years ago he got himself drunk and fell into the river, abandoning Archie and me once again."

Daphne gasped, and Finley's hand bore down, cutting his potato in half instead of peeling it. She reached over and took the remaining half from him, placing a whole one into his hand in its place. Her touch was gentle, despite his earlier attack, her eyes equally soft.

Once again her sympathy brought him dangerously close to the edge. His hand tightened around the new potato as he pulled himself back, tearing his eyes from hers and looking at his motionless knife instead.

"I was eighteen by the time he died, so we would have been all right—better, in fact, without Father's endless debts. I could have easily looked after Archie without Father there to cause trouble. But it was only days after his death when those men first came for us. Nisha saved us, and we've been running ever since."

"So they have something to do with your father?" Daphne asked, perceptive as always.

"I don't know what he did to anger them, but I'm fairly sure it wasn't an unpaid debt. If it was, they would have demanded money, and I would gladly have paid to be rid of them—even if it took me years to earn enough. No, it's something else." He leaned back, looking over the forest and drawing a deep breath. "I just can't imagine what. What could Father have done to make someone so angry that they would seek revenge on his sons for three years?"

Daphne stared at him blankly. "It's incomprehensible."

Finley blew his breath out, looking blankly at the potato still clutched in his hand.

"I've been trying to come up with an explanation for three years, and I still haven't worked it out. That's why I left Archie a few weeks back. I was following a lead, trying to work out what Father had done. If I could only understand the original issue, maybe I could work out how to appease them."

"You've tried asking them, I suppose?" Daphne asked tentatively.

"Of course. The first time they caught us, I asked repeatedly. They wouldn't say a word. It's all so senseless." Familiar frustration boiled inside him. All he had wanted for the last six years was to give Archie a normal, stable life. Why did circumstances always conspire against him?

"And you want my help working out their motivation?" Daphne asked, reminding him of the original purpose of the conversation. "That's why you told me all this?"

"What I want," he said heavily, "is to save Archie without endangering anyone else. But since that seems to be impossible, yes. I'm asking for your help."

"Then you have it," she said without hesitation.

Her ready agreement took him off guard, given his earlier blunder.

She responded to his visible surprise with a shrug. "It's the only logical course. I don't want to spend the next three years on the run."

He regarded her carefully, telling himself to accept her offer and leave it at that. But words spilled out of him anyway.

"We could escort you to the Marleston crossing. Once you've crossed into Sovar, you should be safe. Your cousin is the crown princess there. I'm sure they wouldn't pursue you so far." He didn't breathe as he waited for her response.

Daphne shook her head decisively, not even taking time to consider his offer. "I came to Oakden to find out who I am, and I haven't done that yet. I can't run away."

Relief flooded Finley, along with curiosity. He hadn't earned the right to pry—quite the opposite—but he longed to know what was behind her words. He would have to work extra hard to build up enough trust for her to share more of her story with him.

For now, the important thing was that she was going to stay. He had been given time to earn her trust, and that was all that mattered.

CHAPTER 11
DAPHNE

aphne finished peeling the last of the potatoes with relief, withdrawing to her room with a mumbled excuse about needing a nap. She didn't lie down on the bed, though. If she did, she would immediately sleep. The nap had been an excuse, but it wasn't a lie. Sleep pulled against her, despite her two earlier naps.

But she refused to give in to sleep until she'd had time to think. There was too much to process from her conversation with Finley.

She had guessed that tragedy lurked in the brothers' past, but even so, Finley's story plucked at her heart. When Finley had concluded by asking for her help, she had responded instinctively. Her subsequent excuse about her own self-interest had been a justification after the fact, although it was true enough that she had no desire to spend years looking over her shoulder. She hadn't been able to walk away from Archie's predicament, and she couldn't walk away from the four of them now.

She didn't even want to walk away anymore. Daphne had come to Oakden to free herself from the Legacy—instead, it had immediately ensnared her even further. She felt instinctively certain that if she ever wanted to be free of its heavy weight, she had to untangle the complicated web binding the five companions.

With a sigh, she sank back onto her pillow, giving in to the relentless pull of sleep. A few moments of mental peace, free from her churning thoughts, would be welcome.

But when she woke minutes later, her thoughts took back up exactly where they had left off.

There was no denying the Legacy's effect was stronger. She had hoped her symptoms would lessen with each day she remained in Oakden, but instead the opposite was happening. Daphne carefully traced back over her days in Oakden thus far, concluding that something had changed after she woke Archer.

Instead of slipping gradually from the Legacy's notice, Daphne had attracted its power further, and it had responded with enthusiasm—latching onto her more strongly than ever. Her ability to part thorns might have faded, but in exchange, the Legacy had strengthened her sleepiness.

But to what end? What did Daphne have to do to finally be free of it?

Getting entangled with a sleeping enchantment was the opposite of what she should have done, and yet... If she could go back—knowing everything she knew now— would she act differently? Could she walk away and leave Archer there, knowing he might be condemned to years of sleep while his brother and friends grew older without him?

She sighed and slid to the edge of the bed. They had all made the best decisions they could in the moment, so there was no point bemoaning the past.

Which is exactly what she had been trying to tell Finley. She remained sitting, staring out the small window in front of her. Finley hated his father—there was no other word for it. The memory of his voice and words as he spoke of the man made Daphne shiver. How could he speak of his own father that way?

And how dare he criticize Daphne's mother and father —people he didn't even know! A surge of protective love for her parents washed through Daphne, but as it faded, it left her stomach churning harder than ever. If Finley's judgment of her parents—and of her own attitude toward them—had been entirely wrong, why was it so hard to shrug off his words? Why did she feel so sick?

Voices reached her through the thin wooden walls of the cabin. Nisha, Morrow, and Archer had returned, bringing a wave of conversation with them.

Daphne forced herself to stand. She needed to be focusing on the future, not the past. The current situation was difficult enough without borrowing past troubles as well.

Slipping back inside her usual composure, she stepped out into the main room.

They debated for two days on the best way forward. Nisha wanted to try tracking their enemies, but Finley insisted the trail would already be cold.

"Tracking them will be an impossible job. We've never managed it before. But there's one place where both sides know the other has been recently...right here. If we wait, eventually, when they can't find any trace of us elsewhere, they'll circle back."

When it came to a vote, Daphne voted with Finley. She much preferred their comfy cabin to traipsing all over the kingdom.

"If we're going to stay here and wait for them," Nisha said, bowing to the inevitable, "then we can't let them catch us by surprise. We can't become complacent. We need to be on the watch and ready for them."

"You make us a watch roster," Finley said, "and we'll all follow it."

"Make sure you include me." Daphne grinned. "Just not for any night shifts."

"I don't think we need to cover nights," Nisha said seriously. "They know we were in this region, but not where we are exactly. My hope is that we'll know they're back before they can pinpoint our location, and we can take extra precautions then." She eyed Daphne speculatively. "We'll patrol in pairs for safety, but I'm not so sure about including you. There's no advantage to having a patrol partner if they can't hold their own in a fight. That makes them a liability rather than an assistance."

"But she saved us all last time," Archer protested.

Nisha was unmoved. "That was thanks to the lingering power of the Legacy. We can't rely on that again."

"Daphne is helpful even without the Legacy." Archer sent a reproachful look toward Nisha. "She can peel potatoes twice as fast as the rest of us."

"Thank you, Archer," Daphne said wryly. "You're a salve to my self-esteem. But don't worry, Nisha. I can fight."

She glanced at Finley. Would he back her up? He had appeared at her side in the forest every morning so far, silently joining her training dance. But he said nothing, observing the conversation without comment.

"I see." Nisha sounded polite but unconvinced.

"I could show you, if you like," Daphne offered.

"I'll help with a demonstration," Archer said eagerly, but one look at his face reminded Daphne of the puppy kicking analogy.

Her eyes skipped over Morrow just as quickly. She'd been training most of her life, but she didn't fancy facing off against someone of his size. Which left...A smile grew on her face.

"I'm sure Finley would be happy to help me," she said sweetly.

From Finley's look of resignation, he had expected her words.

Nisha agreed, and they all moved outside.

"I'm not a weapons master like you, Nisha," Daphne said as they gathered on a level patch of forest floor. "And I'm not saying I'm an expert at unarmed combat either. But if someone grabs me, I won't just be a helpless victim. So that's what I want to show you—what I'll do if someone tries to seize me."

"That's fair enough," Nisha said after a moment's thought. "I can't expect you to be able to fend off any imaginable attack since none of us could do that."

"Are you sure?" Archie muttered with a grin, eyeing the array of weapons that bristled all over Nisha.

But she gave him a stern look in response. "It doesn't matter who you are, or how well trained—there's always the chance of encountering an opposing force strong enough to take you down. If Daphne knows basic self-defense, that's enough for me."

Daphne turned to Finley. "Try to grab me."

"From the front or the back?" He eyed her speculatively.

"Either. Or...wait. We'll do both. You choose which one first so I'm surprised."

Finley sighed. "This is going to hurt, isn't it? Hurt me, I mean."

She gave him her sweetest smile. "Maybe."

He sighed again. "I guess I deserve it." And then without any warning, he lunged at her.

Before she had time to sidestep, he'd grabbed one of her arms and spun her around so her back was against his chest. Wrapping both arms around her, he locked her arms at her sides.

Daphne responded on instinct. Using a small jump to spread her stance, she bent her knees, lowering her body. At the same time, she thrust both elbows upward, breaking his hold.

He tried to recapture her, but she moved too quickly. Reaching her left hand across her right shoulder, she grabbed his arm and yanked him onto her back. Continuing in one swift motion, she stepped forward and threw him over her shoulder.

He landed on his back with a grunt and lay there. Daphne instantly let go of his arm and stepped backward.

The four on their feet all stared down at Finley, who wasn't attempting to stand. He waved a hand at them.

"Just...give...me...a minute," he wheezed.

Archer crowed with delight. "Nice work, Daphne!"

Finley finally rose to his feet, shaking himself out. "Do we really have to do that again?"

"Yes," Nisha said. "Now from the front." Her tone was serious, but Daphne glimpsed a laugh in her eyes.

Once again Finley lunged for Daphne without warning. Seizing both her wrists, he clamped down on them with a firm grip. For the second time, Daphne's body responded instinctively, reacting to years of training.

Twisting her arms inward, she rotated within his grip until she could reverse his hold, clamping onto his wrists in just the way he was attempting to do to her. But unlike him, she didn't stop there. Kicking forward in one fluid motion, she only just remembered to soften her blow before her foot connected with his chest.

He let go and staggered backward, rubbing his hand

on the impact point. Daphne winced. At least she hadn't followed up her kick with an elbow to the head as her parents had trained her.

"Do I pass?" she asked Nisha.

"I apologize for doubting you." Nisha spoke solemnly. "I can recognize training when I see it. If you like, I could teach you some knife fighting techniques to expand your capability."

"I suspect I should be honored by the offer," Daphne said carefully. "So I'm thankful. But I'm afraid it's an honor I'll have to decline."

Nisha blinked. "Why?" She sounded like she couldn't fathom anyone turning down such a treat.

Finley, apparently recovered from both windings, laughed. "Do you have to ask? Knife training sounds far too fatiguing for Daphne."

"Precisely," Daphne said. "I'm quite sure that any sort of training with Nisha would be exhausting."

Finley laughed again. "You seem to have worked us all out."

"And we've worked her out," Archer declared. "She's perfect!"

Daphne groaned. If one of the Legacy's effects was going to linger, why couldn't it have been her ability to manipulate thorns and not Archer's puppy love? If it kept going much longer, she might have to kick him next after all.

CHAPTER 12

FINLEY

Finley checked Nisha's schedule the minute she finished it, trying not to look too eager. Apparently she wanted to punish him even more than Daphne had already done in her demonstration because he wasn't paired with Daphne for a single patrol until the fourth day of the repeating schedule.

At least he could join her each morning for her training dance.

But when he slipped away from the cabin the following morning, he was spotted by the one other person in the cabin with an intense interest in Daphne's whereabouts. Finley had only just settled into his pose when Archie popped out of the trees, his eyes widening with joy when he saw Daphne.

"So this is where you both are!" He gave Finley a wounded look.

Finley almost growled at him to go away, but a glance at Daphne shut his mouth. He was no more an invited guest than Archie was, and his brother wasn't going to leave willingly. Daphne valued the moments of peace to start her morning, so Finley wasn't going to be the one to start a disturbance with Archie.

His brother dropped into a vague approximation of their training pose, positioning himself on Daphne's other side. But unlike Fin, he kept up a steady stream of chatter as he did his best to mirror Daphne's movements. Finley ground his teeth together. Didn't the boy ever run out of breath?

After several minutes of nonstop chatter, Daphne started squeezing her eyes shut more than usual and drawing unusually long breaths. Fin snapped.

"If you're going to be here, Archer, you have to keep your mouth shut!" He glared at his brother across Daphne.

Archie looked back at him with wide eyes, but at least he stopped talking. And Daphne's expression of gratitude made any irritation of Archie's more than worth it. Maybe he'd even get sick of the silence and leave.

Despite Fin's hopes, his brother remained, however. He even made it through the session without a single word more, although it looked like a strain. Perhaps it had been enough of a strain to keep him away on future mornings, though.

But Finley had reckoned without the strength of Archie's Legacy-fueled infatuation. Archie wasn't going to give up an opportunity to spend time with Daphne, even if he had to be unnaturally silent while he did it. And by the fourth morning, he seemed to have largely adapted, looking less stressed and more peaceful by the end of the training session. Perhaps he was learning to appreciate the peace that came from the moments of quiet among the trees.

In the meantime, Finley sought other opportunities to spend time with Daphne. The first to present itself was meal preparation the following day, and when he collected the bucket of vegetables for the day's meals, he suggested they take them to the porch as they had done previously.

Daphne agreed readily, and an instant sense of closeness and camaraderie enveloped them as they took the two porch seats, a lingering effect of the conversation they had shared there previously. Finley threw Daphne a glance as he scooped the seeds out of a small pumpkin. If he stayed quiet, would she volunteer any information about herself? He still itched to know what she had meant about coming to Oakden to find out who she was. He'd rarely met anyone as self-assured and confident in themselves as Daphne.

Daphne didn't appear to notice his gaze, her own attention fixed on the nearest tree trunks. She laughed softly to herself. "In all the years I spent planning my return to Oakden, I never pictured myself in a situation like this. I'm going to have to significantly censor my letters to Rosalie and Olivia." She chuckled, her mood light despite her words.

Finley pressed his lips together, giving her another sidelong glance. Did she miss her friend and cousin intensely? Was she finding it lonely being surrounded by virtual strangers and with no other girls her own age?

"What are they like?" He picked up a second pumpkin. "Are they similar?"

"Rosalie and Olivia?" Daphne sounded surprised. "I've never really thought about it. Hmmmm…" She looked down at the carrot she was peeling. "In some ways they are, and in some ways they're quite different." She laughed softly. "Rosalie is—"

"I love pumpkin!" Archie's head appeared between them. "Will Morrow be making pumpkin pie?" He looked at Daphne. "You'll love Morrow's pumpkin pie! It's my favorite."

The rest of Archie appeared as he forced himself between them despite the small table that already stood there. Without hesitating, he removed the bucket of unprepared vegetables from the table and took its place, perching there as if the table was a stool. Holding up a knife, he grinned from Daphne to Fin.

"I found another knife, so I thought I'd help!" He took one half of the pumpkin his brother had hollowed out and began peeling it.

"We'll be finished in no time with three of us," Daphne said lightly, abandoning her earlier conversation.

Finley clenched his teeth, holding in the words he wanted to say to his brother. But more disappointing than the interruption itself was the lack of even a flicker of disappointment in Daphne. She seemed genuinely indifferent about Archie inserting himself between them.

At least the next afternoon Archie was absent completely since he was out patrolling with Nisha. But in the small cabin with Morrow, there was still no opportunity for private conversation. So when Morrow noticed they were low on kindling and suggested the three of them gather some, Finley jumped at the idea. The three of them spread out beneath the trees, but Finley kept track of Daphne as she combed the forest, hovering in her vicinity without actually approaching her.

He knew how difficult it was for her to shake her usual shadow. If she wanted to take advantage of the rare opportunity for some alone time, he didn't want to force his presence on her—he'd witnessed too much of Archie's juvenile obsession to want to subject her to the same behavior from him. But he lingered in her sight line, hoping to reassure her of her safety while giving her the opportunity to approach him if she wanted conversation.

And to his delight, she drifted closer and closer until the two were gathering sticks from the underbrush side by side. She gave him a companionable smile—an expression he couldn't have imagined ever receiving from her when she was first forced to join them—and it emboldened him to speak.

It was a risky subject—one that would inevitably remind her of his past deception—but it was something that had been weighing on his mind.

"Back in Ethelson, you said you had something urgent to discuss with Lorne. I'm sorry that being here with us has made it impossible for you to seek him out."

"Did I say that?" Daphne stooped to pick up a stick. "I'd forgotten."

Finley's brows rose, and his eyes lingered on her curiously.

She laughed, but there was a shaky note to it. "That makes me sound fickle, doesn't it? It felt like an urgent matter at the time, but now..." Her face grew shadowed. Clearly something was weighing on her—something that had happened since their first meeting and that had overshadowed her original mission.

There was one obvious conclusion as to what that might be. Finley's gut clenched. He was the reason for the shadows on her face.

But when she glanced at him, instead of anger in her eyes, he saw amusement driving away the shadows. Her lips twitched. "Somehow being pursued by faceless criminals who want to abduct—and possibly murder—me puts other supposedly urgent issues in perspective."

"When you put it like that..." Finley shook his head, his mouth curving into a smile in response to hers.

If Daphne could laugh about their situation, perhaps he'd been mistaken about the cause of those shadows. Perhaps he had projected his own feelings onto her.

For three years, he'd been plagued by nightmares of Archie being taken by their enemies, and that morning he had woken in a cold sweat from the familiar dream— except this time it was Daphne being dragged away, her eyes terrified and accusing as she screamed his name.

"We'll work out what those men want," he said. "And then I'll help you find Lorne myself." He hesitated. "If you want my help."

She stumbled slightly at his words, and his hands flew out to brace her, steadying her by both arms. He lost his armful of sticks in the process but managed to save hers, the load of twigs and branches clasped between them. He froze in that position, and she looked up at him, her eyes wide, and her lips slightly parted.

His heart rate, which had spiked from the sudden movement, beat even faster. Was hers beating hard as well? A tremble ran through her—he could feel it through the connection with her arms. But she didn't step away.

Her eyes dropped to his lips, and warmth exploded through Finley.

How angry would she be if he dumped her load of wood on the ground? It had to go if he was going to take her in his arms.

"Finley? Daphne?" Archie's eager voice made them both jerk violently away from each other, half of Daphne's gathered armful raining down around her at the sudden movement.

Archie bounded over, his gaze traveling across the wealth of small sticks that littered the ground around their feet.

"I've never seen such a good spot for kindling!" he exclaimed. "What are you doing just standing around?" He began to scoop up the discarded sticks around Finley, his eyes glinting with competitive spirit. "I just got back from patrol, but I'm going to have more than you at this rate!"

Finley stared at him in wordless wrath. "What are you doing here?" he growled.

"I already told you." Archie's arms were already full. "We just got back from patrol, and Morrow said you were out here gathering kindling, so I came to find you." He turned to Daphne. "It's time for you and Morrow to head out for your shift."

"Oh, yes, of course." Daphne's face was red, and she didn't meet either of their eyes as she turned and fled toward the cabin, clutching her remaining half-load.

"Very well done, brother," Finley said through his teeth, stalking toward the cabin in her wake.

"Seriously, Fin?" Archie called, his arms now overflowing. "You didn't even collect *anything*? How long were you out here?" He raced to catch up, shaking his head at Finley's apparent failure.

Finley glared at his brother, but the look of confused pity on Archie's face forced a reluctant laugh out of him.

"Yes, I appear to be remarkably useless," he agreed. "I've been noticing it more and more. Here give me some of those." He took some of the sticks off his brother, and the two strolled back to the cabin in—almost—perfect amity.

CHAPTER 13

DAPHNE

Daphne's thoughts of Lorne receded as the days passed, but not because her problem was resolved. Quite the opposite.

Lorne had been her best hope for answers when her issue had come from her years spent outside Oakden. But her situation had changed. Each day brought an increasing number of naps, and she could no longer deny that the Legacy's power had grown since she woke Archer. As far as she knew, Lorne had no experience with kissing awake a Sleeping Beauty.

The thing that would have kept Daphne awake at night—if she was capable of keeping her eyes open—was the way the Legacy's power continued to strengthen. Her power over thorns had faded quickly, and she sometimes got hints that Archer's infatuation was fading as well, and yet her naps only grew worse.

Daphne had centered the Legacy's forces on herself, and she had no idea how to shake them loose. It was the shadow that hung over her daytime hours as she settled into the new rhythm of their days. Naps were her long-familiar companion, but each one now came with a new intensity, a feeling of desperation that grew more potent each day.

Where was it all leading? Would she sit down to nap one day and not wake up?

At least she had little time to dwell on her fears since she was rarely alone. Both brothers continued to join her during her morning training dance, and she grew accustomed to their presence. With Archer there, the dynamic had shifted. She no longer felt the frightening communion she had felt when she moved in perfect rhythm with Finley. Obedient to his brother's command, Archer remained silent for the length of the exercises, but she could almost hear the strain of the words he kept locked inside.

She no longer found it irritating, however. Archer's presence had become protection from any further moments alone with Finley. Because after the incident gathering kindling, it was obvious Daphne needed a buffer from Finley's dangerous charm.

She had found his charismatic good looks unsettling from the moment she met him, but at first her instincts had placed a barrier between them. She had been certain something else lurked beneath his easy charm, and it made her wary. But ever since their conversation on the porch, her barriers had crumbled.

Finley had opened himself up and let her see the man beneath the facade—and there had been no sign of a conniving trickster. Beneath Finley's outer layer, there lurked raw vulnerability, steely responsibility, and an overwhelming love and protective instinct toward his brother.

That knowledge gave a depth and an edge to every one of his charming smiles, making them dangerously potent. Neither had she overlooked the way his eyes always sought her out. His attention was far more subtle than his brother's, but it made her heart race and her thoughts scatter in a way Archer's presence never did.

But Daphne had come to Oakden with a mission—one that was so far failing spectacularly—and she couldn't allow herself to be distracted by romance. She might be discovering who Finley truly was, but she was failing at discovering her own self—the Daphne she was always meant to be. The Daphne who didn't nap constantly. For most of her life she had been the Oakdenian girl who napped everywhere she went, and nothing had really changed—now she was just the Glandorian girl who napped everywhere. Her old belief that returning to her first home would solve everything now seemed impossibly naive.

But she couldn't avoid being alone with Finley when it came time for their first rostered patrol. It was an unavoidable difficulty, she told herself, even as she dressed with more care than usual, taking time to arrange her hair.

Finley seemed to be in an equally good mood, bolting down his breakfast and indicating his readiness to start patrolling. But out among the trees, with nothing to buffer the full force of his presence, the whole thing seemed like more and more of a bad idea. Daphne wasn't usually prone to blurting things out unintentionally, but Finley had an effect on her she'd never experienced before. If they were truly alone for hours, she wasn't sure what she might end up saying. She had seen men look at her friends the way Finley looked at her, but she hadn't realized how intoxicating it was.

"Daphne," Finley said as soon as the cabin was out of sight.

His voice was low and rough, and it sent a delicious shiver through her. Maybe she didn't need to avoid romance. Maybe—

"Wait!" Archer's familiar voice shouted from behind them, and Daphne turned to see the youth chasing after them, a piece of toasted bread hanging from his mouth. "Wait!"

"Archie." Finley drew the single word out, turning it from a greeting to a chastisement.

But Archer swallowed the last of the bread and grinned at them, his spirits undimmed. "I'm not rostered on until this evening, and I'm too restless to sit in the cabin all morning. Three eyes are better than two, and all that."

"I think we have six eyes between us," Daphne said with a suppressed laugh. She should have known she wouldn't really be left alone with Finley for four whole hours. Not when Archer was around.

Archer inserted himself between them, slinging an arm around each of their shoulders. "We should circle to the west of town and go past the manor house. I'm convinced that's where we'll eventually find some sign of them. It's where they first saw me, after all. And where we first saw them, too."

"Thank you for that insight and wisdom, Archie," Finley said in a tone of long-suffering. "Whatever would we do without you." The last line sounded like it was spoken through his teeth.

"You'd all be a lot duller, that's for sure." Archer grinned at his brother, unabashed.

But a moment later, his expression turned dismayed, and he swiveled to look at Daphne. "But not you, of course, Daphne! You could never be dull!"

"You do know I frequently fall asleep in the middle of conversations, right?" Daphne's lips twitched. "I think that's the definition of dull."

"Oh no," Archie assured her earnestly. "You look too beautiful when you sleep to be dull."

Daphne pressed her lips together, meeting Finley's eyes across Archie. She had expected to share a moment of silent laughter with him, but the look he wore was one of complete agreement with his brother's words. Looking quickly away, she decided Archer's presence was a very good thing after all.

∾

They fell into a settled rhythm as the weeks passed. Nisha's roster continued in an endless loop as they waited for their pursuers to circle back to the area around Lord Castlerey's storage barn.

Daphne would have been far more restless if not for the burgeoning spring. As the days warmed toward summer, the forest came to life around them, ensuring the time spent walking through the trees was always pleasant. After so many years among the endless roses of Glandore, Daphne loved spotting the various flowers that proliferated across the forest floor, and she soon made a game of learning all their names.

She and Nisha had taken over the job of visiting the market, purchasing cloaks in the local style for all of them on their second visit. So far they had attracted no undue attention, but Daphne worried what would happen when the weather warmed enough to make anyone wearing a cloak stand out.

At nights around the fire, the others looked to Daphne to tell them stories of Glandore and Sovar—her tales a source of fresh entertainment for the old friends. In return, they filled her in on the details of their last three years together, the five of them analyzing every memory as they tried to puzzle out the mystery of their pursuers. But that was a game the others had been playing for three years, and the answers continued to elude them.

Daphne continued to monitor her naps, grateful that the rate of increase had slowed down, even if it did continue to creep up. She still worried daily, however, and she debated internally about whether she should raise it with the others.

When she dropped asleep halfway through a short trip to hunt for spring greens, she finally put the question to Fin and Archer.

"Have you noticed that I'm napping more?" she asked as they continued through the forest, searching for anything that could supplement their food supplies.

"You're perfect just the way you are," Archer quickly assured her.

Daphne sighed. Surely his infatuation should have dwindled to nothing in so much time?

Thankfully Fin took her question more seriously. "I think you might be. You napped twelve times yesterday."

Despite the seriousness of the topic, Daphne had to bite back a smile. It had actually only been ten. The day had been wet, keeping them all trapped in the cabin, and two of the naps had been entirely faked—her only recourse to stop herself from snapping at poor Archer who had hovered at her elbow in the small space all day.

A sudden whoop from Archer made her startle, but he didn't notice, peeling away from them to pursue a patch of green some distance away. As he harvested a cluster of spring onion, Fin turned to Daphne, his voice quiet.

"Does it worry you? Your napping. I've noticed you don't talk about it much."

Of course he'd noticed.

Daphne shifted uncomfortably, but his earnest, patient expression—so different from his usual twinkle—undid her. She had been worrying about the Legacy's hold on her for weeks, and for once she longed to unburden herself. What would it feel like to share the load with someone whose broad shoulders could carry the weight?

"I can still remember being normal as a child," she said, "before we left Oakden. But sometimes it feels like those memories are fading. Like I'm losing the last piece of who I was before the Legacy twisted me."

Finley's brow creased, his eyes worried. "Twisted?"

Daphne held up a hand to stop him, not wanting to hear whatever pacifying compliment might come next.

"Ever since the naps started, I've assumed that once I turned eighteen and was able to return to Oakden, the fatigue would lift. I thought I would have a chance to be free."

"But they haven't gone away," Finley said softly. "They're getting worse. The Legacy hasn't released you after all." His jaw tensed. "It's because of me, isn't it? Because I made you wake Archie and entangled you in our problems."

Seeing his distress, Daphne felt a shot of longing to be able to repudiate his words—to deny it had anything to do with him. But the words would have been hollow, and he would have known it.

"I don't blame you," she said instead. "You didn't know. You were just trying to save your brother."

"Archer!" Morrow's loud yell made Daphne turn away, blinking to drive back the tears.

"I need your help!" Morrow bellowed again.

Archer jogged toward them, dropping the greens he'd collected into the basket at Daphne's feet. He hesitated at sight of her, her face still turned away, but Morrow called again, and Archer gave a frustrated sigh.

"I'll be right back," he promised and jogged off.

Daphne and Fin listened to his retreating steps in silence, distantly hearing the murmur of voices as he reached Morrow.

"You're doing it again," Fin said, the annoyance in his voice making Daphne's eyes spring back to him.

"Excuse me?" she snapped, stung. Hadn't she just absolved him of blame?

"It wasn't your parents' fault then, and it isn't my fault now," he said, a little more heat creeping into his voice. "Why are you so desperate to let us all off the hook?"

"And why are you so desperate for me to wallow in pointless resentment and bitterness like you?" She glared at him, cracks running through her control. "Has it made you happy, Fin? Has it changed the past or Archer's situation? Has it achieved anything at all except to make you and everyone around you miserable?"

Fin sucked in a breath, his eyes widening. "I make you miserable?"

"No," Daphne said quickly, putting her hand up to shield her eyes. "That was too much. I didn't mean to say that. I'm not…I don't usually…" Where had her usual calm acceptance of life gone? Why did Finley provoke so much intense feeling in her?

She lowered her hand. "I'm sorry."

"Don't be," he said quickly, and if he was still feeling hurt at her words, he'd hidden it away where she couldn't see. "I want you to let out your feelings. Repressing them only does you a disservice. Eventually, they'll come bursting out anyway."

"I have no desire to wallow," she said tartly.

"Then don't wallow." His challenging gaze wouldn't let her go. "Acknowledge the truth of the situation you're in and what caused it, feel the feelings that creates, and then let them go, if you want to."

It sounded so simple, and yet...

"And what about you?" she asked. "You must want to wallow, then. Since you haven't let anything go."

Part of her wanted to hide from the intensity of the conversation—already fatigue was pulling at the edges of her mind, the emotions draining her. But another part of her refused to back down. If he was going to challenge her, then he needed to prove he could take the same challenge back.

He stood frozen, looking at her.

"I..." he started, only to stop.

She gave a small, tight smile. "That's what I thought. If I need to accept that my parents—and you—have wronged me, then you need to let go of the wrongs done to you. Your father is dead, Fin. The anger isn't serving you."

She thought he would turn away, that he would leave her alone among the trees, but he did neither. Instead, he straightened.

"You're right. If I want you to release the feelings you've repressed, I have to release the ones I've been holding. Or at least, I have to try."

His words were so unexpected they released something inside her. Her hands tightened into fists, her muscles quivering with the effort of remaining still.

"You're right that I'm angry!" Her quiet voice shook with intense emotion. "I'm angry that my parents gave me this burden, and I'm angry that just when I was supposed to be free, you tricked me into entangling myself even further. And most of all, I'm angry at the Legacy! I don't care that it doesn't have a mind or a will. I'm furious with it! I'm sick of my own body and mind betraying me! All I want is to be myself without the Legacy's burden! Is that so much to ask?"

"Not at all," Fin said softly. "And I only wish it was in my power to give you your freedom. I wish I'd never had a part in making your life worse."

His words pierced the haze of Daphne's storming mind, draining her anger liked he'd pulled a plug.

"You don't make my life worse," she whispered, so softly she thought he might not catch the words.

But his breathing quickened, and he stepped toward her, one hand reaching out before dropping back to his side.

"I did this to you," he murmured. "I have no right to..."

Daphne wasn't sure what words came next, and the possibilities scared her.

"What if it's building to something worse?" she blurted, her worst fear leaping from her mind to her tongue in an effort to fill the silence. "What if one day I go to sleep, and I don't wake up?"

Finley's muscles tightened, and this time his hand gripped one of her arms. "If that happens, I will never abandon you. I will do whatever it takes to wake you. You, of all people, know that's true."

Daphne released a shaky breath, moisture tangling in her eyelashes. She didn't know what to do with the fire in his eyes or with the relief his words sent coursing through her.

His voice grew more urgent. "I will make sure you wake up. And I don't need to know who you are without the naps. That was one thing Archie was right about—you're incredible with or without them."

Daphne laughed hollowly, looking down. "We don't know what I'm like without the naps, do we?"

"Daphne." Fin stepped even closer, his eyes trapping hers.

Slowly, his free hand reached out, his fingers brushing down her arm, tracing it from shoulder to wrist. Her skin tingled at the lightness of his touch, her heart thrumming as he reached her hand and wove his fingers through hers.

The weight and warmth of his hand, so firmly holding hers, filled her simultaneously with a sense of security and an unfamiliar excitement. She looked down at their clasped hands. How could so much be communicated with just entwined fingers?

Fin stepped even closer. "I meant what I said. I don't need to know what you're like without them." His voice was low and deep. "You're already the most amazing person I've ever met, Daphne."

Her eyes leaped upward, and her breath caught at the nearness of his face. She could see every one of his long, dark lashes, and her eyes traced the light stubble that lined his chin.

Without thinking, her free hand lifted to run lightly along the sharp line of his jaw. He sucked in an audible breath at the contact, and her eyes jumped back to his. His gaze was locked on her lips.

Her breath tangled and caught, her heart beating so hard it hurt. She should pull away. Any moment, she was going to pull away.

But the warmth and security of his handhold kept her in place.

"Daphne," he breathed again, his face sinking toward hers.

Her breath hitched as his nose hovered beside hers, his eyes dropping closed and his breathing turning rough and pained. Her hands leaped to his chest to push him away, but instead they lingered there, flat against his jacket.

"Daphne," Fin repeated, almost a groan. "Tell me you don't want this, and I'll stop."

She said nothing—could say nothing—and his mouth crashed down over hers. His hands captured her waist, pulling her flat against him, and she sank into the kiss.

They had been dancing around their attraction for so long that the heat of it nearly consumed them, flaring white hot, trying to melt them down and meld them together. But as Daphne felt her heart pull toward him, closing the emotional distance between them as he had closed the physical one, she pulled herself back.

Gasping, she wrenched herself from his arms. He

stood, staring at her, his breath coming in hard pants and his eyes wild.

"What is it?" he asked, voice rough. "Daphne, what's wrong?"

"I...I don't know," she stammered.

"What don't you know?" His voice turned gentle. "You still don't know me? Or us? You don't know about us?"

"I don't know *me*! I'm still not free." The words felt torn from Daphne, and as soon as she'd spoken them, she turned and fled.

"Daphne!" Fin called after her, but she ignored him, fleeing for a quiet part of the woods where no one would find her.

CHAPTER 14

FINLEY

From euphoria to despair in the space of a moment.

Finley wanted to chase after Daphne, to hunt her down and make her understand that he already saw her as whole and valuable, just as she was. But he knew when he wasn't welcome, and he wasn't going to force his presence on her. That would only drive her away further.

But neither could he return to gathering spring greens. He paced back and forth among the trees, reliving the kiss and the expression on Daphne's face as she pulled away from him. How could she look like that after a moment of such intense connection? Finley couldn't remember the last time something in his life had felt as right as the presence of Daphne in his arms.

Eventually he was forced to return to the cabin. To his relief, Daphne was already there. She hadn't fled from them completely, then.

But she was avoiding him—as much as was possible

in the small confines of the cabin. He knew Nisha and Morrow could see it, but mercifully neither of them commented.

After Daphne rebuffed his first few attempts to talk to her, he stopped trying, reduced to watching her when she wasn't looking. She looked tormented, and he longed to gather her into his arms and smooth away the lines between her brows with his fingers.

She continued to avoid him the next morning, exchanging only the barest practicalities over breakfast. But they were scheduled to patrol together, and to his relief, she didn't find an excuse to bow out of it.

Perhaps she was secure in the knowledge that Archie would tag along, as he always did. Finley merely hoped the hours spent together would bring back some of the former ease between them.

As they walked away from the cabin, Archie positioned himself between them, shooting Finley a glance—the first hint that he knew something was going on. But he said nothing, keeping up his usual stream of chatter. And for once, Finley was glad of Archie's words to fill the space between him and Daphne.

Just as he'd hoped, as the first three hours ticked away, she gradually relaxed back into some semblance of her normal self. She laughed with Archie and even replied to Fin's comments with her usual wry observations.

The suffocating band around Finley's chest lightened.

"What about that man?" Archie cried in exaggerated alarm, pointing at a man approaching the village on the main road.

He was easily visible from their position in the trees and was equally clearly not a threat. Daphne sighed, but Finley could hear the amusement behind it, and he could have hugged his brother in thanks.

"I think that one is even older than the last one you pointed out," she said with a small gurgle. "He must be past seventy, and I think he might collapse if he wasn't leaning half his weight on that horse he's leading. If he's an example of your attackers, I'm going to have to question why you're running at all."

"It isn't for my sake," Archie told her earnestly, placing a hand on his chest. "But Fin here is a lot weaker than he looks, and it's my duty as his brother to keep him from any and all threats. Even the...er, weak-looking ones."

"Yes, after all, he might be a master in unarmed combat," Finley said in a straight voice. "And then where would we be?"

"Where, indeed!" Archie nodded. "You wouldn't believe the number of situations I've had to rescue Fin from, Daphne."

"No," she said dryly. "I wouldn't."

"But," Archie added, "now that I've had a better look at his face, I have to admit that man is a total stranger." He turned a wheedling look on Fin. "Don't you think we should just swing by Lord Castlerey's manor before we head back? We've been watching the roads for nearly three hours! They might have arrived early this morning, before we got away from the cabin."

Daphne threw Finley a pleading look of her own,

clearly wanting to indulge Archer, and he was helpless to resist the plea in her eyes.

"Fine, then," he said. "I was planning to walk back that way anyway. There shouldn't be much harm in going early."

"It's a thin line between harm and gain," Archie crowed, rubbing his hands together.

Finley eyed him. "Is it?" he muttered.

How had he never seen the similarities between his brother and their father? He had been trying to ignore it ever since Daphne first pointed it out, but he couldn't pushing the thoughts away. Not if he wanted to be true to what he'd told Daphne the day before.

But it was one thing to speak easy words and another thing to follow them through. Could he really let go of his anger toward his father? Could he acknowledge how much of his father was lurking in Archie's bright person and...possibly even in Finley himself? If only because of who Fin had chosen not to become.

He drew a deep breath. The middle of patrol was hardly the place to be asking himself those questions.

He let Archie take the lead, and he took them through the trees, passing behind the lord's manor and close to the abandoned barn where Archie had slept.

Seeing it always made Finley shudder, remembering his fear the first time he saw Archie lying so still on the barn floor. But then he had found Daphne, and she had saved Archie. She had changed everything—forcing Finley to see a future beyond protecting Archie and dealing with his father's mess. Finley didn't intend to let her go easily, even if it meant finding a new way to see his father.

"Do you hear that?" Daphne hissed silently, grabbing Archie's arm.

Archie responded instantly, falling silent and looking to Fin. Finley strained his ears, listening for anything out of place.

"Voices," he whispered. "We need to get closer."

He moved forward silently, using skills he had practiced so often that they came as easily as second nature. Daphne followed behind, not quite as silent but close. She had improved a lot in the weeks of their patrols. Archie brought up the rear, making as little noise as Fin. Everything Finley knew that might keep a person safe he had forced his younger brother to learn as well.

The voices grew louder, and Finley stopped, keeping himself out of sight of whoever was lurking at the back of Lord Castlerey's property. Peering around a particularly broad tree trunk, he scanned the area. Three men stood huddled together behind the barn.

Archie appeared at his side, pulling urgently at his sleeve. But Finley didn't need his brother's warning to recognize the men. He still didn't know any of their names, but he would recognize their faces anywhere. They were the three who had been pursuing the brothers the longest—the three who had first seized Fin and Archie, back when they were clueless and unprepared.

"Is that them?" Daphne breathed in his ear, her breath sending shivers across his skin.

He nodded.

"Now what?" Archie whispered.

Finley looked away from the men to find two faces trained on his, waiting for instructions.

"Now we wait. We need to see where they go and follow them if possible."

"I told you this is where we should patrol," Archie whispered. "If they were going to circle back to where they last found us, that meant this barn."

"I'm surprised they're lingering so near the lord's house, though," Daphne murmured.

"When they move, I'll follow," Finley said. "You two stay here."

"What? No!" Archie's protest remained soft, but his eyes shouted defiance.

"It's not as easy to follow someone covertly as you seem to think," Finley hissed. "Keeping them from noticing one person will be hard enough, let alone three."

Archie opened his mouth to protest, and Fin played his trump card. "I could let you come with me, but what about Daphne? Do you want to leave her here on her own? Those three won't be alone, and the others could be lurking anywhere in the area."

Archie's eyes darted to Daphne's face, his expression changing to one of resignation. Daphne, on the other hand, was giving Finley an unimpressed look that said she knew exactly what he was doing. But she didn't say anything, accepting the need for the two of them to stay behind. She was always good like that—quick to grasp the practicalities of a situation.

It was one of the many reasons he loved her.

Love. The word echoed through his mind. When had he become so certain of his feelings?

"He's here." The words from beyond the trees made Finley snap back into the moment. They'd been seen!

But no sound of running feet reached his ears, and when he cautiously took another look, all three men were looking toward the manor, not the forest. Did they have another target besides Archie and Finley?

The men began to move, but their steps were measured, and they circled the barn toward the manor. Finley gestured for the other two to remain in place and carefully eased around the tree. His quarries hadn't gone far, stopping on the far side of the barn, but it took Finley longer to weave his way through the trees until he found a place that allowed a view of them while keeping Fin himself hidden.

From his vantage point, he watched a tall, slender man approach from the back steps of the manor. He was dressed in much richer clothes than the men waiting by the barn, and his hair style must have taken at least thirty minutes to arrange. If he was their new target, they had set their sights higher than Finley and Archer.

But the men by the barn made no attempt to approach the newcomer, instead waiting for him to approach them, their faces lined with impatience. Finley frowned. It was even less believable that the men could have business with the lordly man from the manor than it was that they planned to abduct him. What in the kingdoms was going on?

The man from the manor glanced toward the trees,

and Finley caught his first full view of the man's face. He was furious. But he didn't appear to have seen Finley.

His cold fury broke over the waiting men. "*What* do you think you're doing?" he hissed at them. "I have been very clear about approaching me while I'm at the manor. What if it had been someone else who had seen you lurking outside? What if they started asking questions?"

One of the men tried to respond, but the newcomer held up a hand to silence him, and the man fell instantly quiet.

"We must get out of sight of the house. Immediately." He stalked off in the direction of the trees, sending ice down Finley's back.

The lordly man was leading the ruffians directly toward Daphne and Archie—and from their hiding place, they wouldn't have been able to hear the man's words to give them warning.

Finley plunged back into the trees, running as fast as he dared between the trunks, ducking and weaving and leaping over underbrush. His instinct was to run straight back the way he had come, but that path would intersect with the men. Fighting the screaming voice in his head, he aimed deeper into the trees, drawing a wide circle that would take him back to his original position from a different angle.

His breath sawed through his throat and lungs, but he pushed his legs faster. He had to reach Archie and Daphne first.

Running at speed, it was impossible to be completely silent. Some sound must have reached the waiting pair because when they came into sight, they were peering in his direction. And already, behind them, he could see flashes of the approaching men through the trees.

Finley froze, his face a grimace of alarm. Archie responded instantly, looking over his shoulder to follow the direction of Fin's gaze. He went still at sight of the men, only his head moving as he turned back to look at Daphne and then Fin.

"Move! Move!" Finley mouthed, not wanting to speak or move himself in case he drew unwanted attention.

Archie sprang into action, leaping straight into the air and catching a branch above his head. With enviable ease, he swung himself onto it, reaching one arm back down to Daphne. She wasn't usually one for fast movement, but she didn't hesitate. Taking his hand, she let him haul her silently into the tree, her feet scrabbling at the trunk as she moved upward.

Her foot whisked above eye height mere seconds before the men stopped only a few trees away. If they had arrived thirty seconds earlier, they would have discovered Daphne and Archie, and even now, if one of the men scanned the forest canopy, they would be spotted.

Finley eased himself slowly backward, moving silently and carefully so as not to draw any eyes. Safe behind a tree trunk, he peered carefully around it. He finally had a good view of the newcomer, and he intended to memorize his appearance. If Fin ever saw the man again, he would recognize him.

Unfortunately, Finley's new position put him too far from the men to hear more than the general murmur of their quiet voices. It was obvious, however, that the newcomer wasn't happy—and equally obvious that the ruffians answered to him.

Finley waited with growing impatience and fear as the conversation stretched on for what was probably only minutes but felt like hours. Finally the murmur stopped, and Finley peered back around the tree. The man from the manor stood alone, watching with a sour expression as the ruffians traipsed off.

Only when they were out of sight among the trees did he turn and walk back toward the manor. Finley waited until the newcomer, too, had disappeared from sight, and then forced himself to count to one hundred and twenty.

He stepped out from behind the tree at the exact moment Archie dropped to the ground. The two brothers' eyes met, and Archie grinned. Finley had been the one to teach him to always count out two minutes before coming out of hiding.

Finley rushed toward his brother, but he didn't arrive in time to catch Daphne as she slid from the tree. Instead, she dropped into Archie's arms before quickly stepping away.

"Well," she said, dusting herself off, "that was interesting."

"You could hear them." In his anxiety over their safety, Finley had forgotten that the two in the tree were perfectly positioned as spies. "What did they say?"

"Not the key information we want, sadly," Daphne said. "So we still don't know why they want to harm you. But we do now know that the first men are in the employ of that other one. And he's growing increasingly angry at their failure to capture you. I assume that wasn't Lord Castlerey? I had the impression from his words that he's a guest in the manor."

Archie nodded. "Lord Castlerey is older. I've never seen this man before, but it definitely sounded like he was a guest. From the way he talked, I'd say he's been visiting Lord Castlerey for some months."

"A guest?" Finley shook his head. "Who is he? A relative? A wealthy merchant? How did Father get tangled up with someone like that?"

"You know what Father was like." Archie shrugged. "He never cared much about position or wealth. He would talk to the lowliest person he encountered as if they were his long-lost brother—but by the same token, he would just as comfortably have interacted with the king himself in the same way."

Finley groaned. "This could be even worse than we feared." He dropped his voice to a mutter. "And it was already pretty bad. But I didn't know the person after us had connections with the nobility."

"At least we now know how they stumbled on Finley in the first place," Daphne said. "But I guess we were wrong about why they circled back here. They weren't tracking you either time—this is their current home base."

Archie gave a low whistle. "What awful bad luck on my part to run into them by chance! They must have caught sight of me in the village or while I was scoping out the barn."

All three of them fell silent for a moment, considering

the unlucky coincidence. Archie was the first to break the silence.

"There's really only one question left to ask about this incident," he said.

They both turned to him with quizzical looks.

"However did you nap in that tree without falling out, Daphne? Your perch on the branch looked precarious at best. I think my heart nearly burst thinking you were sure to fall."

"You were napping in the tree?" Finley asked. It sounded impossible, even for her.

"I never fall when I'm napping," Daphne said complacently. "I think it's part of the Legacy effect. But that's hardly a relevant issue right now! We finally have a new clue. After all these weeks, the patrols have managed to accomplish something."

"We need to follow that man into the manor and find out who he is and why he's doing this!" Archie exclaimed.

"No," Finley said firmly. "We need to go back to the cabin and make a strategy."

Archie wrinkled his nose. "A strategy to do what?"

"To follow that man into the manor and find out who he is and why he's doing this, of course," Daphne said.

Finley threw her a wry look. "Without being discovered, that is."

CHAPTER 15

DAPHNE

"So all we need to do is infiltrate the manor and question its occupants without being identified as outsiders," Daphne said as she paced feverishly back and forth in the small living space of the cabin.

All three men tracked her with their eyes, Morrow looking a little dizzy. Daphne knew she was panicking. She also knew that the panicked feeling had little to do with the impossible task before them. Daphne had been faced with seemingly impossible situations before, and as far as she could remember, she'd never panicked in her life.

But she'd been feeling the forces of the Legacy closing around her for weeks, and since her kiss with Fin and the discovery of the mastermind behind their pursuers, it was starting to feel like a stranglehold. Whatever the Legacy wanted from her—whatever it was driving toward—it was getting close.

"Tell me again why we can't go in as servants?" She completed another loop of the too-small room.

"Nisha said it was impossible." Archer sounded cautious. Even his infatuation didn't know what to make of her current state. "She said servants all know each other well, and they'd notice a new face straight away, let alone multiple new faces."

"Who knew that Nisha was once a servant herself." Morrow gave a disbelieving chuckle. "Hard to imagine Nisha bowing and scraping and scrubbing floors."

"Why do you think I'm not a servant anymore?" Nisha asked from the doorway.

"Nisha!" Daphne pounced on her. "Where have you been? You know the most about manor houses. You need to tell us—"

"You need to sit down before Morrow gets so dizzy he keels over." Nisha fixed Daphne with a stern look. "Aren't you feeling at all sleepy, young lady?"

Daphne dropped immediately into one of the dining chairs. "Actually," she said. "Now that you mention it, I am."

The exhaustion—held at bay by her frenzy—hit her like a wall. She put her head down on the table and was instantly asleep.

The moment consciousness returned, she propelled herself upright. "What happened? What did I miss?"

"Relax." Fin's hand settled on her shoulder, gently but firmly guiding her back into the seat. "You missed nothing of importance. Nisha is just explaining her plan."

"You have a plan?" Relief washed over Daphne, almost

overriding the warmth that was spreading through her from Fin's touch on her shoulder.

He still hadn't removed his hand, and she didn't point out his oversight or shrug away from him. She needed all the comfort she could get.

"I've been into the village," Nisha explained, catching Daphne up.

"I thought you just went for a walk?" Daphne could vaguely remember Nisha muttering something about needing a walk.

"You lot were talking in circles," Nisha said matter-of-factly, "and I preferred to do something productive."

"It was dangerous to go alone," Fin said quietly. "You should have taken me with you."

Nisha shook her head. "It was easier to get information on my own."

Morrow raised an eyebrow. "And did you get information?"

"Of course." Nisha placed a parcel wrapped in brown paper on the table. "Information and these." She turned to Daphne. "Do you know how to dance?"

Daphne looked back at her warily. "I just spent six months at the Sovaran court, so unfortunately yes."

"Unfortunately?" Archie's brow creased. "How can anyone dislike dancing?"

"I find I can dislike any and all energetic activities," Daphne said. "Consider it a gift, if you will."

Fin's hand tightened on her shoulder, and for a second her calm control nearly cracked. But whatever he said about releasing her feelings, it clearly wasn't the right moment.

"While I tremble to ask," she said calmly to Nisha, "why do my dancing skills matter right now?"

"Houseguests," Nisha answered cryptically.

Finley raised a brow. "I hope that makes more sense to someone else than it does to me."

Only blank looks met his inquiring gaze, so he turned back to Nisha.

"If the local lord has houseguests, that means parties," she said, as if it was obvious. "Lots of them. And parties mean extra help hired from town and purchases made with local suppliers. So I asked around. Turns out the next entertainment Lord Castlerey has planned is tonight—and it's a ball."

She pulled open the parcel and shook out a heavy gown of pink satin. In her other hand, she held up an elegant face mask. "Even better for us, it's a ladies' masquerade."

"A ladies' masquerade?" Daphne asked blankly. She had been to plenty of formal events at the Sovaran court, and even a masquerade, but she hadn't heard of a ladies' one.

"The ladies go masked, but the men don't," Nisha said. "A full masquerade would have been better, but this is good enough. A ball is already the perfect opportunity to get a couple of people into the manor without suspicion. Lots of guests will be coming from out of town, so no one will expect to recognize every face."

She looked directly at Daphne, Fin's hand still on her

shoulder. "Only two of us could successfully pose as a couple, so I purchased the clothing with you and Finley in mind. I hope you can make any necessary adjustments before tonight."

~

Daphne straightened the dress for the tenth time, trying to work up the courage to leave the small bedroom.

"Are you sure it fits all right?" she asked Nisha.

"It does." Nisha prowled in a full circle around her, her critical eye on Daphne's gown as she checked it. "It's a good thing you're handier with a needle than I am."

"I didn't learn as a child," Daphne said, "since my mother much preferred travel to needlework. But Rosalie's mother insisted Rosalie and I learn." She gave a breathy laugh. "We weren't the easiest pupils—Rosalie has about as much patience for it as my mother, and I kept falling asleep in lessons."

"Pure coincidence, I'm sure," Nisha said wryly. "But at least you retained some basic skills, and that's better than me. Now come on, it's time for you two to get moving."

Daphne opened the bedroom door quietly and slipped into the main room. Fin stood with his back to her, his hands on Archer's shoulders. From Archer's sulky expression they were having the same conversation they'd been having all afternoon.

"I'm just saying I should be there, too," Archer said. "I could have gone out and bought myself a formal outfit."

Over Fin's shoulder, Archer's eyes caught on Daphne, and he stuttered to a stop, his face going red. A small smile tugged at her lips. She knew Archer's infatuation wasn't his fault, but his responses were so adorably boyish at times that she couldn't help smiling to herself.

Fin noticed his brother's reaction and turned, looking to see what had caught Archer's attention. He froze at sight of Daphne, and the look that sprang into his eyes filled her with something far more potent than amusement.

"You look beautiful." He spoke as if they were the only two present, and she flushed.

"You look well yourself." It was an understatement. Despite six months in the Sovaran court around well-dressed courtiers, Fin in formalwear took her breath away.

Morrow gave a single resounding clap, finally breaking Fin and Daphne's locked gaze.

"You both look just the thing!" he exclaimed. "No one will question that you're guests of a lord. But has anyone thought to ask if Fin can dance?"

Fin threw him a look. "Of course I can dance."

"If that's what you call it," Archer sniggered, but Fin ignored him.

Nisha handed Daphne the mask, and Daphne tied it securely in place so that it fit snugly across her eyes and nose. Next came a cloak—her own original one, handed to her by Nisha.

"Are you sure...?" Fin asked, but Nisha didn't hesitate as she handed over his cloak.

"You're posing as guests—ones who've traveled from

out of town for the ball—so you shouldn't be wearing local cloaks. But you have to wear something. Daphne can't go strolling through the forest in a ballgown."

Morrow clapped Fin on the shoulder. "Don't argue, lad. Nisha's the one with the expertise. Besides, we should be going."

"We?" Daphne looked from him to Finley.

"I'll be walking you as far as the edge of the forest," Morrow said implacably.

"But then you'll come back?" Fin asked, glancing meaningfully toward Archie.

"Aye, I'll be back." Morrow gave him a steady, reassuring look. "And we won't be listening to his pleading this time, don't you worry."

"Very well." Fin gave his brother a stern look. "Archie, behave. We'll be back before you know it."

"Will you?" Archer looked and sounded more serious than usual.

Fin's voice softened. "Don't worry. Daphne and I can do this. We'll be back, along with some answers."

Archer sighed and looked away. Finley continued to gaze at him for a moment before shrugging and turning to Daphne.

He offered his arm with a flourish, but she ignored it and swept out of the cabin ahead of him. Her heart was already conflicted enough without walking through the forest with her arm through his.

Fin sighed behind her but said nothing. Was she hurting him with her attitude? She didn't want to hurt him, but she was caught in a maelstrom not of her own making, and without a proper foundation—the kind that came with truly knowing yourself—she didn't know where she was being blown. It was better by far for Finley to keep himself free of her.

They walked through the forest mostly in silence, Morrow's presence ensuring there was no opportunity for private talk anyway. Daphne tried to focus on the upcoming mission, but her mind kept slipping sideways to Fin before circling around to her worries about the Legacy. They had to stop twice on the walk for her to nap, lightning fast sleeps that left her less and less refreshed.

What if the unknown man wasn't at the ball? What if he was there, and he recognized Finley? Fin had never seen the man before, only his hired ruffians, but could they be sure the man hadn't seen Finley?

At the edge of the trees, they gave their cloaks to Morrow. Fin gave him a nod and received one in return, and then the large figure of their friend disappeared into the gathering darkness, heading back for the forest.

Fin offered his arm to Daphne again, and this time she took it. It made no logical sense, but Daphne could almost feel the Legacy's whirlwind sweeping her in. And yet, she couldn't draw back. The only way past it was through.

"Are you all right?" Finley asked softly, watching her with concern as they walked through the manor gates.

Daphne didn't even try to put her feeling into words.

"Are you sure we haven't forgotten anything?" she asked instead. "I feel like we've forgotten something important."

Fin chuckled. "That's perfectly normal, don't worry.

It's a trick of the brain. I've felt like that often enough myself."

"And had you forgotten something?"

"Generally I had, yes."

His words surprised a laugh from her, and given his reassuring smile in response, it had been his intention. Something inside her settled.

"Here we go," he muttered, and she lifted her chin.

As long as they stayed away from Lord Castlerey they would be fine. Once inside, any houseguests would think they were staying at the inn, and any guests from the inn would think they were houseguests. They would walk through the crowd as good as unseen.

Golden light spilled out the manor's open front door, inviting them onward. It illuminated a couple entering before them—a couple who were handing a gold-embossed invitation to a waiting footman.

As Daphne's eyes latched onto the invitation, Fin faltered beside her, catching himself before their hesitation could be noticed.

"Ah," he said quietly as they continued forward. "Invitations."

"I knew we'd forgotten something," Daphne said. "Will it matter?"

His hesitation was almost imperceptible. "Hopefully not."

"I could always create a distraction by falling asleep, and you could sneak in. I can be quite dramatic about it if necessary."

Fin laughed softly. "I'd like to see that—on another occasion. For now, I think we can stick to the main rules."

"There are rules? Perhaps I should have learned those before we started the mission," she said dryly.

"Thankfully they're easy, love." The word slipped so naturally off his tongue that she nearly stumbled. "Number one is don't look nervous. And number two is never draw attention to yourself—unless, of course, you want to draw attention." He winked at her.

When they reached the now-vacated door, Finley tipped his chin up, slipping on a haughty air that looked entirely natural. Ignoring the footman, he tried to stride inside, but the man moved to block his way.

"I'm afraid I'll have to see your invitation, sir." The footman's tone was polite but implacable. "There's a strict guest list for this event."

"Yes," Fin said in a strident tone that managed to be simultaneously petulant and domineering. "I can see that. And what I would like to know is why I was left off! I've never been so insulted in my life! I can assure you that I don't mean to take such an insult lying down. If Lord Castlerey thinks he can—"

"Please, sir." A man dressed like a steward thrust the footman aside and bowed low. "I assure you the oversight was unintentional. If you consider for just a moment, you will remember that it is not Lord Castlerey but the Legacy that is responsible for the oversight—and indeed it is the Legacy fueling your anger even now. Remember, only important guests are ever forgotten."

"Well, as to that..." Fin cleared his throat and straightened his jacket, looking as believably shamefaced as he had looked incensed a moment before. "I suppose no real harm has been done." He held out his arm to Daphne again. "Come, my dear, let us put this behind us and enjoy the party."

She took his arm, and the two of them swept into the manor as if they owned the building, walking straight across the entryway and into the ballroom. Brightly clothed people mingled inside, couples already swirling to the music. Within steps they were lost among the crowd.

"And that," he murmured in her ear, grinning, "is how it's done. We can thank the Legacy for that one. Nobles rarely hold an event in Oakden without leaving someone off the guest list. And given how enraged the overlooked guests tend to be, servants usually jump straight to appeasement, rather than enraging them further with questions. Which happens to be very convenient for us."

"You've done that before," Daphne accused.

"Of course." His grin broadened. "But never in the same place twice."

Daphne shook her head, but a shadow of concern marred her amusement. They had used the Legacy to get inside the ball, but at what cost? The last thing Daphne needed was more of the Legacy's attention.

"Fin!" She clutched his arm with both hands, her eyes trained on someone over his shoulder. "There he is! The man from the forest."

"Are you sure?" Fin's eyes tightened, although the smile didn't leave his face.

"Yes, yes, it's definitely him. I was staring at him the

whole time I was in that tree, terrified he was going to look up."

"I'm turning you slowly," Fin murmured, matching his actions to his words, spinning them smoothly so that he faced toward the man instead of her. "I see him. Wearing that distinctive purple coat. That will work to our advantage."

"Should we split up?" Daphne forced her voice to sound level despite how much she disliked the idea.

Fin glanced down at her. "No, I don't think that's a good idea. There's still the possibility we might need to make a quick exit, and I don't want to be on the other side of the ballroom to you if that happens."

"In that case, let's make our way to the refreshment table." She indicated the long table that lay against one wall.

Fin nodded, and they strolled toward it, weaving their way through the crowd. As they walked, they caught snippets of conversation.

"*Such* a lovely event!"

"A bit embarrassing if you ask me. Hardly a decoration in sight."

"Have you tried the raspberry tarts? They're delicious as always. But I'd avoid the lemon ones. Nasty stuff."

"Excellent orchestra! Even better than the one at the last ball I went to—and that was in the capital."

Daphne shook her head. Apparently it would be easy to get people talking—everyone seemed eager to give their opinions.

At the refreshment table she took a lemon tart in a

spirit of defiance. After one bite, she smuggled it back onto the table, subtly wrapped in a napkin. She should have had more trust in the unknown critic.

"You don't want to touch the lemon ones," a woman said in an under voice. "But the raspberry ones are quite nice."

Daphne smiled at the woman. "I'd heard as much, and was just thinking that I should have taken the warning more seriously."

The woman, who was dressed in expensive brocade and wore a slim mask, laughed. "You're just like my daughter. Some of us have to learn from personal experience. I understand completely."

Emboldened, Daphne stepped closer. "I don't know many people here, but you seem like the kind of person who knows everyone."

The woman stood a little straighter. "You've got a good eye, my dear. Despite the tart." She winked at Daphne who smiled back.

"I was wondering about a few of the gentlemen." Daphne indicated a random man in an elaborate suit, his diamond buttons having caught her eye. He looked about ten years older than her and had no woman on his arm.

"My dear!" The woman shook her head. "I can see you set your sights high. But Lord Tremlow is notoriously picky." She gave Daphne a second look. "Not but what I can see you're a beauty behind that mask, my dear. I daresay you have enough to attract any man's attention." She tittered behind her hand.

"Oh." Daphne flushed but pressed on. "What about him, then? Over there in the purple jacket."

The woman turned to look. "Lord Barlowe? Yet more of your discerning eye, indeed. Not but what he's a little on the old side for you, I would have thought. But then much can be overlooked when a man comes with a castle." She winked.

A lord? And a castle? Daphne glanced over her shoulder at Finley, who was trying to look uninterested in their conversation as he filled his plate at random.

The woman followed her gaze, lowering her voice to a whisper that was still loud enough to carry. "I can only assume he's your brother, my dear. No woman who came on the arm of a man like that would have eyes for other men." She let out a hearty guffaw, which Daphne returned with a sickly smile.

"Do you know Lord Barlowe well?" Daphne asked, trying to get the conversation back on track. "Have you visited his castle?"

"Oh, one meets Lord Barlowe everywhere," the woman said. "So I suppose I know him as well as anyone might expect. But you're quite right that it's about time he threw a ball of his own, and perhaps a house party as well. I've heard enough about that white castle by the lake that I've a hankering to see it with my own eyes."

"So you've never been there? Do you know anyone who has? I would love to hear it described in more detail."

The woman smiled at her. "I can see you're a cautious type, and there's nothing wrong with getting all the facts first." She lowered her voice again. "Especially if you're going to give up a man like that." Her eyes lingered on Fin.

"Yes," Daphne said awkwardly, "so if you know anyone who..."

"Try Lady Sartenet." She waved her fan toward a woman wearing bright orange with feathers all over her mask. "I believe I first heard of the white castle from her."

Daphne thanked her and extricated herself from the conversation as gracefully as possible. When she stepped back to Fin, she let out a long breath.

"Very nicely done." His warm smile both teased and affirmed. "We'll make an actress of you yet."

Daphne shuddered. "No, thank you."

"Let me guess," he laughed, "it was too fatiguing."

"Far too fatiguing. But now I have to do it again."

"Lord Barlowe..." Fin murmured, a crease of worry between his eyes. "Connections with the nobility was bad enough, but he's a lord himself with a castle besides? What possible interest could he have in me and Archie?"

"At least we have a name now." Daphne moved them toward her next target. "And hopefully this time we'll get a location for that castle."

But when she struck up a conversation with Lady Sartenet, using flattery to endear herself and then turning the conversation to Lord Barlowe's castle, Lady Sartenet sighed.

"Ah, the white castle on the southern lake with its rows of cherry blossoms. How dearly I should like to see it for myself."

"Have you never done so?" Daphne asked. "Then do

you perhaps know someone who has? Other than Lord Barlowe, of course."

"Hmm, well, let me see." Lady Sartenet hummed to herself. "For that you had best talk to Lady Galsey." She pointed at the woman Daphne had met beside the refreshment table. "I'm sure she's been there."

When Daphne returned to Fin, she was frowning. "That seems strange. Has no one been there?"

"It might be strange," he said, "or it may simply be that the women have faulty memories. It's an easy enough detail to forget over time. The important point is that we have information on its location."

"Not much," Daphne said dubiously.

"There's only one lake on the southern border of the forest. And it's an area known for its cherry blossoms. I've never been to that region personally—it's one of the few I haven't visited—so I can't speak for the truth behind the tales of a white castle. I don't think I've heard of it before, though." He looked thoughtful.

"So we have a name and a location," Daphne murmured. "That's a great deal more than you ever had before."

"But why would a lord be obsessed with seeking revenge on my family?" Fin's voice was laced with frustration. "What did my father do to him?"

"That isn't something that's likely to be covered by noble gossip," Daphne said regretfully.

"So maybe we risk it all." Fin's voice held steady. "Maybe we talk to him directly."

Daphne looked at him with narrowed eyes. "And if he recognizes you?"

"He's never come after us personally, so why should he? And besides, we're in the middle of a ball. What can he do here?"

Daphne could think of several things, but she didn't think any of them would make Finley pause.

"We should wait, at least," she said, not liking the reckless light in his eyes. "Let Lord Barlowe have a few drinks first. It might help loosen his tongue and cloud his judgment."

Fin released a breath and nodded, his eyes drifting to her face. "In that case, we should enjoy ourselves in the meantime." He held out a hand. "Dance with me?"

Daphne put her hand slowly into his, trying to ignore the shiver that raced up her arm in response to the contact. But no sooner had he swung them into the dance than her eyes caught on a snowy-haired figure on the far side of the ballroom.

Gasping, she pulled free of Fin and raced across the room toward the familiar face.

CHAPTER 16

DAPHNE

Dimly, Daphne was aware of Fin trailing behind her, repeating her name in an urgent but low tone. But she was too focused on her goal to stop and talk to him.

When she reached the far end of the ballroom, she came to a stop in front of an elderly gentleman with a slightly bowed back but a bright, keen gaze. He immediately broke off his conversation at her breathless approach, and when she pulled off her mask, his whole face lit up.

"Daphne!" he pulled her into a hug, patting her back in a way that sent tears pricking at her eyelids. Her actual grandparents had passed away before her family's return to Glandore, so Lorne was the closest thing she had ever known to a grandfather.

"My poor girl!" he murmured. "Whatever has happened to you?"

"But what are you doing here, Lorne?" she asked at the same time.

They both broke off and chuckled. Glancing to either side, Daphne gestured toward a convenient alcove in the wall of the ballroom—one half obscured by a large potted plant.

"Perhaps somewhere more private?" she suggested, and Lorne raised his eyebrows but offered no protest.

Fin shadowed them to the alcove, his face closed off and still since her mention of Lorne's name. He made no attempt to intrude on their conversation, taking up a post outside, just out of earshot.

As soon as they were seated, Lorne lowered his voice. "Your companion seems to be standing guard. Should I be concerned?"

"About Fin? Oh, no. He's just making sure we're not disturbed."

"I see," Lorne said in the kind of tone that suggested he didn't see at all.

Daphne laughed shakily. "It's a lot to explain."

"That much, at least, is apparent." Lorne shook his head. "But how do you come to be here tonight? Lord Castlerey knows I'm searching for you and mentioned nothing about inviting you here."

Daphne grinned sheepishly. "That's because we weren't actually invited. Officially speaking. Or, in fact, unofficially either."

Lorne's brows rose. "How very—"

He broke off, his head dropping forward as he fell into instant sleep. Daphne watched him in silence, memories of her childhood rushing back. His sudden moments of sleep had been rare then—so rare she had nearly forgotten about them. And yet they still occurred. She swallowed, trying not to think too deeply about what that meant.

"—thrilling it all sounds," Lorne said, waking abruptly after thirty seconds and resuming his sentence without missing a beat. But when he caught sight of her face, he paused and took her hand.

"My dear Daphne, did I do it again? I assure you there's no need for distress. It's a pesky habit, but it does me no harm, nor anyone else either."

"But you still fall asleep like that after all these years?" Daphne asked. "It never goes away?"

"It fades as the years pass," Lorne said. "But then the itchy feet get the better of me, and I end up popping across the border. I don't travel for long these days, but it always causes the sleeps to flare back up." He smiled, clearly unrepentant. "My poor daughter quite despairs of me, I assure you. But then she never did have the wanderlust."

"I thought my naps would just disappear completely as soon as I crossed the border," Daphne confessed.

Lorne patted her hand. "It happens that way for some, your own parents among them. But the result of returning is different for each person, just as the original burden is different. For those who were away a particularly long time—or who went at a particularly young age—it can linger. And you were so young when you left." He sighed. "Your parents have written to me of your affliction several times. It weighs heavily on them."

"It weighs heavily on me!" Daphne cried, with more

heat than she had intended. "I'm the one who suffers for it. I left my family and friends and came to Oakden to be free of it—but it was no use. The Legacy just keeps gripping me harder."

She dropped her head into her hands, horrified by the tears on her face.

Lorne patted her shoulder. "It is a difficult burden for the young—and for those who didn't choose it for themselves."

Daphne forgot her tear-stained face enough to look up at him. "How could they do it to me, Lorne? My own parents?"

He sighed deeply. "They wanted to return while you were still a toddler, you know. Did they ever tell you that? They endured for years longer, believing it their duty." He sighed again. "But everyone has their limit. If you had been in pain, I believe they would have returned to Oakden, but when it was only sleep that afflicted you…"

"Only sleep?" Words failed Daphne as she thought of the underlying fatigue that had shaped every part of her life. Of the strange looks and whispers that had always accompanied her. "I didn't ask for this," she whispered into the silence.

"No, you did not." Lorne's voice was heavy with grief. "But your parents do love you, Daphne. They are humans —flawed humans—but they love you deeply."

"I know." Daphne wiped away the tears, her voice thick. "They've always done their best to be there for me in every other way. I don't even know why I'm crying." She flashed a look at Fin. "A friend told me recently that I need to let out my feelings more, but I didn't realize it would be so messy and exhausting." She wrinkled her nose at the final word.

Lorne laughed. "That it is. But you will find the feelings ease as you share them. They won't always be so potent."

"I certainly hope not," Daphne muttered, scrubbing away the last evidence of her tears. "I just...I'm just frustrated. I came to Oakden to discover who I truly am, and I'm even further from that than I ever was. Everything is a mess!"

"It does seem a little messy," Lorne murmured with a slight smile. "But what do you mean about discovering who you truly are?"

Daphne shrugged. "I have so few memories from before the Legacy's burden hit me. I want to know the true Daphne, the one unaffected by Oakden's sleepiness. But ever since I arrived, the Legacy's power has been gripping me even more tightly than ever. I can already feel I'll need to nap right here before I can stand again."

Lorne frowned. "It's getting worse? That sounds unusual." He hesitated. "I think you'd better tell me exactly what's happened since you arrived in Oakden. But before you do, I have to ask. Do you truly think that you're not the true Daphne now?" His voice grew even more gentle. "Because I can assure you that you are."

"But this wasn't supposed to be my life," Daphne said. "How can it be the true me?"

Lorne sighed. "A profound question. I'm not saying that what was done to you as a child was an easy thing or a fair one. But there is no person alive who is unaffected by outside influences. We all have people and circumstances that affect who we become—whether we wish them to or not. And it is not granted to any of us to know who we would have been without those external influences. That would have been to live a different life."

"You're saying we have no say over who we become?" Daphne asked, defiant.

Lorne shook his head. "Far from it. We can make choices about how we react to the influences in our life. And sometimes we can do things to change those influences. But sometimes we can't control them—and then our choice is to accept that reality or not. In those cases, we can only wield our influence upon ourselves. You cannot escape pressure, Daphne, but you can choose whether or not it turns you into a diamond."

She let out a shaky laugh. "If I was a diamond, would I pretend to fall asleep to avoid awkward situations?"

"Oh, but that's the very best time to fall asleep!" Lorne winked at her. "I would know."

Daphne's laugh grew more natural. "Does it work for you, too?"

"Quite disrupts the flow of conversation," he assured her. "And see! You're already finding ways to use those naps to your advantage. The napping is just another part of who you are, Daphne. And maybe one day the naps will stop—if you dislike them so much, I hope they do—but the effects of bearing them all these years will linger. They are a part of you now—for good or ill—and your history with them will always be a part of who you are, even as you become a new Daphne. We're all of us constantly growing and changing. Or we should be. The other option is to calcify, and I've never seen the fun in that."

Daphne smiled at him. "No one could accuse you of standing still."

He smiled back but fell silent, giving her space to sit with his words. She let them sink deep into her mind. Hadn't she told Finley something similar? Hadn't she told him that even though his father had wronged him, he had still helped shape who Fin became? If she would never say to Finley that his true self could only be uncovered if he'd never known his father, why was she saying the same thing to herself? But could she accept that her naps weren't obscuring her true self but rather were part of her, as difficult as they were?

She and Fin had promised each other that they would try to see their pasts differently, and she had to at least try. She drew a deep breath, her shoulders straightening and her face relaxing.

"Thank you, Lorne. I should probably have worked that out for myself, but maybe I needed to hear it from someone who had walked the path before me."

"It usually helps, child." He glanced at where Fin still kept watch. "But now, I think we must both tell the other what brings us here, and perhaps we will each know more than we do now."

"You should start," Daphne said, "because I think my story will be longer. How is your son? Is he recovered?"

"He is back to full strength, I'm happy to say."

"What a relief that must be for you!" She beamed at him.

"In fact, he has been out of danger since the early days after the accident, which is why I sent for my housekeeper to relieve me in the nursing duties. You can imagine my dismay when she told me about meeting you on my doorstep and abandoning you there! I returned to Ethelson immediately to find you and was even more dismayed to find no trace of you at all. I've been searching for you ever since."

"You've been searching for me all these weeks? On your own?" Daphne's heart sank. Despite his love for travel, Lorne was growing too old to be jolting all over the kingdom looking for her.

"Not on my own, no." His eyes twinkled. "Some dear friends have been assisting me. But I couldn't do nothing. How could I write to your parents and tell them I lost my goddaughter?"

Daphne relaxed a little, relieved to hear he hadn't been alone.

"I stopped in to see Lord Castlerey," he added, "who is an old acquaintance. And since he was soon to host a ball, he suggested I stay a little longer than planned. And then I turn around and here you are."

"Here I am," Daphne murmured, shaking her head as she thought of what had brought her there. "Compared to your story, my tale may be a little hard to believe. But I swear it's all true." She proceeded to tell him everything that had happened since she had broken into his house and found Finley there.

When she finished, Lorne turned for another look at Fin. When he turned back, his eyes were twinkling.

"I'm extremely fond of all my grandchildren," he said, "but I'm afraid none of them have such rakish good looks."

Daphne blushed. "If only I'd known that at the start of the spring."

"Or perhaps," Lorne murmured, "it's a good thing you didn't know."

"Yes," Daphne whispered back, her eyes on Fin's profile. "Perhaps it is."

CHAPTER 17
FINLEY

Lorne stood and raised his voice. "Young man!"

Finley swung around, fighting down a flash of fear as he settled into his familiar, charming smile. He offered his hand to Lorne who shook it warmly.

"I understand you're Finley. And I believe you might have something of mine."

Finley's eyes widened, and he glanced at Daphne. So Lorne had told her then? She knew Finley had stolen from her old friend?

She merely looked confused, however.

"If I tell you I took it to protect my brother, does that help?" he asked Lorne.

Lorne's face remained stern, but Finley caught a slight twitch of his lips. "Since I take it your intention was to use it on my goddaughter, I'm not sure it does."

"I would never use it on her now," Finley said quickly.

Lorne gave a small chuckle. "No, I suspect you wouldn't. Nevertheless, I would like it back. It was a gift from a good friend." He hesitated and glanced at Daphne. "But perhaps you can return it at a later date. I understand there is still some difficulty ahead."

"I was planning to return it anyway." Finley had decided on that as soon as he realized how much Lorne meant to Daphne.

Daphne stood as well. "Are you talking about your knife? Did you take that from Lorne's study?"

Her eyes narrowed, and Finley held his breath. But she turned to Lorne.

"He really does return the things he takes. I've seen it more than once."

"A most unusual thief," Lorne said, and this time he was definitely smiling. But his expression quickly turned more serious. "But your report of this Lord Barlowe is most concerning."

"Have you met him?" Daphne asked. "Do you know anything about him?"

"I met him for the first time in this house." Lorne frowned. "But I must confess that I noticed nothing of interest about him." He spread his arms. "He seemed a perfectly ordinary person—as much as any lord can be considered ordinary."

"So you've been living here in the same manor with him for a few days?" Finley asked. "And you never noticed anything in all that time?"

Lorne shook his head. "I haven't actually been staying in the house. As I mentioned to Daphne, I have some friends with me, and we've been staying together at the local inn." He frowned. "I could ask them if they've heard anything of this Barlowe. They're more widely traveled than even me."

Finley glanced around the ballroom. "Are they here?"

Lorne shook his head. "They were invited but preferred a quiet night. I'm sure they'll still be awake, though, so I could go immediately and ask them."

"Would you?" Daphne seized his hand in both of hers. "Thank you so much!"

He patted her clasped hands. "Nothing but a trifle, my dear. I'll return as soon as possible."

He disentangled himself and hurried toward the ballroom door, moving in a sprightly way despite his bent figure. Finley and Daphne both watched him go.

"Should we wait for him to return before we approach Lord Barlowe?" Daphne turned to Finley with an expression of concern.

He smiled down at her. "First, we should finish what we started."

He held out his hand, waiting patiently while she stared at it blankly. Then the music swelled, the current song nearing its end, and understanding lit her face. She swallowed, her hand rising slowly toward his. But before it made contact, she paused. Whatever she'd discussed with Lorne was making her more hesitant than she had been earlier in the evening.

And yet, Finley could have sworn some of the tension lurking beneath her surface had eased. But still she hesitated, seeming to tremble on the brink of something he didn't understand.

With a soft sigh, she placed her fingers in his and

looked up at him with the softest of smiles. "I would love to dance with you."

Finley's hand tightened convulsively around hers, his pulse taking off. But his feet didn't move. Instead, he reluctantly pulled something from his pocket.

"If we're rejoining the ball, you'd better put this back on."

"That's where it went," Daphne cried, seeing her mask dangling from his fingers. "I lost track of it."

She smiled up at him expectantly, and he placed it slowly on her face. Her fingers held it in place as he reached around her head to tie the two ribbons together. His face hovered beside hers, his arms stretched around her, and he didn't dare breathe lest he shatter the moment.

It took all his self-control to pull back and offer her his hand again, some semblance of his usual smile on his face. But when she put her hand into his for a second time, he couldn't resist pulling her close, cradling her in his arms as he swept them both onto the ballroom floor.

They had never danced together before, and yet they moved as one, their feet gliding smoothly and their focus locked on one another. A slight pink suffused Daphne's cheeks, but she held his gaze confidently, her posture straight and open.

"Daphne," he breathed, unsure how to put everything in his mind into words.

"Fin," she said back, her voice tinged with affection. His heart leaped and thumped painfully in his chest.

"In the forest that day," he began, and Daphne sighed softly.

"I'm sorry I ran away from you. I told myself I needed to protect you, but I was also confused and anxious. I'd spent so many years expecting to return to Oakden and reclaim my true self. The reality has been...different." He pulled her closer despite the conventions of the dance, and she gave him a dazzling smile that momentarily robbed him of words.

They came back to him slowly, driven by the most concerning part of her confession. "You thought you were protecting me? From what?"

"The Legacy. After everything it has done to me—is still doing to me—I didn't want you to get sucked in as well." She shivered in his arms, and he swung her toward the edge of the dance floor, positioning them behind a potted tree so that he could pull her all the way to his chest and hold her there.

"I already told you." His voice was rough. "I won't abandon you to the Legacy, no matter what."

For a blissful moment, she sunk into his hold. But within mere seconds, she pulled back, an indignant expression on her face.

"I appreciate that you want to protect me, but that means you should understand that I want to protect you too. The Legacy is building toward something, ensnaring me deeper." A shadow passed over her face. "I can feel it. And there's no reason for you to get sucked in as well."

Finley smiled down at her. "I think it's a little late for that."

Could she see the love blazing in his eyes? She must have sensed something because a flush appeared around the edges of her mask.

"I should warn you that I'm finished running away from the Legacy," she said. "I have to accept what it's made of my life and find my way forward despite it. And to do that, I have to face whatever it throws at me next. You're finally on the road to answers and freedom yourself. Are you sure you want to be part of more chaos?"

"If it's your chaos—always," Fin said without needing to think. "If you're ready to stop pushing me away, that is." His chest squeezed painfully. "Are you ready for that?"

Daphne's radiant smile released the pressure inside him, warmth flooding through him in its wake. She leaned into him, her lips hovering near his ear.

"I can live with the naps if I have to, Fin, but I don't want to live without you."

He stared down into her eyes, drinking in her mischievous smile and the sincerity in her gaze.

"Blast that mask," he growled, and then his lips were on hers anyway, and the rest of the ballroom had faded into irrelevance.

When they finally broke apart, he scooped her up and spun her around, nearly colliding with the tree as his laughter enveloped them both.

"My one worry," she said when he put her down, "is how we're going to break the news to poor Archer."

"Ugh, Archie." Finley shook his head. "My patience with that boy has been wearing paper-thin."

"But it's not his fault, poor thing," Daphne said. "It's the Legacy."

"Is it?" Finley's eyes narrowed. "I notice your control over brambles wore off weeks ago. If you ask me, he's been using the Legacy infatuation as an excuse—because otherwise he knows I would have dumped him in the creek by now for the way he moons over you."

Daphne laughed. "In that case, he's probably doing it to rile you up. The poor boy hasn't had any other entertainment for weeks."

"I'll give him *entertainment*," Finley growled, but Daphne laughed again, and his irritation melted into a smile. He was too full of joy to remain irritated with anyone, even Archie.

"Young love," an urbane voice said from the other side of the potted tree. "It's enough to warm anyone's heart."

Finley instinctively stepped in front of Daphne, trying to shield her from the stranger's view. But when the man stepped around the tree and he recognized Lord Barlowe, his mind went completely blank.

"As touching as this display is," Lord Barlowe continued, "I'm not sure it's appropriate for a ballroom. On behalf of my good friend, Lord Castlerey, I'm afraid I'm going to have to ask you to leave."

Finley stared at him, his mind racing. Did the man know who they were? Was he—

"Ah, before you consider protesting your right to remain," Lord Barlowe said, flicking a nonexistent speck of dust from his sleeve, "I should perhaps mention that I was privileged to witness your very...ah, creative entry to the ball."

Finley and Daphne remained silent, and Lord Barlowe smiled. "Very wise. You have had your fun, and if you leave quietly now, no harm has been done. Do you not agree?"

"Certainly we'll leave if we're no longer welcome here," Fin said easily.

Was it a mere coincidence that Lord Barlowe was the one evicting them from the ball? Regardless of his reasons, they could hardly refuse. If they made a scene, they would attract Lord Castlerey's attention, and Barlowe's accusations would be proved.

Their chance to question Barlowe was disappearing before his eyes. They should have been more circumspect. He tried to think of a way to phrase a subtle question, but the situation wasn't exactly propitious.

"Of course we'll leave." Daphne tugged on Finley's sleeve, and he gave in to the inevitable, giving Barlowe a quick, shallow bow.

He let her tug him through the room, skirting the dance floor as they headed toward the ballroom door. They would have to wait outside the manor and intercept Lorne when he returned. Perhaps together they could think of another way to approach Barlowe.

But as they left the ballroom and entered the manor's large entryway, Lord Barlowe trailed behind them. Finley glanced back at him, weighing the risks of speaking versus staying quiet. Perhaps the man had given them just the opportunity they needed?

He hesitated near the front door, looking at Lord Barlowe again.

"My dear sir," the lord said with apparent amusement. "You seem to have something more to say to me. But may I suggest that whatever enlightening words you have to impart, they would be best said away from our interested audience?"

Finley glanced at the two footmen who flanked the door, both watching the odd group in the entryway with interest, and then down at Daphne. Her teeth were set, her wary gaze fixed on Lord Barlowe, but she didn't protest. And for the first time that night, Finley was grateful for her mask. If Finley's identity ended up being revealed, Daphne at least retained some protection.

"Very well, my lord," Finley said. "Perhaps you are right."

Barlowe gestured toward an open door that led into a sitting room, ushering them both through before closing it behind them and perching himself on the arm of the nearest chair.

"If you intend to upbraid me," he said, "I should perhaps warn you that I am not easily put out of countenance."

"No," Daphne said quietly. "I don't think you are."

Barlowe smiled at her, a slow, lazy smile that Finley didn't like.

"A lady of above ordinary perception, I see. If one is forced to have an adversary, is it not more entertaining to have a worthy opponent?"

"Opponent, my lord?" Daphne continued to meet his gaze steadily. "I don't know what you mean."

The lord swung his leg, his lazy smile still fixed in place. "Oh, I think you do, Daphne. I think you know exactly what I mean."

Finley tensed, his thoughts upending in an instant, all his assessments of danger changing. It had been a mistake to bring Daphne to the ball. He never should have considered it.

"I did not achieve my current position by failing to pay attention to details," Barlowe continued. "I certainly would not pursue a man across the breadth of a kingdom for three long years without knowing his face." His eyes lingered on Finley's face, and he laughed softly. "Such a noble face," he murmured.

His gaze snapped to Daphne. "Your face, however, I would be most interested to see..." He trailed off with the faint hint of a question, as if he thought she would remove her mask to satisfy his curiosity.

Finley tensed, ready to intervene if Barlowe tried to approach Daphne, but neither of them moved. Daphne's stony gaze remained fixed unflinchingly on Barlowe's face, and he gave a small smile.

"I'll admit, I wasn't sure how you fit into the game, my dear," he continued. "Especially after I heard of your impressive rescue of young Archer. But after that enlightening display in the ballroom, I think I have a fairly accurate idea of what piece you are in this particular puzzle."

Finley's hands fisted, his blood boiling. He wanted to

push Daphne behind him, to shield her even from Barlowe's gaze. But he had to tread very, very carefully.

"I'll admit," the man went on, "I was impressed to see you here tonight. Even after all these years, I did not expect my own identity to be uncovered. But you see, that leaves us at an impasse because that is not a situation with which I'm comfortable."

He stood, his actions suddenly quick and decisive. "Entertaining as it has been, I think it's time we drew this game to a close. Do you not agree, Finley son of Timothy?"

Finley froze, his brows drawing together. Daphne grabbed his arm.

"What is it, Fin?" she asked softly, and he realized he had never told her his father's name.

"My father wasn't called Timothy." The room seemed to recede, reality dipping and rearranging yet again.

Was it possible that their last three years of flight and terror had all originated from a case of mistaken identity? Had Lord Barlowe been chasing the wrong people?

Barlowe's brows shot up. "Do you really not know? Now that is surprising!"

"What don't I know?" Finley's fists tightened, his patience running thin.

"Your own father, apparently." Barlowe watched him closely. "Do you really not know that your father was the missing Prince Timothy, the youngest brother of our current monarch?"

CHAPTER 18

FINLEY

Finley staggered back, clutching at the small table behind him. "What...what did you just say?"

"You truly didn't know." Lord Barlowe shook his head. "Remarkable. To keep the truth from his own sons. Tut tut. I suppose he didn't intend to die in such a foolish accident."

Finley could barely hear his words, too overwhelmed with the ridiculousness of the claim.

"My father was Garrow," he said firmly. "A wastrel, yes, but an ordinary man."

"I've never even heard of a missing prince," Daphne said suspiciously.

"The royal family don't like to talk about it," Barlowe said. "Embarrassing to lose a prince, I suppose. And they keep popping out so many twins that you can't blame them for struggling to keep track of them all. Although, from what I understand, they had an advantageous marriage alliance arranged for him and were not at all pleased when he declared he would live as an ordinary citizen instead—and proceeded to run off with a serving maid."

"Fin?" Daphne's fingers tugged at his sleeve.

"My...my mother was a serving maid before her marriage," Finley said slowly. "That much is true."

"I assure you it is all true," Barlowe said crisply. "I wouldn't have been pursuing you for years if it wasn't. I don't make mistakes."

"You've been chasing Archer and me because our father was a prince?" Even as he spoke the words, Finley struggled to believe them. "But why?"

"For your blood," Barlowe said simply, and Daphne recoiled.

"Oh, nothing as crude as that," Barlowe assured her. "But the Oakden Legacy is lamentably fond of royalty."

His words shook loose a thought in Finley's mind. They had blamed Archie's enchanted sleep on the date of his attempted heist—attributing the power of the spindle to his turning sixteen. But had it been more than that? Had the Legacy reacted so strongly because he had royal blood? If so, they were fortunate Daphne's vague royal connection had been enough to break his sleep. Perhaps the interest the Legacy seemed to have in her had also helped?

Finley shook his head. What was he thinking? It couldn't be true. His father hadn't been a prince.

"My father—" he began but found he couldn't go on. His father had rarely talked of his past, and Finley had never known his paternal grandparents.

"Your father was, from all accounts, a charming young prince," Barlowe said. "But I don't think he found the adjustment to ordinary life as easy as he expected. I'm sure he did love your mother, but alas, sometimes love is not enough. When it comes to living an ordinary life, habits of economy are also important."

Finley gave a rough, grating laugh. No, his father had never had those.

"Economy is, in fact, a most unpleasant necessity," Lord Barlowe said, "which is why I decided to become a lord. And why I now need your help."

"My *help*?" Finley gave the man a disbelieving look. "Is that what you call it? You have an odd way of asking for help."

"I'll admit that some of my efforts in the past have been regrettably crude," Barlowe said. "But let us put the past behind us and consider, instead, the future."

But Daphne's thoughts seemed stuck elsewhere. "What do you mean you *decided* to become a lord?" she asked. "That isn't something you can just decide."

"Why ever not?" Barlowe smiled urbanely. "I dress like a lord, I speak like a lord, I introduce myself as a lord. Who is to say I'm not one? Oh, I don't push it too far. The capital is—currently—beyond my reach. But there is a perfectly good life to be had in the rest of the kingdom. After three months, my visit here is drawing to a close, but only tonight I've received invitations to two more house parties. I am, apparently, valued for my wit." He laughed softly.

"I suppose it was gifted to you at birth," Daphne said indignantly, "and you've chosen to misuse that gift."

"Have I?" Barlowe raised a single eyebrow. "I have lived in luxury at the expense of others for a decade now, so I would consider it a most excellent use."

"Ten years?" Finley asked. "You've only been chasing us for three..." He trailed off as he realized the obvious truth. "Before that, you were chasing our father."

"He proved even better at eluding me than the two of you," Barlowe said. "You wouldn't believe the trinkets I have been forced to sell to fund the search. It is past time now for it to come to a close."

Daphne and Finley spoke at the same moment.

"What about your castle?"

"You still haven't told me why you were chasing my father and now me."

"What elegant confluence," Barlowe said. "You present the question and the answer at the same moment. I must produce the castle I claim to own, and I must produce it soon. After so many years, questions have begun to be asked—oh only the most subtle, of course. But I have seen how subtle questions can grow."

"It doesn't exist?" Daphne asked. "And you've managed to fool everyone that it does for an entire decade!?"

"Remarkable, is it not, what people will believe if you say something with enough confidence," the false lord said.

Finley shifted uncomfortably. He couldn't deny the

words when he'd made the same observation more than once.

"I will admit that I haven't been circulating through house parties for the entire ten years," Barlowe offered. "For the first seven I acted as companion to an elderly, and extremely wealthy, noble lady. She placed my witty pronouncements slightly above her many lap dogs in terms of my entertainment value—a place of great honor in her household, I assure you. And for the price of excellent meal-time conversation, I was kept in luxury as a permanent houseguest. I knew the arrangement couldn't last forever, so I had already begun my search during those years, but I'll admit it was of a more desultory nature during that time. In the three years since, I have worked with more urgency."

"This is too much." Daphne sank onto the closest armchair, curling up into it and resting her head against the backrest. Her eyes closed.

Finley immediately placed himself between her and Barlowe, wishing, once again, that he had never encour-aged her to walk into the manor.

"So it's true?" Barlowe stepped sideways so he could see Daphne. "My men reported that you had traveled into the region with a young lady who was given to frequent napping, but I doubted their report."

"She grew up outside Oakden," Finley said reluctantly.

He didn't want to tell Barlowe anything about Daphne, but he didn't trust the man's smooth manners. If he thought Daphne was mocking him, he might react badly.

Silence drew out between them, Fin's emotions threatening to overwhelm him. Daphne had challenged him to let go of his bitterness toward his father, and Finley had committed to doing so—or attempting to do so, at least. He had also begun to accept her assessment of the ways in which his father had influenced both him and Archie.

But when she had gently questioned the truth of his perception of his father, Finley had never wavered. He had been so certain that he had known his father, so certain his father had ruined his life.

And yet now it turned out that Finley hadn't known his father at all. He hadn't even known his true name.

Fresh resentment surged through him. Why hadn't his father told him?

Finley could understand wanting to protect Archie, who had been so young, but why not tell Finley? Had his father really thought he was protecting his older son?

His mother had thought the same, though. How many times had she told Fin to remain a child while he still could?

His childhood and youth rolled through his mind, the old events replaying with fresh color. His father's desertion of their family, the subsequent three years of nomadic life—all of it looked different under the new revelation.

Finley had thought they were always fleeing debts, but he couldn't remember now if his father had actually said so. How many of those times had they actually been fleeing discovery —from Barlowe himself or from others who had realized the truth and sought to use his father for their own ends?

He could hear his mother's words in his mind, telling him to forgive his father, telling him that he misunderstood him. But Finley had stubbornly refused to accept her words. Perhaps Finley had not been entirely blameless in the situation himself.

He tried to ground himself, to think it through clearly. Some facts hadn't changed. His father hadn't been a good father. He hadn't loved them well. But perhaps he had been doing his best, loving as best he knew how. Finley could understand that—he knew what it was to try and to fall short.

Something inside him shifted, resentment giving way to something that felt like grief. But there was no more time for processing emotions.

Barlowe still hadn't taken his eyes off Daphne, watching her sleep with far too much interest.

"Enough with the distractions!" Finley snapped, trying to keep Barlowe's attention on him. "Let's speak of matters as they really are. You have been persecuting and attempting to abduct both me and my brother—a child!— for years. But even if our father was a prince, we don't have a castle to give you. We never did."

"No, no, of course not," Barlowe said in a soothing tone that made Finley want to throttle the man. "I have the castle already—or I will have as soon as you clear away a couple of impediments for me."

Daphne finally stirred, rising from the chair and coming to Finley's side. "Let me guess. This castle that you claim is yours belongs to a girl currently trapped in an enchanted sleep, and the brambles protecting her won't let you pass. That's why you need a prince."

Barlowe gave a delighted clap. "You prove once again that you're a lady of more than ordinary perception. You have seen straight to the heart of the matter."

"But that's outrageous!" Indignation flowed from Daphne. "Even if Fin or Archer open the brambles for you and wake the girl, that won't make the castle yours. What of her family?"

"Gone." Barlowe didn't even pretend to sound grieved. "It was the most marvelous and fortunate coincidence that I stumbled on the story. The elderly lady for whom I was companion once knew the father. He was a royal of some description, but an eccentric who lived alone on his estate until a late marriage and a solitary daughter. The wife passed away, so when the girl fell prey to the enchanted sleep, he set off alone for the capital. He intended to find a prince to rescue her, but unfortunately he did not survive the trip. And so the girl has lain there for decades, both her and the castle forgotten by the kingdom."

"Even if she doesn't have a family," Daphne insisted, "when she wakes, the castle will be hers."

"Precisely." Barlowe gave an unpleasant smile. "Another reason why I must liberate the property and its sleeping beauty without delay. I, myself, am only advancing in years."

"You can't mean to marry her," Finley exclaimed, revolted. "If she fell prey to a Legacy sleep, she's likely only just turned sixteen."

"Oh relax, there's no need for all this outrage," Barlowe said. "My interest in the girl is purely for her possessions. Naturally we will remain betrothed until she reaches eighteen."

"That doesn't make it better!" Daphne cried. "And besides, if Fin or Archer wake her up, they'll be the ones she fancies, not you. And either of them would make a more appropriate object for her infatuation than you!"

"Finley will wake her with a kiss somewhere unobtrusive—he can kiss her foot for all I care," Barlowe said, undeterred. "But it will be my face waiting over hers. The first thing she sees when she awakes will be me—her rescuer."

"I'm not sure the Legacy works like that." Daphne sounded uneasy.

"I believe I have studied it more extensively than you have done, young lady," Barlowe said. "My plan will work, and then my position in society will be secure. I can even turn my sights to the capital."

"The entire plan is utterly despicable." Daphne's voice dripped with ice.

Barlowe merely smiled. "Is it? You will find me unmoved by your outraged virtue. I care far more for my own comfort than for your useless scruples. And surely the girl is better off awake and mistress of her own castle than sleeping for all eternity? It's not as if I intend to assassinate her." He turned his eyes on Finley. "So what do you say? Come with me, open some brambles, wake a girl from her sleep, and our business will be complete."

"That's really all you want from me?" Finley asked

carefully, as Daphne stiffened beside him. "If that's all, why didn't you just ask me to help in the first place? You could have offered to pay me."

Barlowe raised a brow. "And would you have agreed? I don't like to take chances when a certainty can be achieved instead. That option would also have required me to reveal myself—something I had no intention of doing. But since you have proved more elusive than I expected, and have even succeeded in unmasking my identity, the rules of the game have shifted. A new approach is needed. You will find I am an eminently adaptable man."

"You can't do it, Fin," Daphne whispered, her voice distressed.

But he already knew that. There was zero chance he was going anywhere with Barlowe when it would mean leaving Daphne alone.

But when he spoke, he said, "I really think we should consider it, Daphne."

"Fin, no!" she exclaimed.

Finley glanced at Barlowe and drew Daphne aside, pulling her to the other side of the room for some semblance of privacy.

"If I go with him now, this will all be over," he said, watching Barlowe from the corner of his eye. "I have to think of you and Archie."

Barlowe watched them with a small smile, as if he thought the game was already won.

"You can't be serious, Fin!" Daphne hissed, and Finley smiled at her, pulling her into an embrace.

"Of course I'm not serious," he breathed in her ear. "And I'm very sorry in advance."

"What?" She pulled back, but he had already launched into movement.

Unlatching the window at his elbow, he thrust it open, scooped Daphne into his arms and threw her through the opening.

CHAPTER 19

DAPHNE

Daphne flew through the air, tucking her elbows as the night sky flashed across her vision, replacing the lamplit warmth of the manor house. She landed in a clump of bushes, the foliage breaking her fall, even as it scratched her arms and tore off her mask.

Above her, Finley grabbed the windowsill and vaulted after her, his leap taking him clear of the bushes that held her. Daphne struggled free of the clinging branches as Finley landed in a crouch, his whole body jarring from the impact.

He spun, looking for her, but she was already running toward him, stuffing the mask into a concealed pocket. When she reached him, she seized his hand and kept running, tugging him along behind her. Glancing back, she saw a smile spreading over his face, but beyond him, Barlowe stood in the open window, watching them flee.

His back was to the light, making his face impossible to read.

Finley's longer legs overtook Daphne, and he shifted the grip of their hands so that he was the one pulling her along. Together they raced past the abandoned barn and into the trees beyond.

"Fin!" Archer's familiar voice made her falter, pulling back on Finley's grip.

Finley stopped and spun, scanning the trees around them. Archer stepped from between two of the trunks, his face lined with worry.

"What is it?" He stared behind them. "What are you running from?"

"Barlowe," Daphne panted, struggling to catch her breath after the unexpected flight.

"Who?"

"It's a long story." Fin frowned at his brother. "But what are you doing here? You shouldn't be here!"

"I couldn't just sit back at the cabin and wait." Archer's expression was defiant. "I wasn't going to burst into the ballroom or anything. I just thought I'd wait out here and...and provide backup if you needed it."

Fin drew a deep breath, but whatever he wanted to say to his brother, he suppressed it. "Morrow and Nisha?"

"I went to bed early and snuck out the window," Archer confessed. "I knew you'd be furious, but—"

"Actually, this is a good thing." Finley's words caught both Archer and Daphne by surprise.

She frowned at him. A good thing? She clutched his hand tighter, foreboding filling her to the fingertips.

"If you're here, it changes everything." Finley turned from Archer to Daphne, taking both her hands in his. "There was no way I was walking off with Barlowe and leaving you alone back there. But with Archie here..."

"No, Fin." Daphne shook her head stubbornly. "Don't do it. Don't even think about it."

"But if I don't, this will never end."

Daphne's lips pressed together. "We'll report him. We know who he is now. We'll go to the guards and—"

"And what? Tell them we've been chased for years by a *lord*? He'll say the whole thing is nonsense, and they'll believe him, not us. Given Archie was robbing Lord Castlerey only weeks ago, we're not exactly going to be considered reliable witnesses. If we had proof, it might be different, but..."

"We might not have proof," Daphne said, "but neither does he have proof of being a lord. We can challenge him, demand he produces proof of who he claims to be."

"And when he laughs in our faces and walks away, do you think they'll force him to respond?" Fin sighed. "He's been keeping up this ruse for ten years, and he said he pays attention to details. Who knows what false proof he might have accumulated in all that time?"

"What in the kingdoms are you two talking about?" Archer broke in. "Who's a fake lord?"

Fin looked at him, a shadow in his eyes that made Daphne's heart contract. Archer still didn't know the truth about their father or why they'd been pursued for so long.

Would Finley tell him immediately? Archer needed to

know, but he deserved to be told with more sensitivity than Barlowe had shown Fin.

"There's no time." Finley sounded anguished. "Barlowe isn't going to just let us go. He's not the sort of man to pursue us himself, but he'll send those ruffians after us without hesitation. Unless I go with him."

"What? No!" Archer grabbed Finley's shoulder. "What are you talking about, Fin? You can't just hand yourself over to him! Why would you do that?"

Finley squeezed Daphne's hands, looking down into her face, his own gaze steady. "You have to tell Archie for me—the truth about our father, everything."

"You should tell him yourself." She clung to his hands even harder.

"So you found out what Father did to this Barlowe fellow?" Archie asked. "Tell me! What is it? Can we fix it?"

"Yes." Finley pulled himself free from Daphne's clasp. "If I go back now and help him."

"No!" Daphne threw herself at him, winding her arms around his chest and holding on tight, her face pressed against his chest.

"Daphne," he said gently. She didn't move. "Daphne," with more urgency. She still didn't move.

He sighed and took her firmly by the shoulders, holding her away from him so he could see her face. "I don't want to leave you, either of you. But this is the only way I know how to protect you. I can't let you spend the rest of your life running. They just want me to go through the brambles and free the castle. Just like you did for Archie. No problem."

He smiled, but it didn't reach his eyes. He had to know it wasn't going to be that simple. But she could see on his face that he was going to try anyway. For Archie—and for her.

"I'm sorry, Daphne." He pulled her closer again, kissing her firmly and quickly—like a seal but also a farewell. "I love you."

Archer's mouth dropped open, but Finley was already clapping him on the shoulder.

"Look after her for me, Archie."

He strode away, heading back toward the house. Daphne watched him go, oddly numb.

Archer seized her arm, his voice urgent. "What's going on, Daphne?"

She turned to him, plans forming in her mind. "We have to follow him."

"I still don't understand where he's going," Archer said, eyeing her doubtfully, "but do you really think we can drag him back if he's determined to go?"

"No, that could be disastrous. But we can hide nearby and watch what happens, at least. I need to see how Barlowe treats him. I need to see if he's a prisoner or a guest."

"A prisoner?" Archer asked in alarm. "Who is this Barlowe?"

Daphne hesitated. "Come on. We need to get moving. We have to stay in the trees, so we'll have to take a longer route to reach the front of the manor. I'll explain as we walk."

It wasn't the ideal setting for telling Archie the truth

about his past, but she couldn't keep it from him. As they walked she told him everything they had learned about and from Barlowe—including the true identity of Archer's father. To her surprise, he accepted it easily, responding with a grin.

"Father always told me I was special—that Fin and I both were. Fin thought it was empty talk, but I knew better. I never dreamed I was a prince, though!"

"Your father was," Daphne corrected. "I don't think you are—officially speaking. You have cousins who are princes and princesses, though."

Archer waved her objections away with an airy hand. "*Official* isn't what matters here. I'm a prince!" He sobered. "But I would like to officially register my objection to Fin putting himself in the power of this Barlowe. He doesn't sound at all trustworthy."

"He's not," Daphne said flatly.

"Then why did you let Fin go?" Archer exclaimed.

Daphne gave him a look, and he sighed. "Fine, you did your best." His eyes darted back to her. "What was that back there, by the way? Between you and Fin. What exactly happened at that ball?"

Daphne flushed. "That's not what's important right now."

Archer looked like he wanted to argue, but something caught his eye, and he froze, grabbing her arm.

"Look!" His exclamation was whisper quiet.

Between the trees, they could just see the manor's front drive and its ornate gates. The gates themselves were merely decorative, since the manor had no surrounding wall, but the road from the manor to the village ran through them. Passing through the gates, moving in the direction of the village, was a group of people.

Daphne barely held in her exclamation of dismay. Barlowe strode alone at the front of a collection of rough men, and in their center walked a single straight figure. Finley looked unharmed from a distance, but his hands were tied and two men flanked him, their hands on his shoulders.

Archie growled, and Daphne only just managed to dive forward and catch at him before he launched himself out of the trees after his brother.

"No!" she whispered fiercely. "No, you can't! Look at how many of them there are! You'd have no hope on your own. We have to go back to Morrow and Nisha. Together we can come up with a plan to free him."

Archer's body remained taut, his muscles straining as he leaned toward Finley. But he didn't use his full strength to break free, and as the seconds ticked by, he slowly relaxed. He still looked mutinous, though, and his eyes hadn't left Finley.

Daphne blew out a slow breath. She would have liked to race out there and attack Barlowe herself, but she didn't intend to hand him Archer along with Finley. Finley might have told Archer to look after Daphne, but it was Daphne he was trusting to make sensible decisions.

She kept a tight grip on Archer's arm as she crept closer, keeping within the shadow of the trees. A carriage drew up just beyond the gate, but her spark of hope was immediately extinguished when the driver nodded at Barlowe. The two exchanged a few murmured words she couldn't catch before Barlowe turned to look at Finley. Fin met his eyes defiantly.

"Yes, yes, you quite detest me. I know." Barlowe's voice carried in the still night air. "But it's safer this way." He smiled. "For me, at least."

He looked at his men. "Given the look in young Finley's eyes, I think we could do with a little insurance. If you head for the trees, I'm confident you'll find the girl from the ball hiding there, watching us. Find her and bring her to me."

Fin shouted in outrage and tried to lunge at Barlowe, but the men on either side of him held him back.

"Archer," Daphne said, already backing up. "We have to run. Now!"

She whirled and fled blindly into the trees. Already she could hear footsteps behind them—Barlowe's men had spread out and two of them had lucked on the right direction.

"There!" one shouted, sounding close behind. They'd caught sight of her pink dress through the trees.

The pace of the pursuing footsteps picked up, and more joined them, converging from further back. Daphne risked a quick look behind, just as Archer's long legs overtook her. He checked his pace, and she tried to wave him on. He didn't respond, matching his steps to hers.

"Go!" she gasped out. "Run as fast as you can. Don't worry about me!"

He continued to keep pace beside her.

She tried to increase her own speed, but she was already sprinting as fast as she dared through the trees. Behind her, the steps were getting closer. They didn't have enough of a head start.

"Keep going," Archer shouted, wheeling around and coming to a stop, facing their pursuers.

"Archer!" Daphne slowed and turned. Was he planning to hold them off while she escaped?

She couldn't let him.

Or maybe that was their only hope. If she could get away and reach Morrow and Nisha, they could rescue both brothers. She should keep running.

But her feet didn't listen to logic. She couldn't leave Archer to face them alone. Her trembling fingers drew out her mask and tied it back onto her face. It was probably a futile gesture, but the concealment gave her a thin layer of false confidence.

She took one step toward Archer before her mind seized, a wave of exhaustion hitting so heavily that her legs gave way. She sank onto the forest floor, barely registering that her eyes were fluttering closed.

Daphne came awake abruptly, pulled to her feet by rough hands. Her head spun at the rude awakening, her thoughts confused. She had never fallen asleep like that—in the middle of such a dire situation—and the nap had left her disoriented.

The hand holding her jerked her forward, and she stumbled. A second man seized her from the other side, steadying her as they pulled her along faster.

The terrified energy of her flight still coursed through her, and the thought of a nap strong enough to override it scared her more than even Barlowe and his ruffians. But she pushed that fear aside and took stock of the situation.

Archer had been seized as well and was being pulled along in the same direction. A cut on his arm bled sluggishly, but he still had his feet under him, and his head was turned in her direction. He looked relieved to see her awake.

"Look, boss," one of the men called as they broke from the trees. "There were two of them."

Finley groaned, his eyes running up and down both of them, checking for injuries. Daphne shook her head at him, not even sure what she was trying to communicate.

"Archer!" Barlowe exclaimed. "What an unexpected pleasure! This rather changes the picture."

He looked speculatively between them as his men dragged their two new prisoners closer. "Archer is an even better hostage than the girl since he can both ensure Finley's compliance and also complete the necessary tasks himself if necessary."

Archer met his brother's eyes, his shoulders slumping as he mouthed the words, "I'm sorry."

Finley lunged forward abruptly, trying to break his captor's hold. He managed to tear himself free, lurching toward Barlowe until he came to an abrupt stop at the point of a sword. Barlowe held the tip steady against Finley's chest, a smile still on his face.

For a horrible, unthinking second, Daphne expected

him to run Finley through. But Barlowe's wrist made only the smallest of lazy flicks, leaving a shallow scratch along the underside of Finley's chin.

For a drawn-out moment, the two men stood looking at each other. Then Finley swayed.

Daphne flinched between her captors as he stumbled sideways once and slumped to the ground.

"Fin!" Archer struggled against his captors, but after Finley's brief escape, they had taken Archer in an even firmer hold, and he couldn't wrest himself free.

Barlowe turned toward him, his Oakdenian blade still held ready. Daphne watched, frozen, unable to think of a single thing to do to prevent what was coming.

"Don't think we'll help you now," Archer spat out, glaring at the advancing Barlowe.

Barlowe just smiled. "I think your brother will do whatever I ask if it means saving you." He glanced toward the men holding me. "We don't need her, after all. You can dispose of her in the forest."

"What?!" Archer began a fresh round of pointless struggling against his captors until a fist in the stomach sent him onto his hands and knees, retching.

Barlowe paused, eyeing him in disgust. "Did you think I would leave her behind to run and warn that enormous brute of yours? Or to go spilling my story to anyone who will listen? There's no point in my having the castle if the truth gets out another way." His eyes narrowed as he addressed his men again. "When you've dealt with her, find the other two and dispose of them as well."

He stepped toward Archer, but a burst of light and sound from the manor door made him pause. Distant voices swirled around Daphne, background noise to her racing thoughts. She had one chance to get free, and if she failed, she died.

CHAPTER 20

DAPHNE

aphne's parents had trained her in self-defense, but she had little hope against the two burly men who held her on either side. There was, however, one thing Daphne did better than unarmed combat.

Sleep.

"What do we do, boss?" one of the men asked, his voice edgy. The noise and voices were growing louder.

Without waiting to hear Barlowe's response, Daphne dropped into a nap, slumping toward the ground. She wasn't really asleep, but she knew perfectly how to fake it, and her captors were taken completely off guard. Unprepared for her sudden dead weight, their grips faltered, and she collapsed into a heap on the road.

"She's asleep again!" one of them exclaimed in disgust, just as a chaos of fresh voices broke over the scene, this time from the village side of the gate.

"Look! There!" shouted an unfamiliar man.

The words were followed by an enraged bellow that reminded Daphne strongly of Morrow. A barrage of orders, shouts, running feet, and carriage wheels flooded Daphne's senses.

"To the carriage!"

"Get him in!"

"No! No! Forget that one!"

"Kill them all!"

The last made Daphne's eyes spring open. She caught a glimpse of Barlowe, half hanging out the window of the moving carriage, shouting his orders back to the men he had left behind.

The ringing sound of drawn weapons came from above her, and she rolled forward, losing her mask in the process. Legs moved in all directions, and she jumped to her feet, several steps away from her captors.

Archer had already recovered from his retching and was on his feet as well, a dagger in his hand. When she popped up beside him, he seized her wrist, swinging her around so they stood back to back. Barlowe's remaining men surrounded them, the circle drawing in closer as they took in Archer's single blade and Daphne's empty hands.

A wordless shout of challenge made the closing circle falter. The guests departing from the ball had stopped in confusion and were milling some distance away, but pounding feet sounded from the direction of the village, and the shout came again.

Archer grinned. "Morrow."

Barlowe's men sprang into action at the name, stampeding forward to seize Archer and Daphne. Daphne grabbed the arm of the first man, using his own momentum to send him spinning past her onto the ground.

As she twisted, she caught a glimpse of the approaching runners, one head standing out above the others, the man's shoulders drawing as much attention as his height. At his side ran a slim woman with a blade in both hands.

Daphne didn't have time to smile before she faced her next attacker, and this one carried a sword. Using the long blade to protect himself, he seized her, holding her against his chest with an arm around her neck, like a human shield.

Another of Barlowe's men approached them, his own blade held threateningly in their direction.

"I'll be taking her," he growled, making it obvious why he had turned on his comrade. There weren't enough hostages to go around.

Her captor spat something in reply, and Daphne seized his momentary distraction to bite down hard on his hand. He screamed and pulled back. Using the same maneuver as she had used on Fin all those weeks ago, Daphne threw him over her shoulder—directly into the second man.

"Morrow!" she screamed as she ran toward the approaching rescue party. "Nisha!"

Two of the remaining men were fighting Archer, but another lunged forward, catching her wrist and jerking her back so hard she nearly fell, her shoulder screaming in pain. But he was too late. Morrow had reached them.

Daphne twisted her arm, breaking free of her captor's

grasp before she whipped her arm back to smash the side of his head with her elbow.

"Daphne!" Morrow followed her blow with a second one that downed the man.

Nisha reached her next, a drawn sword in either hand and her teeth bared. Behind her followed an unfamiliar man with his own drawn sword, his expression dangerous despite his young age. He was accompanied by a woman whose face niggled at Daphne's memory, although she couldn't immediately place her.

"Don't let them flee!" an older voice called from the back of the group, and the two strangers broke off to pursue the two men making for the treeline.

"Barlowe ordered all of us killed—even the two of you," Daphne panted out to Morrow and Nisha, warning them of the danger.

But from the expressions on both their faces, they welcomed an attack. Daphne stepped back, letting them surge ahead of her. If someone else wanted the fight, she was more than happy to leave it to them.

Within minutes, the flurry of fighting was over. Two men groaned on the ground at Morrow's feet, his threatening expression keeping them from any attempt to stand. Nisha had returned her swords to their scabbards on her back and was hauling a third man to his feet.

"Do you have any more rope?" Archer called to the two strangers, sounding almost cheerful as he restrained a kneeling man.

The two who had accompanied Nisha and Morrow had the attempted escapees bound by the wrists and were leading them back toward the rest of the group. The woman nodded and handed her prisoner to the man, hurrying over to Archer with a fresh length of rope.

"Always trust a merchant to have what's needed," Lorne said from the road behind them, a chuckle in his voice.

"A merchant?" Daphne looked at the woman again, finally remembering where she had seen the brown-haired young woman before. "Avery? What are you doing here?"

The roving merchant girl had stopped in Daphne's Glandorian hometown more than once, although she'd traveled alone then.

"I'm the friend Lorne mentioned." Avery gave a cheerful smile. "And you must be Daphne. From Thebarton in Glandore, right? I meet a lot of new faces in my travels, but the ones who've moved kingdoms are few and far between, so they stand out." She squinted her eyes in an effort of memory. "You napped a lot, yes?"

Daphne nodded. "I still do."

The man approached, his eyes running over Avery in concern. "Are you all right?" he asked quietly, and she gave him a reassuring look that shone with so much love Daphne had to look away, feeling like an intruder.

From the wedding band on Avery's finger, she had acquired a permanent companion in her travels since Daphne last saw her.

"Daphne!" Lorne pulled her into a reassuring embrace, and for a second she let herself rest before voicing the thought that had been ringing in her mind since she opened her eyes from her false nap.

"Where's Finley? Did you see what happened to him? Barlowe put him to sleep with an Oakdenian blade, but I didn't see..."

"They hauled him into the carriage." Archer pulled the knot he was tying extra tight, his voice grim. "With a crowd approaching from both sides, Barlowe abandoned me and fled for his carriage, but Finley was closer and already incapacitated. Two of Barlowe's men managed to load him in before the driver got the horses moving. Barlowe escaped with Finley and a carriage full of his men."

"At least they didn't get you both," Lorne said gravely. "I take it you're the brother."

Archer nodded. "I'm Archer."

"And I'm Lorne. The two with me are Avery and Elliot, roving merchants and friends of mine. I left the ball to consult them, but they insisted on hurrying back with me right away. It was a good thing they did—and an even better thing that we met these two on the way." He nodded toward Morrow and Nisha. "They're a distinctive pair, so I took a guess they were the friends Daphne had described and hailed them."

"But what happened?" Avery asked, surveying the six captured men, all now bound. "Lorne said he left you in the ballroom!"

"Barlowe recognized Finley." Daphne explained briefly about their flight and Fin's subsequent return, leaving out the information about his father's true identity.

"Fin should never have trusted Barlowe." Archer sounded angry. "He's always getting himself into trouble with his misguided determination to protect me."

"Maybe he wouldn't feel the need to protect you if you didn't sneak out of windows and run off on your own every chance you get," Nisha said caustically.

Archer had the grace to look shamefaced.

Morrow shook his head. "It's our fault, really. We should have guessed what he was about as soon as he said he was going to bed early."

"You discovered he was gone and came after him?" Daphne asked, and Nisha nodded.

"And now we'll go after Finley." Morrow said the words matter-of-factly. "Do you know where Barlowe's taken him?"

"He'll be heading for his castle." Daphne frowned. "Or the castle he's been claiming as his, anyway. But Fin's the one who knew where it was." She looked at Lorne. "Something about a southern lake and cherry blossoms? Supposedly there's a white castle on the lake."

"That must be on the southwestern border of the forest." Lorne's brow creased. "The road from Ethelson to the capital passes just to the east of the lake, so I've been through the area several times. I don't remember a white castle, though."

Before Daphne could explain about the sleeping girl and the wall of thorns, the milling group near the manor door finally worked up the courage to approach. As they took in the scene and the six bound men, their exclamations and questions grew louder and louder, attracting a growing crowd from inside the manor.

Lord Castlerey pushed through them. "Now, now," he called, "what's this?" He looked disapprovingly over the group until his eyes fell on Lorne. "Lorne! What are you doing out here? What has happened?"

"I'm afraid this group of men attacked my goddaughter, Daphne." Lorne drew her forward. "They were threatening her with swords when we luckily arrived on the scene."

Several women screamed, and a fresh burst of chatter broke out among the watching guests.

"It was Lord Barlowe," Daphne said loudly. "He was the one who told them to do it. He ordered them to kill me!"

"Lord Barlowe?" Lord Castlerey frowned. "Nonsense! Why, he was called away on an urgent family matter some time ago. He isn't even here. If these men have been bandying his name about in an effort to save their own hides, I shall see them suitably punished."

Daphne growled under her breath. No wonder Finley had been reluctant to approach the lord with their story.

Lorne put a steadying hand on her arm and spoke to his friend. "If you could have these ruffians delivered to the nearest guards, I would be in your debt, my lord. It has been a terrifying experience for my goddaughter, and I would like to get her back to the inn and warmed up as soon as possible."

"Of course, Lorne, of course," Lord Castlerey said. "It's no wonder she's overset. A most troubling business!

Attacking my guests as they leave my ball—I never heard of such a thing! We have the villains well in hand, don't you fear." He signaled to several footmen, and they hurried forward to take charge of the prisoners.

"I suppose we needn't worry about what the men might say," Daphne said dryly as they turned away, "since it seems Lord Castlerey has decided what happened for himself."

"I suspect it's for the best on this occasion," Lorne murmured. "I believe this is a matter best handled by ourselves."

He put his arm around her shoulders and led her down the road, toward the village. Archer followed close behind, flanked on either side by Nisha and Morrow.

"What happened to Avery?" Daphne checked over her shoulder at the people still milling around Lord Castlerey and the six prisoners, but there was no sign of the two merchants there.

"She and Elliot already headed back to the inn," Lorne replied. "They're a capable pair, so I'm sure they'll have a private sitting room ready for us by the time we arrive—hopefully one with a roaring fire. I really do want to see you warmed up, my girl. That dress isn't made for the night air, and I don't want you going into shock."

Daphne stopped abruptly, pulling him to a stop with her. "I'm not the one we need to be worrying about right now."

"I assure you I have top class worrying skills," Lorne said with unimpaired cheer. "I can worry about a staggering number of people all at once."

"Is that something to boast about?" Archer asked. "My mother always advised me not to worry."

"A wise woman," Lorne said. "But we all need occupation in our old age, and since I can no longer travel much, I sometimes dabble in other hobbies."

Nisha spoke up from behind them. "If we're going after Finley, we'll need transport. And better directions than just *southwest*. The inn seems as good a place as any to strategize."

Archer stepped up to Daphne's side and slung an arm over her shoulders. "And they have lovely, comfortable chairs as well. How could you resist?"

"How indeed?" She shrugged out from under his arm, giving him a repressive look.

But her knot of worry loosened slightly at sight of the concern and impatience that lurked at the back of his eyes. She wasn't the only one eager to be off after Finley.

Lorne resumed walking, and the rest of them followed. "At the inn, we'll consult a map and plan what we can from there."

When they finally reached the brightly lit building, they found everything just as Lorne had predicted. Daphne gratefully accepted the warm drink handed to her, but she didn't dare sit in one of the armchairs by the fire. She would be asleep in seconds if she did.

With everyone gathered, Daphne told the evening's story again, this time with full details. Her audience exhibited a satisfying amount of shock at the revelation of the true identity of Finley and Archer's father.

"Their father was Prince Timothy?" Avery seemed to

be the only one who recognized the name. "And he's deceased? King Vesper will be sorry to hear it. The last time I was in the capital, he confided his brother's story to me—confidentially, of course. He regrets his father's firm stance on the matter and asked me to keep an eye out for Prince Timothy in my travels." She glanced at Elliot. "We'll have to adjust our plans and visit the capital before we move on to Halbury. I can't leave Oakden without telling the king the news of his brother's death."

"Of course." Elliot put a comforting arm around her. "We said we'd be in Halbury in the summer, but not exactly when. We can take as much time as you like."

Avery seemed to draw strength from the contact, her manner turning brisk. "For now, however, we have more pressing matters." She produced a map of Oakden and laid it across the room's large table.

Everyone crowded around as Daphne searched for a lake that fit Finley's description. It wasn't hard to find it.

"There." She placed her finger on the spot. "That's where Fin thinks Barlowe's castle is. Except it's surrounded by brambles and forgotten by the world. I think the Legacy has helped with the forgetting, but it must have been cut off for at least a generation."

Avery rolled up the map, speaking with decision. "Once we're there, we should be able to find something as big as a castle, brambles or not."

"You're coming with us?" Daphne asked.

"Of course," she replied, and her husband laughed.

"If you can keep Avery from jumping into a rescue with both feet, please let me in on the secret."

"I appreciate your enthusiasm as always, Avery," Lorne said with a smile. "Are you volunteering your wagon?"

The three of them began to discuss logistics, but Daphne wasn't listening.

"You would be just as capable of opening the brambles as Finley," she murmured to Archer.

He made a thoughtful sound at the back of his throat. "We'd have to get there before them. Can we do it?"

"Barlowe and Finley are in a carriage, so if we go on horseback..."

Elliot's voice broke through her thoughts. "Brilliant as your plans may be, Avery, those two seem to have a scheme of their own." He nodded in Daphne and Archer's direction.

"Daphne? Archer?" Lorne raised his brows, looking concerned.

"We need horses," Archer said. "Fast ones."

"You want to get there before Barlowe and Finley," Nisha said slowly.

Archer nodded. "Barlowe has already shown he's willing to kill to keep his secret. So what do you think he'll do to Fin once Fin opens those brambles and wakes the girl? We have to get to that castle before they do—Fin's safe until then. I can open the brambles enough for us to get in, and then we can take Barlowe by surprise when he arrives and rescue Fin."

"Unfortunately the stables of this inn aren't exactly brimming with riding horses of sufficient speed and stamina," Nisha said.

Elliot exchanged a look with Avery. "There's Nutmeg, at least," he offered when she gave a small nod.

"Is that your cart horse?" Archer sounded skeptical.

"She's not exactly a normal cart horse, though, is she?" Daphne asked, remembering her previous encounters with the chestnut mare. "I always thought she seemed… different."

Avery laughed. "She certainly is, but you're observant to have noticed. Most people don't."

"How unusual is she?" Archer asked, brightening.

"Very," Elliot said dryly. "Avery has taken her so many places over the years—sometimes into places brimming with Legacy power—and it's changed her. She's far smarter than any horse has the right to be, for one. Like the parrots in Glandore or the mice in Sovar. And she doesn't tire nearly as quickly as she should."

"She can manage the ride," Avery said decisively. "Elliot knows that from experience."

Daphne raised her eyebrows, looking between them. At any other time, she would have been interested in the story behind that statement. But she couldn't think about anything but rescuing Finley.

"Just how extraordinary is Nutmeg?" she asked instead. "Could she manage the ride with two riders?"

"That depends on the second rider." Avery glanced at Morrow. "Extraordinary or not, she's still a horse, so if one of them was Morrow here…But I assume you mean yourself and Archer? In that case, she should manage."

Nisha frowned. "But what can the two of you do on your own?"

"We'll come up with a strategy on the way." Archer spoke with the confidence of extreme youth. "We'll have the element of surprise, remember. And you can all follow behind more slowly to provide backup."

Daphne didn't share his confidence, but neither was she going to say anything to discourage the scheme. They had to take the risk and try to rescue Finley. And for once they would be the ones a step ahead instead of Barlowe.

Archer glanced at Daphne. "Fin wouldn't want you to go with me, though. He would want you to stay safe."

"If Fin was here, he would get a say," Daphne replied tartly. "Since he's not, I'm going."

The two faced off for a moment before Archer grinned. "If you're sure, I won't be the one to stop you. Fin can grumble about it all he likes once he's safe himself."

"I don't know why I'm agreeing," Lorne muttered, "except that I don't think we could stop you if we tried."

"I know that we wouldn't be the first choice to go usually," Daphne said quietly. "We're not exactly the strongest fighters of the group. But we are the lightest, and we have something else going for us besides."

Lorne met her eyes, understanding in his. "The Legacy," he said simply, and she nodded.

They were heading into an area rich with Legacy power, and of all the people present, she and Archer were the two to have most recently attracted the Legacy's attention. Daphne had been decrying the effect ever since, but it was time for her to make use of her position instead.

"You'd better come and meet Nutmeg, then." Avery led

the way to the inn's stables where they were greeted by a chestnut mare who whinnied at the sight of Avery.

She seemed reluctant to take Daphne or Archer on her back at first, but after some chiding from Avery, she settled and accepted her new riders.

"We'll hire a cart horse in the morning and follow as quickly as we can," Avery promised. "So don't get your-selves killed in the meantime."

Daphne only had time to nod before Nutmeg took off as if she wasn't carrying any riders at all.

CHAPTER 21

FINLEY

Finley woke to rough jolting. He was sprawled awkwardly on the floor of a carriage that was driving too fast down an uneven road.

He groaned and received a kick to his middle.

"Now, now," said Barlowe's amused voice. "I'm sure violence isn't needed. Finley is an ally now."

Finley slowly maneuvered himself into a sitting position in the crowded space. Barlowe and three other men already sat on the two bench seats, all of them watching him. At least his hands were no longer bound.

"Strange behavior for an ally," he said grimly, rubbing the back of his head.

"My apologies," Barlowe said smoothly. "Consider it a miscalculation on my part. As you can see, I changed my mind and brought only you, as agreed."

Finley glanced suspiciously around the carriage, but unless Barlowe had Archer stashed on the outside seat with the driver, he really had left him behind.

"What did you do to them?" he demanded suspiciously.

"Nothing, I assure you. I didn't touch a hair of their heads. I left them by the manor." Barlowe's smooth smile put Finley's back up, but he had no way to test the truth of the man's words.

Barlowe continued to watch him, his smile never faltering. "If you want to ensure the ongoing safety of your brother and that beautiful young lady, then you know what you have to do. My requirements are perfectly simple."

Finley nodded, reluctant acquiescence on his face, despite his racing mind beneath. Clearly his only option for the moment was to play along. Thankfully, Barlowe wasn't the only one with experience at false smiles and charming masks.

His mind wanted to dwell endlessly on Archer and Daphne, but he refused to give up hope. He had equipped Archer the best he could, and Daphne was smart, quick, and knew how to fight. And neither of them were alone. They would protect each other if they possibly could.

If they had survived the encounter with Barlowe, they would go to Morrow and Nisha, and then they would come after Finley. Given the way Barlowe had treated him, he was confident of that. Whatever smooth words Barlowe said now, he had already shown his true colors. Nothing he said could be trusted.

Of course, Finley had been the one to walk straight into Barlowe's trap. But there was no time to bemoan his past foolishness. He needed to focus on his next step. He would play along while looking for a way to slow them down, if possible, so his friends would have time to catch up.

Since biding his time meant continuing to bump along the road on the floor of the carriage, squeezed between the legs of the other four passengers, it was an uncomfortable night. At least the driver slowed down to a safer pace, unable to push his horses at top speed for hours at a time.

They changed horses at an inn once, but no one inside the carriage dismounted, giving Finley no opportunity to seek help or carry out any sabotage. And after the inn, the journey grew even rougher.

Despite the slower pace, the new set of horses pulled less smoothly than the previous pair. The motion suggested one of the new animals was poorly trained and unused to pulling in harness, and Finley resigned himself to a long night. Even so, to his surprise, he managed to doze on and off until the carriage finally came to a halt.

Morning had broken, and Finley climbed out onto a deserted road, his muscles complaining with every movement. No other travelers could be seen, and neither were there any buildings in sight. Apparently Barlowe wanted to stretch his legs but didn't trust Finley near other people. Finley's hope of a hot breakfast receded.

Cherry blossoms in bloom crowded the road, creating a beautiful riot of color and beauty. Their presence suggested they were nearing their destination, but Finley could see no sign of brambles nor any distant hint of a white building.

Examining his surroundings more closely, Fin realized

the forest still stretched away from the road on either side, hiding behind the rows of cherry blossoms. They had reached the southwestern region of the forest but not the forest's border or the lake that lay there. He still had time.

The men grumbled quietly among themselves as they walked up and down, stretching their legs, although they made sure not to do so in the vicinity of Barlowe. Finley traced their steps, keeping his distance from the others without straying far enough to raise alarm. Outnumbered seven to one, whatever he attempted would need to be more strategic than making a run for it in the middle of the forest.

He wheeled around at the outside limit of his self-assigned path, heading back past the horses. The driver had moved away from them—taking his own chance to stretch his legs—and as Finley passed, he was momentarily the only one standing near them.

A quick visual examination confirmed his earlier suspicion. As he had expected, the far horse appeared little more than a yearling, twitching at every noise from the forest. Finley adjusted his course, walking close enough to the near horse that he could touch it as he passed.

"Sorry, old boy," he murmured as he twisted the poor horse's ear. "You don't deserve this."

He strode quickly on as the horse whinnied and danced in place. The creature's movement jostled the flighty young horse harnessed beside him, and the year-ling broke into movement.

The older horse whinnied louder, and the driver shouted, but it was too late. The yearling lurched off the road, dragging the other horse and the carriage with him, and a splintering crash heralded the destruction of one wheel and part of the harness mechanism.

Barlowe and his men converged on the carriage, all speaking over the top of each other and blaming the driver for his momentary absence. But when the chaos subsided, Barlowe was looking at Finley.

Finley looked back, a polite, blank expression on his face, although he was relieved to see both horses were unharmed. Barlowe's eyes narrowed.

"It seems we'll be going the rest of the way on foot," he said.

"It seems we will," Finley replied coolly.

Barlowe gestured to one of his men and murmured something quietly to him while his eyes remained on Finley. The man ran off and returned with a length of rope.

"I'm sure you'll excuse the discourtesy," Barlowe said as the man rebound Finley's hands. "I've never been the trusting sort."

Finley said nothing, forcing himself to appear calm as the man did his work. Barlowe wasn't happy, but neither was he truly alarmed at a delay, and that made Finley more afraid than he had been since he woke up. Barlowe had no serious fears of pursuit.

What exactly had happened to Archer and Daphne after he was forcibly put to sleep?

CHAPTER 22

DAPHNE

Daphne cantered down yet another endless road, grateful for Archer's presence at her back. Despite the simmering tension that drove her forward, she kept slipping into short naps. And though she usually kept unlikely balance during her Legacy-fueled naps, she didn't like the idea of napping alone on the back of a racing horse.

When they finally stopped for a few snatched hours of sleep beside the road, she slept deeply and dreamlessly.

"At least we don't need to worry about meeting Barlowe on the way," Archer commented once morning dawned. The hard night's ride hadn't diminished his usual cheer. "Even my optimism doesn't like our chances if we try a direct attack."

Avery had shown them a route on the map that kept them away from the main carriage road, leading them on paths that were less smooth but more direct.

"This route also avoids the town on the eastern side of

the lake, though," Daphne said. "Which means we won't be able to collect reinforcements."

"I doubt we would have been successful at gathering them even if we tried. We still don't have any proof, and I don't exactly look the part of a prince on his way to wake a Sleeping Beauty."

Daphne grimaced at the thought of what she herself must look like after a night divided between horseback and the forest floor.

When the first cherry blossom tree appeared, Archer urged Nutmeg into a faster pace. It wasn't long before their path approached the lake from the north, disgorging them onto a much wider carriage road that ran westward along the north side of the lake. Cherry blossom trees lined the road on either side, and they thundered along between clouds of blossoms.

Despite the size and beauty of the road, the surface was rough and pitted, as if it didn't see regular use and hadn't received upkeep in years. Daphne drew encouragement from the indication that they'd reached the right place. If this part of the road ended at the castle, as they hoped, it must have long ago fallen into disuse.

Nutmeg, already having proved her ability as far beyond any normal horse, tossed her head, neighed, and increased her pace without urging, galloping toward two distant white towers. Neither Archer nor Daphne made any attempt to slow her.

They rounded a corner, and a solid wall of brambles came into view, towering above them. It blocked the end of the road completely, although it wasn't quite tall enough to obscure the white towers beyond.

Nutmeg came to an abrupt halt before the brambles, and Archer swung down from her back. He turned to offer assistance to Daphne, but she was already sliding down on her own, her eyes glued to the wall of greenery.

"We beat them," she murmured, sure Barlowe would have had Finley remove the entire wall if they'd already arrived.

"Do you really think I can move all that with a single touch?" For the first time Archer's usual confidence faltered.

"The volume of brambles doesn't matter." Daphne spoke confidently, having experienced it for herself. "It's hard to describe. Just touch it, and you'll understand."

He reached out, and she quickly spoke again. "Just remember we only want a small hole. We want to get ourselves and Nutmeg through, but then you have to close it up again. We don't want to remove them all yet."

Archer rolled his eyes. "I know. It would be hard to forget considering that's the only part of the plan we've worked out."

"In my experience, youthful boys aren't always good at details," she muttered, as he reached out to touch the closest vine.

The greenery in front of them burst into movement, slithering over and under as it unwound itself. It shrank away from them, creating a tunnel that arched just above the height of their heads, leaving just enough room for Daphne to lead Nutmeg through.

"Nice work." Daphne retrieved Nutmeg's bridle and gestured for Archer to lead the way.

"You were right—it was easy." Archer grinned, his confidence restored. "And it should be just as easy to get it to close again. It's incredible, actually! I wonder how long my power over it will last."

Daphne frowned. "Long enough for Barlowe and Finley to arrive, I hope."

Archer wasn't listening, too busy gazing at the scene on the other side of the brambles. A small white castle rose before them, enclosed on all sides by the wall of greenery.

"You can close it now," Daphne said when he showed no sign of noticing that she and Nutmeg had stepped out of the tunnel of brambles. "Archer?"

He jerked around and stared at her. "What? Oh, right!"

He hurried back to touch the closest bramble, directing it to close again behind them. Daphne watched him with a crease between her brows. Was his abstraction a result of the Legacy power? Was it already driving him toward the girl waiting in the castle?

Someone had to wake the girl up—Daphne didn't deny that. But given her own experience in a much less power-filled situation, she had grave concerns about what would come after the waking.

Ever since she had woken Archer, she had felt the power of the Legacy lingering around her, growing increasingly strong. But she had never felt it as strongly as she did inside the wall of brambles. She only hoped she could direct its power in a way that helped them all rather than falling prey to it.

Archer bounded up the front steps to the closed door of the castle. It opened easily beneath his hand, swinging wide to give them access to the entryway beyond.

They both stepped inside and stopped short. Daphne had been inside manors and castles before, but this entryway was far more crowded than any she had yet seen.

A large staircase gave access to the upper levels, and an enormous fireplace stood along one wall, an old woman slumped on a chair beside it, asleep. But those features were mere backdrop to what stood in the center of the space. Dominating the entryway completely stood a large canopied bed holding a sleeping girl, her head cushioned on a soft pillow.

Daphne wasn't close enough to get a proper look at her face, but a golden plaque attached to the bed spelled out her name: Gabrielle.

"He brought his daughter's bed down to the entryway?" Daphne shook her head in disbelief. "I know Sleeping Beauties can't be moved, but that seems excessive. I suppose he didn't want anyone who made it this far to miss her."

"Well, you certainly couldn't do that," Archie snorted.

"I suppose the woman by the fire must have been a servant here when the girl was enchanted." Daphne gave the slumbering woman a sympathetic look. "Do you think there are other servants sleeping around the castle?"

Archer shrugged, already moving toward the girl. "I suppose we'll find out after we wake her up."

Daphne caught his sleeve, slowing him down. "Are we

sure about this?" she asked uneasily. "Maybe we should come up with a strategy first?"

Once the girl was woken, the ticking clock would begin on Archer's control over the brambles. And with such an ostentatious placement of the bed, it would also make their interference immediately obvious to Barlowe.

But, once again, Archer hardly seemed to hear her, his eyes focused on the girl.

"Archer!" she said more sharply, and he finally looked her way.

"Are you ready for this?" she asked. "She's going to be...confused about you when she wakes up."

Archer reached the side of the bed and looked down at the sleeping girl. "We can't just leave her asleep. I was a sleeper myself once, remember." He swallowed. "I sometimes have nightmares where you never woke me up and I'm still stuck there, asleep, while my brother gets older and older."

Daphne softened. "I didn't know that." She hesitated. "Do you remember those first moments after you woke up? How strong was the enchantment you felt toward me in those moments?"

"Overpowering," Archer said promptly, still looking down at the girl.

"I'm worried about how long-lasting the infatuation has been." Daphne frowned. "Your sleeping enchantment was so much weaker than hers, and yet there's been nothing weak about your infatuation. What will it be like for this girl?"

Archer grinned mischievously at her. "I suppose now

would be the right moment to confess that the effect gradually weakened over time and completely wore off weeks ago."

"Archer!" Daphne glared at him.

He continued to grin unrepentantly. "I needed something to entertain myself, and Fin's reactions were too priceless for me to stop. Plus he clearly needed me to spur him on." He shook his head. "He isn't usually so bloodless and cautious." His grin reappeared. "And it worked, didn't it? I saw what happened after the ball."

"That wasn't because of you, infant." Daphne sighed, gazing down at the girl. "What do you know of love?"

"Nothing, thankfully," Archer said cheerfully. "You can tell that to the girl if she gets too attached."

"I can try," Daphne said dubiously.

"Gabrielle," Archer read off the girl's name plaque. "It's a nice name."

Up close the girl looked just as young and innocent as Archer had looked while asleep. It seemed impossible she was as old as sixteen, and yet Daphne had thought the same thing of Archer. She just wished the girl had some family to stand at her side and greet her when she woke, as Finley had done for Archer. Perhaps that was the silver lining of the Legacy's infatuation. Perhaps it would soften the blow the girl was about to receive as she learned of the death of her only family member.

Archer dropped to one knee at the side of the bed and picked up one of the slender hands that rested against the coverlet.

"Well, here goes," he muttered to himself and lifted it to his lips.

CHAPTER 23
DAPHNE

The girl remained still, Archer frozen beside her with her hand still in his. Daphne stared at the two of them, waiting for something to happen.

"Should I try again—" he started before breaking off as the girl's eyes fluttered open.

She blinked several times, frowning at Daphne before catching sight of Archer.

"Oh!" Her pink lips formed a perfect circle, and her eyes lit up.

Archer quickly dropped her hand and stepped backward.

"Welcome back to wakefulness, Gabrielle," Daphne said into the breach. "I'm Daphne."

Gabrielle's eyes remained fixed on Archer, her face flushing a delicate rose. "What's his name?"

"Lady Gabrielle!" The loud cry from the fireplace saved Daphne the need to answer.

The sleeping woman from the fireplace ran across the room with surprising vigor and threw herself on the neck of the young girl. "You're awake! You're awake!"

She began to sob.

Archer seized the opportunity to back several more steps away, his expression one of mild horror.

Gabrielle wriggled out of the woman's hold with difficulty. "Have I been asleep long, Nanny?" She glanced around the entryway. "Why, whatever is my bed doing down here? Have I been asleep a terribly long time?"

The old woman's tears paused, her expression arrested. "I...I don't know, Pet." She looked at Daphne.

Heartened by the obvious connection between the woman and the girl, Daphne replied to the clear question in the woman's gaze.

"It has been a long time, I'm afraid. I don't know how long exactly, but we believe it's been decades."

"Decades!" the woman said sharply. "Then the old lord...?"

Daphne gave a reluctant nod. "From what we understand, he left to seek help for his daughter but didn't survive the trip. You've both been sleeping here ever since."

"Oh, how awful!" The woman turned on Gabrielle again, wrapping the girl in a fresh embrace. "My poor dear!"

Gabrielle, who was now on her feet, protested loudly at being grabbed in a watery hug for a second time.

"Your poor Papa," the woman said, her words catching Gabrielle's attention as Daphne's had not.

The girl tore her eyes from Archer—who had retreated even further from the bed—and frowned at her nanny. "What about Papa?"

"He's dead, my lady," the woman said. "Apparently we've been sleeping for decades."

"Papa is dead?" the girl repeated blankly. "But..." She frowned. "But you are still here, Nanny."

"You know I would never leave you," the woman said, her voice firm. "I've been sleeping with you, as is right and proper."

"Have I really been sleeping for years and years? How strange." She looked around the entryway again. "And there isn't even any dust. Are you sure?"

"I think that might be part of the enchantment." Daphne tried not to sound impatient. After being afraid of the girl's response to her news, it wasn't fair to feel irritated with the girl for not reacting enough.

"The old lord was a kind man," the nanny said in a quiet, almost apologetic aside to Daphne, "and he doted on his daughter. But he didn't know much about children, let alone youth, and he was quite elderly. Lady Gabrielle fretted at being kept here without others her own age, and he never knew how to talk to her."

"Has she no other family?" Daphne asked. "Is there no one we can contact on her behalf?"

The woman's expression grew fierce. "I'm her family. Her mother passed birthing her, poor lady, and I raised Gabrielle with as much love as if she was my own. There's no one who can take better care of her than me."

"What of you, then, ma'am?" Daphne asked. "Do you have family for us to contact?"

"Call me Nanny, dear." Nanny patted her on the hand. "Everyone does. But I'm afraid I have no one to send you to either. I was a serving maid here as a girl, and my husband was an undergardener, which is how we met. We never had children of our own, which might be why the old lord assigned me to the nursery after Lady Gabrielle was born. He was always good to us after that, seeing the way his daughter had attached to me. My husband rose all the way to head gardener before he passed. My family now is Lady Gabrielle, as I am hers."

"There must have been other servants," Daphne said. "Did they sleep as well? Are they somewhere inside the castle?"

"There were other servants, of course." Nanny frowned around the entryway. "It's a big place. But the others didn't stay overnight. They weren't caught in the enchantment, so I can only assume they moved on long ago."

"I've never seen such beautiful eyes," Gabrielle said, oblivious to their conversation. She gave a wistful sigh.

"What's that, Pet?" Nanny sounded confused.

"You're going to be embarrassed about this later," Daphne murmured, although she hadn't actually noticed any perceptible embarrassment in Archer since his infatuation had worn off.

"Oh, Nanny!" Gabrielle seized her nanny's arm. "Isn't he the most beautiful boy you ever saw?"

"Who?" Nanny looked so honestly bewildered that Daphne burst out laughing.

"But he is! He is!" Gabrielle's voice rose, and Daphne was surprised she didn't stamp her foot.

"Do you mean that young man over there?" Nanny began searching in one pocket after another until she finally located her glasses and placed them on her nose.

She frowned in Archer's direction. "He's quite pleasing looking, I suppose," she declared after an extended examination.

"Pleasing looking!?"

"Do you not think so?" Nanny asked, even more confused.

"He's far more than just pleasing!" Gabrielle declared. "I love him!" She hurried across the entryway toward Archer, who was backing away with a fresh look of alarm.

"Love!" Nanny exclaimed in alarm. "Whatever is wrong with her?"

"Archer is the one who woke her up," Daphne explained. "Considering he's young, good-looking, and was the one to rescue her, I suspect she was always going to be inclined toward him. But the Legacy is enhancing it into a full-blown infatuation. It might also explain her calm reaction to her father's death."

"Oh dear." The older woman watched Gabrielle latch onto Archer's arm and stare up at him with an adoring expression.

Looking at Archer's face, Daphne couldn't quite suppress another laugh. After a moment, Nanny chuckled as well.

"Maybe you're right, and there's a blessing to be found in this infatuation," she said. "I can see this Archer isn't one to take advantage. He's certainly not using the opportunity to ingratiate himself with an heiress at any rate. If it will help ease the strangeness of it all for her, it might be a good thing."

Across the entryway, Archer tried to shake Gabrielle off his arm, but she had latched on too tightly and wouldn't let go. The girl glared back at Daphne whose eyebrows shot up.

"I'm not sure what I did," she said mildly, "but your Gabrielle doesn't seem too inclined toward me."

"You're mine," Gabrielle declared loudly enough for Daphne to hear. "She can't have you. She's too old."

Daphne grinned. "I most certainly am," she called back. "You're quite welcome to him."

Gabrielle beamed, closed her eyes, and rested her head against Archer's arm. He made a strangled sound in his throat and threw Daphne a look that was clearly asking for a rescue. She just laughed again. He shouldn't have confessed that he'd been playacting toward her for so long if he wanted a quick rescue from her direction.

"No," she said to Nanny. "You don't need to worry about him trying to ingratiate himself with her."

And she didn't need to worry about Archer coming under the influence of the Legacy himself. Now that he'd finished the task of waking Gabrielle, his horror at her hero worship seemed to have counteracted any Legacy pull toward her.

"But who is he?" Nanny asked. "While we appreciate

what you've done in waking us, how did you come to find us in the first place? If it's been so many years..."

"He's the son of Prince Timothy," Daphne said, watching for a reaction.

"Oh!" The woman's eyes lit up. "I remember the young prince! He was such a charming scamp. He was only a few years older than Lady Gabrielle when I accompanied her and the old lord on a visit to court. But that was back when she was just a young mite herself." She shook her head. "And that's his *son*, you say!"

She fell into silence for a moment, pondering the enormity of the lost years.

"So you've come from court, then?" she said at last.

"Actually, we haven't." Daphne hesitated. "It's a long story, and we might not have much time. I should tell you both at the same time."

"Archer, bring Gabrielle over here," she called, and he hurried to her side, trying unsuccessfully to outstrip Gabrielle.

"You have to rescue me," he said in a desperate whisper when he reached her. Daphne just grinned at him.

"We'll be more comfortable in here." Nanny gestured them through a door off the entryway that gave into a comfortable sitting room.

Like the entryway itself, the room had been well preserved, protected from the ravages of time by the sleeping enchantment. Daphne selected the hardest looking seat in the group of chairs, determined to keep herself awake, and Archer quickly sat on a single armchair.

Gabrielle looked disappointed but settled for pulling her chair as close to his as she could and gazing at him adoringly.

Nanny frowned at her charge before sighing and looking to Daphne. "Now, what's this urgent matter? Does it have to do with Lady Gabrielle?"

"I'm afraid it does." Daphne outlined the facts about Barlowe and his quest as quickly as possible.

Nanny gave a shriek at hearing Barlowe's intentions, but Gabrielle merely wrinkled her pretty nose.

"Of course I wouldn't marry some old man who only wanted my castle."

"Very right, my dear," Nanny said firmly. "And so we'll tell him when he arrives."

Daphne and Archer exchanged dismayed looks.

"I'm afraid it might not be as simple as that," Daphne said.

Archer snorted. "Simple? If they try that, it will be quite simple. He'll take one look around, see there's no one but a girl and an old lady in his way and run them both through."

Nanny screamed again, and Daphne gave Archer an exasperated look. But she didn't refute his words.

"Barlowe has already shown himself to be a violent man without scruples, so it's a legitimate concern. And he already has Archer's brother as his prisoner. If you have any gratitude toward Archer for waking you up, I hope you'll also give some concern toward his brother. I think we need a more sophisticated plan."

"I must get Gabrielle away immediately!" Nanny said.

"Abandon the castle?" Gabrielle frowned, momentarily distracted from Archer. "But it's my home! I won't just let him take it!"

Nanny wrung her hands together, clearly torn. Her primary concern was protecting her charge, but protecting Gabrielle also meant protecting her interests. If they fled, they would be two women alone in the kingdom, even displaced from their own time.

"We don't mean to let Barlowe get away with it," Archer assured Gabrielle firmly, and the girl immediately relaxed. Apparently she had full confidence in Archer's ability to deal with the situation.

Daphne turned to Nanny. "I do agree that the best thing you can do for now is to take Lady Gabrielle away. From what you said about Prince Timothy being a few years older than Lady Gabrielle when you went to sleep, I think you must have been sleeping for about thirty years. Surely there would be someone in the nearest town who would still remember the two of you? Once they realize who you are, you can report the situation to the local guards and ask for help. It was difficult for us to do so since we have no claim here, and the Legacy had made most people forget you. But now that you're awake, it's a different matter."

Nanny immediately brightened. "That's an excellent idea."

Archer nodded fervently. "Daphne and I will stay here and protect Fin if Barlowe arrives before you get back."

"No!" Gabrielle cried so sharply that they all jumped.

"We have to protect Archer! We can't leave him here alone and in danger."

"Alone?" Daphne muttered, but she didn't bother protesting more loudly. At least Gabrielle had now learned the name of the boy she so desperately loved.

The girl began a spirited argument with her nanny, which Daphne ignored, her mind busy on an idea.

"You might be right," she said, and both women turned to her with fierce nods, clearly thinking she was talking to them. "Archer should be the one to take Gabrielle into town. Nanny can stay here and help me."

"What?" Archer shook his head vigorously. "Of course I'm not going to abandon you here, Daphne! Why would you suggest that?"

"I think it's an excellent idea," Gabrielle declared before pausing. "There wouldn't be any risk of harm to Nanny, would there?"

Daphne hesitated. "I think there would be very little," she said cautiously.

"Do you have a plan in mind?" Archer asked, his curiosity caught.

Daphne drew a breath. "We need to get Gabrielle to safety, and we need her to fetch the guards. She's the property's owner, so she's the one with the right to call on them. Since she's clearly not going to go without you, you need to be the one to take her. But we can't just abandon the castle in the meantime. If Barlowe arrives and it's empty, he'll have no need for Finley."

"He would kill him on the spot," Archer agreed, his face and voice serious. "Get rid of the witness."

"Exactly." Daphne kept her voice steady and her face impassive. "We need Barlowe to think his plan is working. That means that when he arrives, we need not just brambles but also a sleeping girl." She drew another deep breath, feeling the weight of what she was about to say.

It had been looming over her for weeks, and now her dreaded fate had arrived. The Legacy had won.

"I need to take Gabrielle's place."

CHAPTER 24
FINLEY

Finley trudged down the road, long since immune to the beauty of the cherry blossoms. His plan had seemed a lot cleverer several hours ago.

The man carrying the rope attached to Finley's bound hands gave yet another vicious tug that made Fin stumble. Apparently his captors shared his feelings about the forced march.

At least Barlowe had been forced to leave the driver behind with the horses, so there were only six men accompanying Finley rather than seven. Not that it evened the odds much.

When two white towers finally appeared in the distance, the mood lightened, and everyone's steps quickened. Everyone except Finley, who felt a twist of tension in his gut at the sight.

"At last," Barlowe breathed, an ardent light in his eyes. "After all these years."

"You can't really think this plan is going to work,"

Finley said, unable to keep quiet. "The girl isn't just going to accept you."

"Of course she'll accept me. I'm her rescuer—her hero."

"Some hero," Finley muttered.

Barlowe whirled on him, the lines of his face cold but his eyes burning. "I've planned everything," he hissed, "and the Legacy is finally going to realize I'm the hero, not the villain."

Finley cocked his head, his brow quirking as he processed Barlowe's words. Gradually the pieces came together.

"You saw me arrive at the ball, and you recognized what I was doing to gain entry," he said slowly. "Because you've done it before yourself, haven't you?"

Barlowe straightened his jacket with fingers that twitched slightly.

"You weren't the first one to come up with the idea. I used it to enter my first noble party over ten years ago." He smiled reminiscently, but the expression quickly faded. "When I did it again and again, the Legacy's power built around me. It propelled me to enormous success over the years that followed—the Uninvited Guest who was catered to and given a place of honor."

"If you've had so much success in that role, why are you taking this so far?" Finley asked.

"Why?" Barlowe stared into the distance. "Would you want to be nothing more than a guest for a decade? Always a stranger in someone else's home, a figure in the background. The Legacy thought it could force me into that role, but it has me wrong. I'm not a villain, I'm a hero. And now it will have to acknowledge me as such—and give me the resulting rewards."

Finley stared at him, but Barlowe barely seemed to remember Finley was there, his bright eyes fixed on the towers ahead. For once Finley didn't doubt the truth of Barlowe's words. Everything else had been a polite, amused mask, a cover for cold plans and cold ambitions. But now Barlowe was burning from the inside out.

This was the motivation at the heart of it all, and it was nothing more than ego—just as it had been for the original uninvited guest. Barlowe thought he was escaping that role, but he was only sinking more deeply into it. And like the original guest, he was going to heedlessly tear down the lives of others along the way, whether they'd wronged him or not.

Unless Finley managed to stop him.

Barlowe didn't speak again, and the remaining path to the white castle disappeared beneath their feet far too quickly. In what felt like minutes, Finley stood gazing up at an impassable wall of thick brambles that grew to an unnatural height, curving away from them in both directions.

Barlowe turned to Finley, the eager light in his eyes tucked away behind his mask once more. He smiled slowly.

"Your moment has come, Prince Finley."

"I'm no prince." Finley didn't step toward the brambles.

"I think you'll find you're close enough for the purpose." Barlowe gestured toward the wall of green.

Finley hesitated for a moment longer before shrugging and stepping forward. If he refused, Barlowe would have no more use for him, and he didn't think he wanted to see what would happen after that. He lifted both bound hands and brushed his fingers across the closest length of bramble, sucking in a breath at the feeling of power and control that instantly flowed through him.

A small part of him had still doubted the whole thing, thinking that Barlowe had made a terrible mistake—that he had the wrong brothers. But with the merest thought, Finley set the whole wall of greenery quivering. It snaked away from him almost too fast to watch, the brambles sinking into the ground in front of them. The effect flowed outward on both sides as the huge circle of brambles came undone, sinking back into the ground, into nothingness.

Barlowe had spoken the truth. Finley's father must have been a prince.

"See," Barlowe said. "That wasn't so hard, was it?"

Finley didn't respond, his eyes on the building that was now exposed before them. He had suspected Barlowe of being pretentious in calling it a castle, but it was undoubtedly the first word that sprang to mind. The structure soared above them, its square towers of gleaming white stone lined with battlements. And beyond, he caught a glimpse of sunlight on the surface of the lake. With the brambles gone, and the cherry blossoms in bloom, it was an enchanting sight.

"Do you like my home?" Barlowe asked with satisfaction. "I'll be planning my first party here soon—one that will put every doubt to rest."

"It isn't yours yet," Finley bit out, but Barlowe merely laughed.

The man holding Finley's rope tugged, sending Finley stumbling forward again. He went without resisting, Barlowe several strides ahead, his eyes fixed on the castle.

When they reached the front doors, Barlowe almost leaped up the steps to reach them. Pulling them open with a dramatic gesture, he let sunlight flood the vast entryway beyond.

Finley stepped in after him, his eyes darting around the space. It was larger than he'd expected, a vast foyer that soared two stories above them. But it contained an excess of furniture—most notably a large, canopied bed in the middle of the space.

Barlowe's eyes moved straight over the odd addition to the room, dwelling instead on the luxury of the furnishings and the gilt edging of the mantelpiece. As he had said, he had no interest in the girl herself, only her possessions and the position she could provide. And he didn't even seem to notice the old woman slumped in a chair by the large, cold fireplace.

"Hurry!" Barlowe's smooth voice held a greedy note as he gestured to the man holding Finley's rope.

Finley was once again tugged forward, this time all the way to the side of the bed. He looked down at the face of the sleeping girl, and his world upended, spinning wildly around him.

It was Daphne. The girl lying in the bed was Daphne.

CHAPTER 25
DAPHNE

Despite the certainty—almost the inevitability—with which Daphne had outlined her plan, she still hesitated when she actually stood beside the bed. Her hands clenched the skirts of the gown Gabrielle had given her.

She had spent so long trying to escape the Legacy's unnatural sleep. Could she really voluntarily lie down and let it sweep her away completely?

"Are you sure Barlowe never saw your face at the ball?" Archer sounded worried. "Are you sure about all of this?"

"Yes," she said, and as she said it, it became true.

Lorne had shown her that she had to accept the way her naps had shaped her past. And now she had to face the way her fear of them could shape her future. She had to face the worst of what she feared her naps could become and come out the other side.

Because she did believe she would wake again. Just as

she was willing to risk everything to save Finley, he would never abandon her to the Legacy's clutches.

Even so, her legs trembled as she climbed into the bed and slid under the coverlet. Already the familiar weight of sleep was dragging at her, trying to pull her into unconsciousness. But she had to resist it. She needed to sleep for longer than a few minutes. She needed to sleep until Finley woke her.

"Here you go," Gabrielle said in a subdued voice, holding out a freshly spun length of yarn.

Nanny had talked her through making it while Archer urged them on to hurry. But it had to be made by Gabrielle's hands alone. None of the rest of them dared touch it, even for a moment. The effects of yarn made by a Sleeping Beauty on the spindle that had put her to sleep were the most potent of all sleep effects—even more so than the prick of a Sleeping Beauty whittled spindle.

As soon as Daphne took the rolled circle of yarn into her hand, the darkness grew too heavy to fight. It forced her eyelids closed, and she barely felt her hand land back on the bed, the yarn still clutched tight in her fingers.

CHAPTER 26
FINLEY

How could the girl in the bed be Daphne? Finley tried to force his spinning mind to make sense of what his eyes were seeing.

He had left Daphne behind with Archer. She couldn't be here unless...

Unless she and Archer had used the extra time he had bought them. If they had arrived at the castle first, Archer could have made a path through the brambles. He could have woken the real Gabrielle whose name was written on the bed before him. And they could have left Daphne in her place.

Finley watched the rise and fall of her chest, her unmoving, closed eyes. Was she really asleep or only pretending?

Fear seized him at the idea of Daphne sleeping here, alone and vulnerable. But wound through it was unmistakable awe at what she had done.

He glanced at Barlowe, his bound fists clenching at the

way the man's eyes were roving over Daphne's face. But there was no flicker of recognition in his features. Was that possible?

Finley thought back over the ball and their interactions. Barlowe had never seen Daphne without the mask. And if Finley—who knew her face as well as anyone's—had found it hard to believe she was really there, Barlowe would be even less likely to suspect it.

It had still been a staggering risk. His heart swelled with a wild mix of emotions. Daphne had risked everything for him, trusting that he would be true to his promises. And now it was his turn to risk everything for her. No matter what the consequences of obeying Barlowe, he couldn't turn back now.

"Kiss her," Barlowe ordered, and Finley leaned willingly toward Daphne's face.

"No!" The rope jerked him back. "Kiss her foot," Barlowe snapped, his usual urbanity fraying. "Stay out of her sight."

Finley straightened and held out his hands. "Cut my ropes."

Barlowe's eyes narrowed, but Finley's gaze didn't waver. "Cut my ropes, or I'm going to fall all over the girl. There are six of you and one of me, surely they aren't necessary."

"Fine." Barlowe waved at one of his men. "Cut him loose."

The man obeyed, letting the ropes fall to the ground at Finley's feet. Finley massaged his wrists as he took his designated place at the foot of the bed.

Flicking back the corner of the coverlet, Barlowe exposed Daphne's right ankle. As Finley leaned toward it, a ridiculous bubble of laughter fought to escape his throat. Barlowe remained deadly serious, however, positioning himself beside Daphne's face, where he blocked her view of Finley.

"Now!" Barlowe said, impatience in his voice.

Finley pressed his lips to Daphne's ankle. He pulled back and waited without breathing, counting the seconds.

Five ticked away, then six, then seven.

"Why isn't she—" Barlowe began only to cut himself off as Daphne finally stirred.

She lifted a hand to her head. "What has happened?" she asked in a clear, sweet voice. "Papa?"

Hands grabbed Finley from behind, pulling him roughly away from the bed. The bodies of Barlowe's men formed a wall, further preventing Daphne from getting any glimpse of him.

His stomach clenched. Did she realize he was there, or did she think Barlowe had actually woken her? Did she fear Finley was already dead?

"I'm so sorry, my dear," Barlowe said in tones of deep, but false, sympathy. "Your respected father is no longer with us."

"What...What do you mean?" Daphne asked, her voice wavering. "But I just saw him."

"I'm afraid you've been in an enchanted sleep, Gabrielle," Barlowe replied. "But I'm here now, and I will protect you. You don't need to worry about a thing. Here, let me help you up." The rustle of bed linen sounded as Daphne sat up and slid out of the bed.

The men dragging Finley across the entryway had nearly reached the door. Finley knew what was waiting for him outside, but he still didn't regret waking Daphne.

"Stop what you're doing, you nasty brutes!" called a loud voice from beside the fireplace. The men dragging Finley froze in surprise, and the voice continued in strident tones. "Why are you dragging that nice young man away?"

The old lady by the fire had woken in line with Daphne, springing up and pointing dramatically at Finley and his captors.

"Nanny!" cried Daphne, pushing past the unwary Barlowe and fleeing to the old lady's side.

Finley had no idea what was happening, but he responded instantly, pulling his arms free of his confused captors' grip and bowing courteously to the two ladies. The men around him looked to Barlowe, clearly unsure how to respond.

Barlowe hurried to the fireplace and recaptured Daphne's hand. She allowed him to do so, making Finley's skin crawl. He kept his face impassive, however.

"Who are those awful men?" Daphne shrank toward Barlowe with a believable level of fear. "What are they doing?"

Barlowe visibly hesitated. If he claimed the ruffians as his men, he might drive her away. He had chosen to fool his way into the role of hero, and now he was discovering the limitations of that position.

"They were dragging that nice young man away," the old lady said. "You must protect us from them, sir!"

"I'm afraid to say that nice young man is actually a thief," Barlowe said with a solemn air. "We found him stealing from your home while you slept, so my men were removing him from the premises for you."

"A thief?" Daphne looked up and met Finley's eyes for the first time.

Her face gentled immediately, her eyes shining at him, and his heart squeezed, his pulse leaping. It was all he could do not to race across the entryway and pull her into his arms.

Barlowe's face hardened. He still believed Daphne to be Gabrielle, but he had bargained a lot on her not getting a look at Finley. Fin was the one who had woken her and the true target of her Legacy-fueled infatuation.

"Oh no," the nanny said firmly. "He couldn't be a thief. He looks just like a young lad I used to bounce on my knee as a baby. He probably just popped up from the local town to check on us."

"I agree," Daphne said in a shy voice that sounded nothing like her usual self. "He doesn't look like a thief at all." She gave Finley an equally shy smile, and he could almost hear Barlowe's teeth grinding together.

"I know!" Daphne said brightly. "We'll make him turn out his pockets. Then we'll see the truth of it."

Finley immediately responded, turning out his empty pockets before Barlowe could think of a reason to protest.

"It's all a misunderstanding, my lady," he said as he

did so. "I haven't stolen a thing from this castle, I swear it."

"There you are!" Daphne cried in satisfaction, smiling happily at Barlowe. "Just a misunderstanding."

She gazed at Barlowe so trustingly that he hesitated, clearly unsure how to remove Finley without turning her against Barlowe himself. She had seen Finley, which was a disaster, and yet she still seemed drawn to Barlowe as well. He hadn't lost hold of the situation, so he clung to the role he had assigned himself.

"These men are only here to keep you safe, Gabrielle," he said. "If you want them gone, you need only say the word."

Finley held his breath, but Daphne shook her head. "Oh no, they should all stay. Even him. We enjoy welcoming visitors to our home." She smiled at Finley again, and he realized why she hadn't taken the opportunity Barlowe had offered.

If she sent Barlowe's men away, he would be sure to send Finley off with them. Which left them at an impasse. So far, Daphne had managed to fool Barlowe, but he still had strength and numerical superiority on his side. How long could they draw out the charade before he found a reason to get Finley away from her?

"You should apologize to our new guests, poppet," the nanny said in a chiding voice, as if she hadn't been the one insulting them the loudest. "You must never forget your good manners."

"Oh, yes, of course." Daphne hurried across the room toward Finley and the men who surrounded him.

He tensed as she approached and felt them do the same. But Barlowe glared from behind Daphne, clearly wanting his men to play nice, so they subsided.

Just as she reached them, Daphne tripped, nearly falling to the floor before she managed to right herself. Finley responded instinctively, leaping toward her, but a growl from Barlowe made him freeze. If he pushed Barlowe too far, it could result in disaster for both him and Daphne. He had to trust that Daphne had a plan beyond taking Gabrielle's place.

"Oh dear!" Daphne looked at something on the ground near the feet of the closest man. "I've dropped my yarn." She beamed at the man. "Would you pick it up for me?"

"Of course he will." Barlowe started toward them, gesturing for the man to do so.

With a pained smile, the man bent to retrieve the length of plain yarn. He handed it back to Daphne quickly, nearly losing his own balance in the process.

"Thank you." Her brow creased with sweet-looking concern. "You look a little shaky there. Let me help you."

She reached out to steady his arm, but he stumbled into her, making her stagger sideways and nearly topple. She collided with another of the men, the yarn trailing from her hand and wrapping over his wrist in the process.

"Oh, I'm so sorry." She unwound it as the first man collapsed to the ground.

Two of the others hurried forward to examine him, and Daphne followed close behind them.

"How terrible," she exclaimed, looking toward

Barlowe. "Is he...drunk?" Her eyes widened at the terrible idea, and Barlowe swelled, staring from one to the other of the remaining men accusingly.

"I'll just check," Daphne said, ignoring Barlowe's protests as she bent close to the downed man.

The yarn still trailed from her hand, and one of the remaining men became tangled in it, cursing as he hopped on one foot, trying to untangle himself. Daphne gave a fresh round of apologies, whipping the yarn off him and managing to fling it on the other man bending over his downed fellow instead.

A wordless cry of warning from behind her sounded as another man collapsed. Barlowe gave a cry, finally realizing something was wrong, and charged forward.

Daphne's sweet air of confusion fell away, energy filling every line of her body as she set her sights on the remaining two men. Leaping forward, she swung the end of the yarn around, whipping it across the face of one of them. He bellowed in protest and batted at it, but Daphne had already pulled it back.

She faced the remaining man, but he had finally realized what was happening. Backing away, he grabbed for his sword hilt, pulling it free. Finley lunged for the man's legs, bringing him crashing to the ground before he could get his blade into position. Daphne darted in, pressing a length of the string against his arm.

The man struggled for only a few more seconds before he, too, went still.

"What have you done?" Barlowe asked in a terrifying voice, made all the more terrible by its quiet volume.

Finley rolled to his feet and pushed Daphne behind him.

"They should wake up in a day or two," Daphne said defiantly, her previous false mannerisms gone. "None of them fit the right profile for a Sleeping Beauty, so they shouldn't be affected too severely."

"I thought you paid attention to every detail, Barlowe." Finley stooped to retrieve the dropped sword. "Do you really not recognize her?"

Barlowe's eyes slowly widened as he looked between Finley and Daphne.

"No," he breathed. "It can't be. We left you behind. You can't be…"

"The real Gabrielle was woken before you arrived." Daphne stepped out from behind Finley to stand at his side. "She said to tell you that she has no interest in marrying an old man and no intention of letting anyone steal her home."

"You little—"

Finley lunged forward, sword outstretched, forcing Barlowe to cut off his curse and jump backward to avoid him.

Barlowe pulled out his own blade, and Finley heard the sharp intake of Daphne's breath. They were both all too aware that Barlowe carried an Oakdenian blade.

Barlowe backed up further, returning to the fireplace where the older lady still waited. He shoved her in front of him, holding his sword point against the small of her back.

"Put down your sword," he ground out, every bit of his

smooth charm gone. "Unless you want to see me gut the old lady."

"Put it down," Daphne urged quietly, her eyes on the woman.

Finley reluctantly obeyed. He couldn't let Barlowe hurt the woman, especially not when it was obvious she had been a willing part of Daphne's charade.

"You nasty man!" the woman exclaimed. "Going after my Gabrielle! At least she's safe out of your clutches."

"It's not too late for me to find her, I assure you," Barlowe hissed, but his face was white and his eyes wild.

Fury swept over the woman's previously placid features, swelling her from the inside out. She pulled something long and wooden from her skirts and turned on Barlowe, stabbing wildly at him.

"Nanny! No! Be careful!" Daphne cried, starting toward them.

Barlowe responded instinctively, slashing the tip of his blade across the woman's arm as she swung at him. Her attack faltered, and she fell to the ground.

As she fell, Finley finally saw what was in her hand. A wooden spindle.

The woman hit the ground, managing one final effort of movement as she flopped down. Flinging out her arm, she sent the spindle rolling across the floor toward Daphne.

Daphne didn't hesitate. Throwing herself forward full length, she slid the final distance to snatch the rolling spindle from the floor. Barlowe shouted in rage and raced toward where she lay stretched out and defenseless on the ground. But Daphne didn't even look at him, turning back toward Finley instead.

Seeing Daphne's response, Finley thought of the spindles Archie had carved and knew instantly what Daphne held. He knew also what she would do next, their teamwork instinctive. Reaching forward, he caught the spindle he already knew she would throw to him.

Snatching it from the air, he lifted his arm and threw it like a javelin, piercing Barlowe's shoulder just as the man reached Daphne.

Barlowe shouted in pain, staring at the wooden spindle protruding from his shoulder as he swayed in place.

"You...you..." He didn't manage to finish the thought before he crashed to the ground.

Daphne clambered to her feet and rushed to meet Finley. He reached her in two strides, lifting her off her feet and swinging her through the air.

"Are you truly all right?" he asked as soon as he put her down. "Barlowe's men didn't hurt you? I've been thinking..." He swallowed, not wanting to voice the terrible thoughts he had fought to keep at bay. "How did you get here so quickly?"

"I've been even more scared for you!" She buried her face in his chest for a moment, babbling a list of events almost incomprehensibly. "Lorne arrived back at the manor in time to save Archer and me. He'd brought everyone with him, so Barlowe fled with only you. Archer and I came after you as quickly as we could. Avery loaned us her horse."

"Who's Avery?" Finley asked, bewildered, but then decided he didn't care.

The nanny would wake up at any minute, and then reality would intrude, and Finley would have to work out what to do with the other sleepers. Finley had only a few precious seconds of solitude with Daphne, and he much preferred to spend those seconds kissing her rather than talking about the mysterious Avery, whoever she might be.

He wrapped his arms firmly around Daphne and kissed her hard. She must have felt the same way because she kissed him back without hesitation.

CHAPTER 27

FINLEY

Nanny hadn't been awake for long before Archer and Gabrielle arrived back, a squad of guards with them. From the excited babble of the guards, it quickly became apparent that the whole town was agog with Gabrielle's reappearance.

"It's insulting, really, that they'd forgotten all about us," Gabrielle complained to Nanny. "I mean, surely they could see the brambles across the lake!"

"That's the work of the Legacy, I'm sure," Daphne said, but Gabrielle only sniffed.

"I'm sure it was the Legacy's fault," Archer agreed. "You shouldn't hold it against them."

"You're right, of course," Gabrielle agreed with a beaming smile. "It's the only explanation that makes sense."

Finley frowned at Gabrielle, but Daphne walked away with a laugh, coming to his side and letting him slip an arm around her.

"Don't hold it against her," she murmured. "She'll be embarrassed by her own attitude soon enough."

Finley relaxed. He was too relieved at having Daphne in his arms again to stay upset at anything—especially something that Daphne laughed off so easily.

Thankfully, the guards were able to remove the sleeping men from the castle entryway—proof that they hadn't qualified as Sleeping Beauties and would likely wake before too long. But they would wake under lock and key.

Since the enchantment had preserved the state of the castle and even the food inside, Gabrielle and Nanny welcomed Archer, Finley, and Daphne to stay the night. All three accepted with gratitude, exhausted after barely sleeping the night before.

Nisha and Morrow arrived the next day with Lorne and two others in tow. Nisha and Morrow were disappointed to hear they'd missed all the fighting, but the young woman driving the cart seemed more happy to be reunited with her horse than anything else.

Lorne soon introduced her as the mysterious Avery—who Finley still knew nothing about—and the man as her husband, Elliot. Finley thanked them both for their roles in rescuing Daphne and Archie, as well as their loan of Nutmeg, and Avery entered wholeheartedly into their plans for the future.

"King Vesper is your uncle," she said decisively when Finley expressed uncertainty about Avery's suggestion that he and Archer go with her and Elliot to the capital. "I'm not saying you have to live a life at court, but shouldn't you at least meet him?" Her voice softened. "You should be the one to tell him about your father's passing, not me."

Since there was no response to that, Finley was forced to agree. It didn't hurt that Archie was full of enthusiasm for the idea.

Finley's feelings toward his father remained mixed, but he owed it to him to at least meet his father's family and inform them of his death himself.

Gabrielle was devastated to hear of their upcoming departure until Avery suggested that she accompany them to court as well. Her devastation was immediately replaced with raptures, and she bounded away to tell Archie the good news.

"I'm not sure he'll see it as good news," Daphne said, clearly trying not to laugh. "You won't have a friend in Archie for making that suggestion, Avery."

"We can't just leave her here with only Nanny," Avery said, clearly unworried by Archie's future ire. "I've been talking to Nanny, and even before Gabrielle's enchanted sleep, her father kept her here, away from the world, without any other young people. She needs a chance to see the kingdom a little and meet others her age." She glanced wryly at Gabrielle who was now bouncing up and down in front of Archer, begging him to join her in some activity he clearly didn't want to do. "Perhaps meet some other sixteen-year-old boys besides your poor brother?"

Finley, however, felt no such sympathy for Archie. He was well-served getting a taste of his own mischief.

Gabrielle's pleas grew loud enough to hear, and Finley gathered that she wanted them all to go outside.

"What a lovely idea!" he called across the room. "We would all be delighted to enjoy some sunshine and admire the cherry blossoms for an hour or two."

"Finley!" Daphne chided in an undertone, but he just grinned at her.

"Admit that it sounds delightful," he said.

She laughed. "I suppose it does."

No one else protested, so Finley and Daphne led the way outside, everyone else following except for Nanny who was overseeing the newly hired servants from the town.

The moment they had settled themselves outside on the gently sloping grass that ran down to the lake, Gabrielle approached Archie, a blush on her cheeks.

"I picked these for my rescuer." Gabrielle brought a bouquet of daisies out from behind her back and presented them to him.

He scrambled backward, trying to get away from the flowers.

"Oh, no...thank you," he stammered. "I don't need flowers."

Gabrielle's face fell. "Chocolate, then?"

She gestured, and one of the new servants rushed forward with a tray bearing a selection of chocolates. For a second, Archie looked tempted. Then his expression firmed, and he shook his head.

"Really, Gabby," he said, "you have to stop offering me things. I've already told you that I don't need anything."

For the first time, Gabrielle looked irritated by something Archie had said.

"Don't call me Gabby!" she snapped.

Beside Fin, Daphne held her breath, but Gabrielle's expression immediately softened. "Even if you don't need anything," she said, gazing at Archie lovingly, "I need you. And you deserve everything."

Archie's eyes bulged, and he looked desperately at Daphne.

"Please, save me," he pleaded. "Tell her to stop."

"Ha!" Daphne said. "Hahahahahahaha." She stopped to breathe and then kept going. "Hahahahaha—no." She smiled sweetly at Gabrielle. "Keep going, sweetheart. I think you've nearly won him over."

Gabrielle immediately brightened. "You'll find the feelings fade in a week or two," Daphne continued, "but to really give him what he deserves, I would recommend keeping it up for at least a month."

"I could gaze at him for a year," Gabrielle sighed, and the rest of them burst into laughter at Archie's despairing wail.

"And we thought Archie was bad," Nisha murmured.

Finley grinned. "Gabrielle explained it to me this morning: He's just so pretty. How can she resist?"

His arm snaked out, circling Daphne's waist and drawing her to his side.

"I don't know why you're talking," Nisha said. "You two are nearly as bad."

"But look at her," Finley crooned. "How could I resist when she's so *pretty*?"

Daphne laughed and whacked him lightly on the shoulder. "Stop that! Archer may deserve it, but Nisha and Morrow haven't done anything wrong."

Finley laughed. He couldn't seem to stop laughing since Daphne had come back to him.

In the chaos of everything, they'd barely had the chance to be alone, but he didn't even mind. She was alive, and now they could have the lifetime of moments he had dreamed about.

But as everyone spread out beside the lake to enjoy the sunshine, he took her hand and led her away from the others, walking along the shore until they were out of earshot.

He gathered her into his arms, resting his chin on her head and gazing across the water. "It's so peaceful here," he murmured. "But we'll be leaving for the capital soon, and everything will change."

"Not everything." Daphne's arms wrapped around him. "My love for you isn't going to change."

He dipped his head to give her a kiss, marveling that he was finally free to do so.

"It has occurred to me," he said when he came up for air, "that there's something we haven't specifically talked about. But I'm sincerely hoping that when you said you didn't want to live without me—and then stole someone's horse to ride across the kingdom to rescue me—you meant you were willing to marry me. Will you marry me, Daphne?"

Daphne laughed. "I didn't steal Nutmeg!"

"That isn't an answer," he said sternly.

"Yes." She smiled at him, freeing one of her hands so she could trace the line of his jaw. "I would love to spend every day of the rest of my life at your side, Finley. Even if that means staying in Oakden forever."

Finley's mood dropped. "I know you miss Glandore," he said quietly. "Are you sure you're really all right with being trapped here with me?"

"Oakden was my home first, and I love many things about it," Daphne said. "I'm not all Glandorian or all Oakdenian, I'm a bit of both. I can be happy here. The naps have even started decreasing in frequency finally, ever since my long sleep in Gabrielle's place. I certainly don't want to force a burden onto you, just so I can live in Glandore."

She sighed. "I'm starting to understand how my parents came to make the decisions they did. It's infuriating to be so constrained by the Legacy's mindless whims!"

"Maybe you won't always have to be." Avery strolled up to them, a smile on her face.

Daphne flushed and tried to push away from Finley, but he didn't let go. She had just agreed to marry him, and he didn't care who saw them hugging.

Daphne chuckled under her breath, shaking her head and relaxing into his arms again.

"Ah, new love," Elliot proclaimed with the air of a venerable grandfather. "We wouldn't know anything about that."

Avery laughed, and he caught her around the waist,

planting an enthusiastic kiss on her mouth while she tried to fend him off.

"Actually," Avery said when she managed to extricate herself, "we believe there may be a way to remove someone's tie to their birth kingdom. Elliot managed to do it with his tie."

"What?" Daphne pushed out of Finley's arms and turned fully to face Avery. "That's possible?"

"It's something we've only recently discovered." Eagerness lit up Avery's voice and face. "There were reasons that made it particularly urgent in Elliot's case, but it left us thinking that maybe there are others who would benefit just as we did. And meeting the two of you is confirmation of that."

"How did you do it?" Daphne asked, just as eager.

But Elliot put a hand on his wife's shoulder. "My situation was unique, but we're researching the possibilities now. It's why we came to Lorne in the first place—we wanted to make use of his library and his vast personal experience. We were planning to travel into Halbury next to follow up some leads there, but when we discovered Lorne frantically looking for you, we had to help."

"I haven't properly thanked you for that," Daphne said. "I appreciate it more than you can know."

"We both appreciate it," Finley said.

Daphne nodded. "And if you do find a way for us to free ourselves from our birth kingdom, we would be even more grateful."

"If we find anything, I'll be sure to send word straight to Lorne," Avery promised. "I think he has a large network of people who would be very interested in that piece of information."

Avery and Elliot continued on around the lake, walking hand in hand.

"If it's ever possible," Finley said when he was alone with Daphne again, "I would move to Glandore for you without hesitation." He paused. "Once Archie is eighteen, of course."

"It may well be longer than that before we hear anything from Avery again anyway," Daphne said. "Possibly much longer. But just knowing it's a possibility...!" She breathed a happy sigh, and Finley's heart swelled to see the joy on her face.

He didn't care if he built a future with her in Oakden or Glandore or both. He just knew his future looked infinitely brighter than it had before she came into his life.

EPILOGUE

DAPHNE

Daphne gazed out the carriage window, unable to keep the smile off her face. "I never thought I'd be so happy to see nothing but roses."

She beamed at Fin beside her, and he smiled back. As always, he took delight in her joy, reminding her how fortunate she had been to find him.

"You really missed Thebarton," he said.

She nodded. "I missed Rosalie more." She hesitated and put a hand on his knee. "Thank you for doing this."

He laughed. "You've already thanked me five times today. I told you when we crossed the river—you've been enduring this for most of your life. I can do it for a month."

"From what Lorne said, it shouldn't have any lasting effect if we're only out of the kingdom for a month," Daphne said.

"Do you think we'll make it back in a month?" he

asked. "We barely managed to get away from the Sovaran court, and from everything you've told me, I'm expecting Rosalie to be even worse."

Daphne laughed. "Two months at most?"

But she knew Fin didn't mind, despite the ache he said he could feel in his bones at all times—like the weariness after a long day. It had hit as soon as they crossed the river into Sovar, but he bore it without complaining.

There was no way Daphne could ask him to live like that forever, though, so she was pinning her hopes on Avery and Elliot. They had left for Halbury before she and Fin left Oakden, and they had been the ones to encourage her to take Fin on a wedding trip to meet her family and friends.

Lorne had added his voice to theirs. "After the life you've lived, it's good for your husband to see a little of the kingdoms. And to experience firsthand what it means to bear the Legacy's burden. A month or two isn't too high a price to pay, so you should trust him when he says he's happy to pay it."

She still wouldn't have suggested leaving Archer for so long if she hadn't seen his obvious joy at court. The king had welcomed his long-lost nephews with open arms, tearing up at their close resemblance to their father. And Archer had blossomed in the presence of a vast extended family.

The boy had been born to live the life of a courtier, apparently, and Lorne had promised to remain in the capital to keep an eye on him. He would be keeping an eye on Gabrielle at the same time since Nanny clearly needed assistance in the task.

The Legacy infatuation had worn off, and she had turned on Archer with the same vigor she had once adored him with—fueled, Daphne was sure, by embarrassment. And yet, despite their constant bickering, they didn't use the size of the court as an opportunity to avoid each other. Instead, Daphne rarely saw one unless the other was somewhere nearby.

She had her own suspicions about where that relationship was going, but for now they were still young and enjoying the crowd of young people at court. Between Archer's feud with Gabrielle and his delight in his new, royal family, there was no room for him to miss his brother while he was away.

"Are you sure you're not going to miss the Sovaran court?" Daphne asked Fin, a teasing light in her eye. "I know how much you love the Oakdenian one."

Unlike his younger brother, Fin had not taken to court life—much to Daphne's private relief. While his charm made him an instant favorite, he had little patience for the frivolities or the falseness of many of the courtiers. Every evening, when they finally escaped to their own suite, he told her again that he much preferred the company of the one person who had always seen behind his pretense.

For Daphne herself, if she was going to live in a palace, she would have preferred to live in Sovar with her cousin Olivia. But far more than either court, her heart longed for the home of her youth—Glandore was the kingdom that called to her the most, and she desperately missed the sister of the heart she had left behind there.

"Daphne!" Rosalie's scream reached her ears before the carriage had even stopped.

Laughing, Daphne pulled open the door and tumbled out, straight into her friend's arms. For several minutes there was too much laughter, too many tears, and too many shouted exclamations for anyone to make sense of anything.

But when Rosalie stopped talking, Daphne was finally able to get a word in. She took Fin's hand and pulled him forward.

"This is Finley," she said, "my husband." It was still new enough that she blushed at the word.

"But he's gorgeous!" Rosalie exclaimed. "Not that I'm surprised since you're so gorgeous yourself. But when you wrote describing his jawline, I thought maybe it was your love coloring the description."

"You wrote to your friend about my jawline?" Fin asked, clearly trying not to laugh.

"It's a very nice jawline," Daphne said, unrepentant. "Any true friend would want to know about something like that."

"About my jawline?" He was definitely laughing now.

"Of course," Rosalie said loyally. "I wanted to know everything. Daphne has been gone SO long. Are you exhausted from your trip?" She shook her head. "What am I saying? You're Daphne. Of course you are!"

"I'm sorry I can't stay," Daphne said, the smile falling

off her face for the first time since she'd heard Rosalie's voice.

"That's all right." Rosalie gave her another hug. "You know I understand. And we can hold out hope that Avery will find a solution. If anyone can, I'm sure it's her. I wrote to her after I got your letter and invited them to stay here any time they'd like. If they ever get sick of traveling—of if they want a home base of sorts to travel from—they would both be a welcome part of our little community. I'll certainly never forget what she did for me and Dimitri. Ooh!" Her eyes lit up. "Now that you're here in person, you can tell me all about this Elliot. Somehow I never pictured Avery getting married. She seemed so independent and content."

"I think she was until she met him." Daphne happily let Rosalie lead her down the sweeping, tree-lined drive that led to Dimitri's manor, telling her friend all about her interactions with Avery and Elliot.

They walked past a beautiful riot of garden, although the only flowers filling it were roses. The sight of them brought memories flooding back to Daphne, and she fell silent as they reached the building. In appearance, it was as much a castle as Gabrielle's home, although the stone that formed it was gray rather than white.

But it wasn't truly a manor anymore. Dimitri and Rosalie had turned it into a community, and it was Daphne's first chance to see how the building had been transformed since her friend's wedding.

In the entryway, she paused, looking around, once again assailed by memories.

"Do you need a nap before we do a tour?" Rosalie asked, clearly trying to be considerate despite her own brimming impatience.

Daphne smiled. "I knew you would want to drag me everywhere as soon as we arrived, so I napped most of the drive from Sovar. Marriage can't have changed you that much."

"But has my enthusiasm ever stopped you from napping?" Rosalie asked with a laugh. "I am eager to do the tour, though. I want to show you everything."

"Marriage hasn't changed her at all." Dimitri strode into the entryway, his face laughing but his eyes soft as they rested on his wife.

"Dimitri!" Rosalie hurried over and threw her arms around him.

But she only embraced him for a moment before stepping back and frowning. "You said you'd be back before Daphne arrived. I want to introduce you to Finley. He—" She looked around and noticed for the first time that he wasn't with them. "Where is he?"

Daphne looked back through the open door and stifled a laugh. "I'm afraid your brothers found him."

Rosalie groaned. "If those terrors have scared him off before we have a chance to win him over, I'll—"

"Don't worry," Daphne said. "He'll like you. Of course he will. I've already told him he has to."

Dimitri gave a startled laugh, but Rosalie took the reassurance at face value. Leaning out the door, she watched the triplets with narrowed eyes as they escorted Fin up the steps and into the manor.

Vernon had his arm slung over Fin's shoulders and was speaking earnestly, one of his brothers flanking them on either side.

"We're just saying," Vernon said, "that we're fifteen now."

"And there are three of us," Ralph interjected.

"Exactly," Vernon agreed. "There are three of us, so if you hurt Daphne—"

"Or do anything to break her heart," Oscar added.

"We'll have something to say about the matter," Vernon concluded.

"Ha!" Rosalie stared them down, hands on her hips.

They took one look at her and slunk away, all three smiling at Daphne as they filed past her.

"As if we need them," Rosalie muttered as they disappeared. "I would deal with him before they ever got a chance."

"Welcome to Oakden," Dimitri said to Fin, shaking his hand. "I apologize for the...ahem...enthusiasm of my family."

"They care about Daphne, and that's all that matters to me," Fin said. "I know they're like family to her, as much as her own parents. And besides, I have a sixteen-year-old brother of my own, so you have my deepest sympathy." He shuddered. "Three!"

Dimitri laughed. "It's never boring, I can say that much."

"Daphne's told me a little about what you've done here," Fin said, looking around the entryway. "I'm looking forward to seeing it for myself. Using an enormous place like this for a whole community—one that can create a thriving hub for the region—is an inspired idea. I know a girl back in Oakden with a home far too large for one person, so I'm planning to learn as much as I can while we're here and suggest the idea to her in the future."

Daphne glanced back, eyebrows raised. She hadn't realized Fin was thinking of suggesting the white castle become a community like the Thebarton manor had become. It was a good idea, though.

The tour took so long that Daphne snuck in a nap along the way. But she enjoyed every minute of it. Her complaints when they crossed into the third hour were a mere matter of tradition.

Rosalie's family had their own apartment, and Daphne's parents would be moving in the following month. They had put off their move in order to travel into Oakden to attend their daughter's wedding, and they had taken the opportunity to visit friends while in the kingdom.

It had been an emotional reunion on both sides. She'd had time before their arrival to work through the anger Fin had encouraged her to release, but seeing them had brought up fresh waves of emotion. Her love for them remained—a bond forged over a lifetime—but after Daphne's travels, she saw them with the eyes of an adult instead of the blind emotion of a child.

Her parents had been emotional as well upon hearing Daphne's unusually candid reflections on what the Legacy's burden had cost her. But the honesty had also begun building new, deeper connections—ones that hadn't been possible when Daphne had been holding herself back.

"We still need to prepare the rest of the individual apartments," Dimitri explained, "and Rosalie is determined to save one for Avery and Elliot. But we have some ideas about who else might be interested in moving in."

The conversation continued around the enormous dining table as they ate the evening meal, words and laughter flying across the table in every direction. Daphne took a moment in the middle of the chaos to arch an eyebrow at Fin. He grinned back at her, clearly more relaxed and happy here than he had been in either court.

Daphne smiled and slipped her hand into his beneath the table. She didn't know exactly what the coming years would bring, but whether they were surrounded by friends and family in Glandore or Oakden, they would always have each other.

It had been a long road to lead Daphne back to her birth kingdom, but she didn't regret any part of it because it had led her to him—and to a life that wasn't like the one she had planned but was instead far fuller and richer than she could have imagined.

Note from the Author

Daphne now has her own story, but there are more adventures to explore in the kingdoms of Legacy as Avery and Elliot search for an answer to the Legacy's burden. The next installment, Legacy of Gold, will be coming in 2026. In the meantime, if you missed the start of Avery's quest, you can read her story in Ties of Legacy, a Kingdoms of Legacy companion novel.

To be informed of my new releases, as well as new bonus shorts, please sign up to my mailing list at www.melaniecellier.com. At my website, you'll also find an array of free extra content for my various worlds.

Thank you for taking the time to read my book. I hope you enjoyed it. If you did, please spread the word! You could start by leaving a review on Amazon (or Goodreads or Facebook or any other social media site). Your review would be very much appreciated and would make a big difference!

Acknowledgments

Daphne has been the most fun character to write in Kingdoms of Legacy, but sometimes that can be difficult when it comes time for that character to be the center of their own story. And, as expected, Daphne gave me quite a few difficulties. But I also loved seeing her journey grow and develop, as well as writing her chemistry with Finley. I only hope you enjoyed reading it just as much!

As usual, I'm grateful to the team who help bring my books into being, and on this occasion, I have to give the first thanks to my amazing family for letting me hide myself away and write so I could get a first draft on paper. And then another big thank you to my editor, Mary, who helped turn that first draft into the finished product.

Thank you also to my betas, especially to Rachel, who has been my most loyal and thoughtful beta for many years now. I appreciate all your time and effort, and all your feedback.

And a thank you also to my dad and to James for poring over the draft, looking for errors. And for the first time, I'm excited to also be able to thank my daughter who's finally grown old enough to love reading young adult books and who has become my most enthusiastic error checker.

And the final thanks goes to God who is with us in weakness as well as in strength.

About the Author

Melanie Cellier grew up on a staple diet of books, books and more books. And although she got older, she never stopped loving children's and young adult novels.

She always wanted to write one herself, but it took three careers and three different continents before she actually managed it.

She now feels incredibly fortunate to spend her time writing from her home in Adelaide, Australia where she keeps an eye out for koalas in her backyard. Her staple diet hasn't changed much, although she's added choc mint Rooibos tea and Chicken Crimpies to the list.

She writes young adult fantasy including books in her *Spoken Mage* world, her *Mage's Influence* world, and her various *Four Kingdoms* and *Kingdoms of Legacy* series that are made up of linked stand-alone stories that retell classic fairy tales.